Esther Campion is from Cork, Ireland and currently lives in north-west Tasmania. She attended North Presentation Secondary School in Cork and has degrees from University College Cork and the University of Aberdeen, Scotland. Esther and her Orcadian husband have lived together in Ireland, Scotland, Norway and South Australia. They have two grown-up children in Adelaide and the youngest at home in Tassie. Esther loves sharing her life on a small property with an over-indulged chocolate Labrador, a smoochy cat and a couple of ageing mares, all of whom she firmly believes are living proof that dreams really can come true. Esther's heartwarming debut novel, *Leaving Ocean Road*, was followed by *The House of Second Chances*.

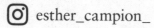

f  esthercampionauthor

⊙  esther_campion_

Also by Esther Campion

*Leaving Ocean Road*
*The House of Second Chances*

# Esther Campion

# A Week to Remember

hachette
AUSTRALIA

hachette
AUSTRALIA

Published in Australia and New Zealand in 2021
by Hachette Australia
(an imprint of Hachette Australia Pty Limited)
Level 17, 207 Kent Street, Sydney NSW 2000
www.hachette.com.au

10 9 8 7 6 5 4 3 2 1

Copyright © Esther Campion 2021

A catalogue record for this
book is available from the
National Library of Australia

ISBN: 978 0 7336 4551 8 (paperback)

Cover design by Christabella Designs
Cover photograph courtesy of Trevillion
Author photo: Michelle DuPont
Typeset in 12.1/18.6 pt Sabon LT by Bookhouse, Sydney
Printed and bound in Australia by McPherson's Printing Group

MIX
Paper from
responsible sources
FSC® C001695

The paper this book is printed on is certified against the
Forest Stewardship Council® Standards. McPherson's Printing
Group holds FSC® chain of custody certification SA-COC-005379.
FSC® promotes environmentally responsible, socially beneficial
and economically viable management of the world's forests.

*To Mike Thomson*

'The most valuable thing for life never changes by time or place – it is to be honest and cheerful, to find happiness in what you have, and to have courage in hardships.'

LAURA INGALLS WILDER

# Prologue

'Katie Daly!' Miss Dorgan, their English teacher, swayed at the top of the steps of the West Cork Hotel. 'You're like a swan,' she slurred before Mr Cashel, the head, took her by the arm, probably saving the woman from a tumble that would have brought the graduation dance to a standstill before it even got going.

'She's half-cut already,' said Conor, who Katie had hardly been able to look at since he'd arrived at her home to collect her, armed with a beautiful rose to pin on her dress and a box of chocolates for her mother. In his brother's car, the poor boy had tried his best to make conversation as they sat apart in the back seat. Transformed as he was with that snazzy haircut and the mandatory tuxedo he'd complained at having to wear, he'd gone from simple gangly country boy to James Bond understudy. Other girls had insisted their partners wear coloured bow ties and matching triangles of handkerchiefs, but Katie made no such demands. After months of agonising over how she would ever find a partner who wasn't one of the male cousins suggested by her mother, not to mind listening to the conversations at school of the girls who had it all sewn up and thought they knew who every one of the boys would end up with, Conor Fox had done two miraculous things in one night – he'd asked her to dance at the hurling club disco and he'd asked her to the ball. Not that he was a hurler. Although happy to support his brother and the local team from the sidelines, the game held no great interest for him. The clash of the ash, they called it. A fierce fast-moving game, the ash sticks held aloft, belting a leather ball at lightning speed, not a helmet between them. No, Conor was refined, happier with a book in his hand. The only boy in her year to bring coffee to school. She would watch him at lunchtimes in the canteen as he queued at the urn, dispensing measures of coffee, milk and sugar from tablet containers and a little medicine bottle. He told them he was recycling. To her, at least, it was cool.

'Sure ye're only gorgeous,' Martin had sneered from where she'd wished he would stop looking at her in the rear-view mirror and keep his eyes on the winding road. She'd never been so delighted to get out of a car. To say the brothers were like chalk and cheese would have been an understatement.

Fizzing with excitement, she thought she might burst out of the full-length white taffeta number she and her mother had found in a dress hire shop in Cork City. What an excursion that had been, trawling the shops for dresses and the glamorous white high heels in which she was now desperately trying to stay upright. And the white nylons; she'd already laddered the right thigh of them, but there was a spare pair in her bag along with money, lip gloss, a small palette of eyeshadow and tissues her mother never let her leave home without.

Conor took her hand and gave it a squeeze. When she looked at him, his eyes travelled over her face and down that dress that had to be back in the hire shop next week. She knew he was taking it all in: the light makeup Bernadette had helped her apply, the upstyled hairdo where her sister had tamed her cow's lick and weaved it all into a pair of French plaits that met at the nape of her neck, the drop diamante earrings her mother had surprised her with the week before.

He gave her a wink and bent his tall frame so their faces were level.

'Don't be nervous,' he told her. 'You're the belle of the ball.'

# Chapter One

'We could have gone to Bali!' Aisling was on one of her moaning rolls as the two friends strode along Freers Beach under a milky blue sky that promised another hot day in Tasmania. 'Why did I let Mick's family decide how we'd spend our anniversary?'

Heather was already well versed in the circumstances that had led to the latest drama in the Fitzgeralds' lives, but Aisling went over it again just to blow off steam.

'The indignity of it! Spending a week in the bogs of Ireland when we could be in some idyllic resort, drinking cocktails at one of those swim-up bars.' But as Aisling knew only too well, the gift from her in-laws, or outlaws as she liked to call them, was as much a present for Mick's forthcoming fortieth as it was for their anniversary. If it had been left to her, there'd have been a big party. But no, Lilian Fitzgerald had other ideas. She'd give her son a holiday in West Cork and she'd have a few weeks with the grandchildren all to herself in Tasmania. Aisling had all manner of fantastic ideas for

surprise parties, but although she was loath to admit it, Mick
would have hated that. So in the end, Lily Fitz got her way.

'It's not as if I could have said no,' she said, snatching a
good breath as they kept up a steady pace along the shore.
'I don't know why I ever agreed to marrying him on his
birthday.'

It had felt like the most romantic thing at the time when
he'd told her he wanted to wake up beside her on every mile-
stone, celebrate each passing year of his life with her. And
for a fella who wasn't prone to gush or go overboard with
romantic gestures, she'd known he'd meant it.

'It's bloody winter over there,' she huffed. 'Why did I have
to get married in winter?'

Heather would outstrip anyone in a competition for Listener
of the Year. There was no doubting the neighbour who had
become her best Australian friend was a great support. She'd
been bearing witness to the highs and lows of Aisling's life for
the best part of five years. God knows, Heather had heard it
all as Aisling had regularly let rip about everything from her
stressful job, to her relationship with Mick Fitzgerald and their
kids, to gripes about all manner of her multitude of relations.
That was the problem with their trips home to Ireland – she
always came back feeling in need of a holiday. There were
Mick's three brothers and their families with a rake of kids
that ensured there was always a christening or a communion
depending on when they travelled home. Then there was the
One Foot in the Grave Brigade – the older relatives who absolutely had to be visited in case it might be the last time. And
her own siblings of course: the younger sister who had their

father in her pocket, and the brother she loved but who had married the sister-in-law she couldn't stand. Heather had met every one of those who had made it to Tasmania and witnessed the fallout of every visit. But wasn't that what friends were for? Helping pick up the pieces when things went pear-shaped?

'It will be lovely to have Lilian nearby,' Heather was saying as they tramped along, their trainers making oversized footprints in the soft sinky sand near the boat ramp. 'You're so lucky to have a mother-in-law to keep the show on the road.'

That was Heather. Ever since she'd moved into the beachfront house two doors up from the Fitzgeralds, she'd been the voice of reason in their private conversations. While Aisling might have preferred to vent without judgement, Heather would consider the fairness of her arguments and gently weigh in when she went too far, defending Mick and anyone else in the firing line. She had that knack of reminding her that the Fitzgeralds really were decent people. It was probably why Aisling had made no mention of Brett Goodstone. Heather had a quality about her that made Aisling wish she could live up to her standards.

'You'll have a ball, Ash,' Heather told her now. 'Remember all the times you've gone home and been, to use your words, "demented going from pillar to post"?'

'Exactly.' Aisling was defiant. 'It won't be much different this time. I'll still have to see all the rellies . . .'

'At least you can see them and then have a whole week to yourselves in a beautiful part of the world.'

'I suppose,' she conceded. 'Although knowing my luck, it'll lash rain the entire time and we'll be blown into the Atlantic.'

'Bloody oath, you'd think you were going to Kabul,' said Heather.

A wry smile spread across Aisling's face. 'I'd take a week in Kabul with George Clooney, and Amal could have Mick in West Cork.'

They laughed over the sound of seagulls and the small waves that swallowed up their footprints as they headed towards home.

～

'Who put that black pants in the wash with a tissue still inside the pocket?'

Aisling didn't care if the neighbours could hear her. The walls of the weatherboard beach house were that thin, they probably knew when she farted, at least when Mick farted. His grandfather hadn't nicknamed him Rear Gunner Fitzgerald for nothing.

'I'm fed up of telling you all. Check your flipping pockets.'

Unsure if any of the three of them were even listening, she pummelled the trousers with a lint roller. Why did this kind of stupidity always happen at the eleventh hour, when you were just about to go out the door?

'Mick!'

No answer from her husband, who was down in the bedroom, no doubt dressed and ready with only his toilet bag to fling into the suitcase.

'Mick, where did you put that hard clothes brush?'

Aisling looked out the laundry window and caught sight of a couple with an all-terrain pram and a dog heading down to the beach. Another perfect summer's evening with locals and visitors soaking up the weather. *Typical*, she thought as she wrestled with the tissue bits that may as well have been superglued to the fabric, *I'm missing out on half the summer here and heading into cold, dreary winter in Ireland.*

'Give it to me here.' Mick came in armed with the brush. Taking the pants from her, he set to work. She hesitated for a moment, but his face was stern. 'Ash, get moving. I think I can be trusted with this job.' He eyed her from where he was bent over the garment. 'We're going on holiday, you know.'

She hesitated for a second, considering a last rant about why in the name of God she'd let himself and his family railroad her into this trip in the first place, but remembering the time, turned on her heel and sprinted to the bedroom. For the hundredth time, she ran through the three weeks she'd organised to the letter. The CEO was fine about her taking leave; Brett in Melbourne would cover both states in her absence. She'd hoped it would be someone else, but it was done now. At least she could go away confident at having steered the Tasmanian stores through another successful Christmas. Her house was in order, clean and tidy with a fridge and freezer full to bursting, though God only knew what her mother-in-law would feed her children. She'd stopped short of leaving the meal planner she'd prepared on the fridge. *Too prescriptive*, Mick had said in that firm tone he used when she crossed the line between care and control.

At the small regional airport, Aisling felt the buzz she always got when leaving the island. Too bad she was about to bypass the bright lights of Melbourne and connect with the late-night long haul to halfway across the world. But the bright lights of Melbourne were the problem. She couldn't turn back the clock. Somehow, she'd have to get through this with Mick. She may have joked about Bali with her friend, but after what she'd done in Melbourne, romantic holidays in exotic destinations were simply unthinkable. Ireland would be bad enough. The time with their families would go quickly. It was the week in West Cork she was dreading.

'No doing donuts around Hawley now.' Mick winked as he handed the car keys to Evan.

The comment snapped Aisling back to the moment. They'd never gone on holiday without the children. Surely they wouldn't go mad in her absence. They'd only be alone for the one night, then they'd motor down to Launceston tomorrow to collect their grandmother. Evan had his Ps. He was a responsible boy, wasn't he? And Natalie would behave herself when her grandmother was around and not throw any hissy fits, wouldn't she? Aisling had them well warned. They'd be messaging her every hour of the day and night anyway to tell on each other. She'd be demented, but they were booked and going now. She couldn't turn back.

'Don't worry about us, Mum.' Natalie slipped an arm around her waist and let her head rest against Aisling's chest. 'We'll be fine with Gran.'

Stroking the soft lengths of her daughter's fair hair, Aisling bristled inwardly. Why should Lily Fitz get all the quality time? These moments with Natalie had become rare. Okay, so it wasn't just because she was twelve and becoming a bit hormonal, but her own crazy work schedule took its toll. The warmth of her baby girl made her want to stay. But in her heart, Aisling knew she'd have worked all summer anyway and only begrudgingly taken her foot off the pedal for a week before the two went back to school. She'd worked her backside off to rise up the ranks in that company. It occurred to her now as she kissed her kids goodbye that maybe all that going the extra mile might be her undoing.

'The eagle has landed,' Mick announced, smiling at his phone as they sat in Dubai Airport, Aisling beside him rifling in her new travel bag for a painkiller.

'I still don't know why your mother insisted on going all the way to Tasmania to mind our two,' she huffed.

'Ah sure, 'tis a holiday for her,' Mick replied, 'and won't we get a couple of weeks with her when we get back into the bargain?'

He didn't need a response to sense her seething into the bowels of that overpriced handbag he hoped she'd got free through her work. Aisling had never been his mother's biggest fan. His dad, God rest him, had loved Aisling's spirit, but warned him early on she mightn't be the easiest woman to live with. Jack Fitzgerald could be laughing somewhere now at the irony of the pair of them heading off to West Cork and his mother having landed Down Under. By rights, his dad should have been enjoying the trip with her. There wasn't a day went by in the two years since he'd passed when Mick didn't think of him and wish he were still around. 'Apple of your mother's eye' Jack used to call him. As the youngest of their four boys, maybe he was a bit spoilt, but he wouldn't swap his mother for worlds.

'She's a great bit of stuff,' he said, mostly to himself as Aisling closed her eyes. 'Are you all right, Ash?' he asked.

'Just tired, Mick,' she said, turning her head away.

She'd been saying that a lot of late. Being promoted to state manager of one of Australia's biggest retail chains had been a huge boon for them financially. But it had come at a price. He'd always been happy to keep the household running while Aisling travelled or put in the long hours, but as a paramedic, he had his own share of stresses. He'd just come out of a crazy Christmas and had been flat out with the influx of tourists. They could both do with a break. He'd been blown away by his family's kindness when they'd clubbed together for this holiday. Although he didn't labour the point, he'd mentioned to his parents a few years back that he'd always wished they could spend longer in Ireland when they came home and explore places they'd never had time to visit. It wasn't without a twinge of sadness that he acknowledged they were travelling in part on his dad's life insurance policy.

It mightn't be the kind of dream holiday Aisling talked about, but they'd have a decent break together. He nodded off himself, imagining the guesthouse in West Cork his mother had booked, the smell of the sea, the cooked Irish breakfasts and the time alone with his cranky, overworked, overtired but amazing wife.

# Chapter Two

Lilian Fitzgerald drove the small Toyota into the service station at Shearwater. She'd been given instructions to use Mick's runabout and had just managed to drop her granddaughter off at a friend's when the orange fuel light turned red. Mick had apologised for not having filled up in the rushed handwritten note that had lain beside the keys on the otherwise clear kitchen bench. Lilian wasn't sure which surprised her more, the fact that there was something on the bench or that her super-organised daughter-in-law had over-looked the task of refuelling the car.

Which pump was it now? The blue or the yellow? Natalie would have known. But it wasn't as if she could leave it until she collected the child from her friend's. There was no way she'd risk getting stranded. Jack would have known, of course. He'd been the driver on previous visits. But she had been learning to cope, changing light bulbs, unplugging drains. How hard could it be to fill a car with fuel in Australia? She glanced over her shoulder. A man towing a boat was filling up at the pumps opposite. *The dumbest question is the one you don't ask*, she reminded herself.

'Excuse me,' she called out.

The man looked up. Lilian caught the smouldering expression and hoped it was more ageing good looks than annoyance. *I'll never see him again*, she reasoned.

'I'm just at a loss as to which colour I need.' She smiled hopefully.

He gave the car a critical look-over. 'Blue's cheaper.'

'Thanks,' she said, but he'd already returned his attention to the meter on his own side.

*Could have been a bit more friendly*, Lilian mused as she filled the tank.

Inside, the attendant didn't look too cheery either.

'Having a busy day?' she ventured, handing over the card Mick had left on the bench.

The young man grumbled something incomprehensible through a handsome black beard, but the weariness in his face said yes, a very busy day. God love him. He didn't look like he was from here either. Indian, Pakistani? How would you know? If she mentioned the wrong one, he might get offended. Aussies were funny about being called Kiwis, she remembered Mick telling her. And didn't Canadians go mad if you thought they were American? Let's face it, if anyone called her English, she'd be a bit peeved.

'Where are you from?' The safest option.

'I'm from India,' he said, his shoulders squaring as he handed back Mick's card.

'Oh, that's one place I'd love to go.' Did every customer who'd never been to India tell him this? 'The festivals . . .' It was the only thing she could think of apart from Lady Di outside the Taj Mahal on her thirtieth birthday.

The shoulders slumped again. 'Today is a big festival. You know the harvest one?' She smiled to encourage him despite not having the first clue. His hands circled above the counter. 'Whole family come together, eating . . .'

What a beautiful smile, Lilian thought, from the pearly white teeth framed by the thick beard to the dark shining eyes. If she looked closely, she fancied she might see India in them.

'Oh God love you and you here working while they're all partying at home.'

He shrugged.

'My son and his family live here,' she went on. 'They hate working on St Patrick's Day. I've heard –'

The bell tinkled as the door opened behind her. 'I'd better go. We'll talk again . . .' She looked at his badge. 'Sanjeev.'

As she went out, the boatman shuffled past, without as much as a nod.

Declan Byrne sat in his surgery typing up the last of his notes on a difficult root canal where the patient had wasted ten minutes of his precious consultation time needing to be reassured that the procedure was necessary. Ungrateful bastard, he thought, hovering the mouse over the Other Comments section before leaving it blank. There was a time when a patient said 'Hello', 'Goodbye' and let you get on with the job you were highly trained to do. But in this age of equality and entitlement, they all thought they were experts. Half of them probably googled their procedure before they came in. No wonder they were terrified.

Declan had seen firsthand a rise in what he viewed as a misplaced empowerment in patients. In his mid-fifties, and in some ways at the height of his career given his experience, he wasn't sure he could face another ten years before retirement. Glancing over at the framed degree and diplomas on his office wall, the class of '87 popped into his head as it had done so frequently in recent months. He'd discovered the graduation photo in his latest house move, his classmates smiling in their gowns, throwing mortarboards in the air. Heady days, he remembered, before the grind of life descended and they all became cogs in the wheel. Should probably be grateful, he thought. Some of them were no longer around.

'Declan.' Siobhan, the dental nurse whose job was as much to maintain a sense of calm as give technical support in the treatment room, came in holding out a brochure. 'Colette from downstairs dropped in a few of these. Mags thinks you could do with a break.'

'Does she now?' He eyed her over his glasses.

Margaret Logan had been trying to run his life for twenty years. He'd inherited her from old George Powell when he'd retired and sold up. George had assured him he wouldn't find a better dental assistant and insisted Mags be kept on in the practice as part of the handover. God knows, there'd been times he could have happily reneged on his promise, like when she'd got the promotion to practice manager, wheedling away at him while trying to make him think it was all his own idea. But she'd been loyal. You couldn't buy that nowadays no matter what you offered. He just wouldn't share the belief with Mags.

Taking the brochure from Siobhan, he saw the stone farmhouse with its brightly painted green front door and white-sash windows, a garden path sweeping down towards the sea.

'Escape to West Cork,' he read aloud, but Siobhan and her ever-expanding bump had already left him to it. Maternity leave: that was another item on the never-ending to-do list. Why did people have to have babies? As his heart began to race in his chest, he reached down to the bottom desk drawer for something to calm the anxiety, but the brochure held his attention. Whether it was the lure of the rugged coastline or the comforting image of the house, he wasn't sure, but he couldn't remember the last time he'd taken a holiday.

At The Elysian, Declan parked the Lexus in the iconic building's underground car park and took the lift to his tenth floor apartment. Nestled between neighbours whose faces he never saw long enough to recognise, he tapped one of his regular orders into his Uber Eats app. Finding the last clean glass in the cupboard, he poured himself a red wine. It was a weeknight; he'd keep it to the one bottle. Throwing himself on the sofa, he flicked through Netflix for the latest series of Scandi noir he could binge-watch. When the door buzzed, he hauled himself up to collect his dinner, but as he went to resume his position, the guesthouse brochure caught his eye from where it had spilled out of his laptop bag on the coffee table. Distracted, he hardly tasted the meal and lost the thread of the episode. Despite the cold, he took his wine and ventured out onto the balcony. Ignoring the seldom-used furniture where leaves decayed in rain pools, he took in the vista he was paying through the nose for.

On the crisp dry night, he could see all the way to the North Side to where the red-lit cross on the Gurranabraher church glowed amid the city's silhouette. So, Mags reckoned he needed a holiday? He'd caught them, Mags and Siobhan, on more than one occasion, exchanging meaningful looks, talking about him in hushed tones. Idle talk, office bitching, he'd told himself, but Mags was above that and Siobhan, to be fair, was his longest-serving nurse. So many young, enthusiastic girls hadn't stuck around. One hadn't even served her notice. Shelly, that was her name. A tall leggy girl with a head of ebony hair he used to imagine brushed out over that olive skin instead of constantly tied back in a work bun. Not that he ever mentioned such a fantasy directly, but he remembered now how she'd flounced into his office, accusing him of being the most arrogant, chauvinistic man she'd ever met and declaring she quit. If he wasn't nit-picking about small errors in her work, she'd told him, he was hitting on her or one of the other girls.

It wasn't his fault if he liked to have a couple of pretty women to brighten up his practice. He was only human. But technicians, other dentists, had all moved on too. Even Malouf, the easygoing Syrian their patients loved, had recently mentioned the possibility of moving to Dublin. Things were starting to slip. Patient numbers were down. Only last week one had asked how to go about making a complaint.

He'd always prided himself on the impeccable stand-ards and excellent reputation of Declan Byrne & Associates. Leaning on the balcony, he looked down over the lights and lines of cars passing back and forth and wondered how things had got so bad. Even his sons didn't want much to do with him anymore. As much as he hated to admit it, he should have seen it all coming the day Karen Byrne walked out.

━

In his shop in West Cork, Conor Fox undid the top and bottom bolts and pulled open the old narrow doors to let in his first customer of the day.

'Morning, Orla. You're in early,' he greeted the woman he'd known since childhood. Like himself, she was one of those residents who'd received every sacrament that punctu-ated their lives in the local church, save marriage of course. At fifty-five, he'd accepted that to be a most unlikely prospect.

''Tis nearly a day's work I have done, Conor,' she said, lifting the plastic cover of the buggy to reveal a sleeping Ava, the youngest of her growing squad of grandchildren. 'Between the farm, the house, her nibs here, not to mind helping out with the bit of housekeeping down at the neigh-bours . . . I'm run ragged.'

She parked Ava to one side of the shop and helped herself to a shopping basket.

'Aren't you very good to be giving Ellen O'Shea a hand on top of it all?'

'Ah d'you know it gets me out of the house,' she said, digging her list out of the pocket of her jacket. 'Sure isn't it the most exciting thing to happen around these parts in a winter in years?'

'Can't argue with you there, Orla.'

The imminent opening of the new guesthouse was indeed a great source of interest in the small community. Summers could always be relied upon to bring in the tourists, guaranteeing a much-needed cash injection for local businesses, but Conor had spent enough lonesome winters here to appreciate what Ellen O'Shea and her partner Gerry were trying to do. They were his new best customers, sharing much of their patronage between himself and the food producers around the area. Lizzie O'Shea would be proud. Long dead now, she'd raised her four children in that farmhouse. Ellen's father and an aunt in America were the only ones left. He remembered Ellen standing here in his shop only a year before and she on a rare visit from Australia. Always a lovely girl, he'd known she was genuine when she'd told him how she loved that house. Hard to believe how much she'd done in a year, enlisting her builder brother and an interior designer friend to transform the place.

'So how is it going down there?' he asked, taking the heavy basket Orla had filled to the gunnels and lifting it onto the conveyor.

'Oh, 'tis fabulous,' she said. 'Ellen is like a hen with an egg getting ready for opening on Saturday, but she has nothing to fear. She's after buying beautiful ware and the linen . . . you wouldn't get it in the Waldorf Hotel.'

Conor had to smile. Between Netflix and a recent first holiday abroad, Orla was full of references to people and places far beyond the old O'Shea farm.

'And how is Eamon coping with the prospect of so many neighbours?'

'Don't talk to me about him,' she began. 'You'd swear 'twas Downton Abbey they were running.'

Leaning her considerable weight on the other end of the counter, she launched into one of the stories Conor dreaded when the shop was full of customers but welcomed on a wintry day in January like this when only a handful of souls would come over the door.

'You should've heard him up at home last night,' she was saying. 'Gave them all a good talk about keeping up the standards of the place . . . "There's to be no drama, no screaming and bawling from any of ye," he said.' She shook her head and deepened her voice as she continued to quote her husband. '"Our house and farm will be non-intrusive elements in this idyllic landscape, not a sideshow."' She gave a drawn-out roll of her eyes. 'A sideshow! Can you believe it?'

Her tale was interrupted by Matt from the kennels, almost a local himself if it wasn't for that funny accent of his.

'G'day,' he said, breezing in with the jacket open and the sleeves of it pushed up like it was a fine spring day.

'Do you not feel the cold at all, Matt?' Orla asked.

He smiled and shrugged the shoulders of his lean frame. 'Too busy, I reckon.'

Conor imagined the comment might be enough of a spur

to get Orla moving, but she stayed where she was, watching as Matt handed over an A4 sheet.

'Another mutt in need of a home?'

Matt sucked in a breath. 'Afraid so. But they're not always this handsome.'

Orla peered over the page where a chunky bassett hound looked into the camera with a pair of the most doleful eyes Conor had ever seen on a hound.

'A real heartbreaker, that one.'

'Don't fall for it, Conor,' Orla warned. 'You have enough to be doing without taking in a stray.'

'I'll put him in the window for you,' he told Matt. Orla was probably right.

'Lovely boy,' Orla remarked as soon as Matt left the shop. 'Funny how he ended up here.'

'He is indeed.' Conor made himself look busy, hunting in a drawer for Blu Tack and going to the window to display the poster. Taking the hint at last, Orla assembled her shopping bags on the handles of the buggy and tucked in the knitted blanket around her granddaughter.

'I'd better get home and make his lordship his Starbucks,' she said.

Conor laughed and shook his head as he saw her out. Orla was gas, always up for a chat and a laugh. The polar opposite to the shy, retiring Eamon O'Shea but the perfect foil, he had no doubt. Those two had been together since high school. Sometimes he envied them their long and happy relationship. There'd been a time when he'd have imagined having the same.

—

In her basement apartment in Brooklyn, Katie Daly undid all seven locks on her front door and picked her way up the icy steps where the sun wouldn't make an impact until later that morning. She let herself in to the hardware store at ground level and waited for Chad Verebeau to finish his casual conversation with a customer she didn't recognise. He could have been a client of her own, one of the many people whose money worked its way into her bank account in that contactless, impersonal way that suited her just fine.

Chad's youngest raced out from the back of the shop, which, along with the upstairs, made up the Verebeau family home. Spotting Katie, he slowed down, hooked an arm around his father's leg and gave her a shy smile. She looked at him from under her trilby but didn't smile back. She paid her rent, gave them no trouble and avoided any unnecessary overtures that might make her appear as a convenient babysitter.

'Just dropping in the key in case you need to get in,' she told Chad, setting the key on the counter and ignoring the nod from the departing customer.

'Sure,' he said. He picked up the child and beamed at her. 'You have a safe trip now, Miss Kate.'

He wasn't the worst of them, she had to admit. His parents had run the store for all of their married lives before retiring and moving into a small house out of town. The younger Verebeaus had been kind enough to let their arrangement with Katie stand.

'I'll be back in under two weeks,' she said. 'Keep an eye on the pipes.'

He shook his head and smiled. 'I sure will, Miss Kate.'

A couple of years before, she'd gone to her friend's for Christmas and had had to extend her stay while the fallout of a burst pipe in the basement was sorted out. A terrible inconvenience. Just as well her computer had been up high enough so as not to lose all her files. Sometimes she thought the hours spent at her desk in that basement running her business were the only thing keeping her sane.

As she walked along the streets of what had been her long-time home, the smart black suitcase snagged on lumps of ice and snow that was turning into a dirty mush. With her breath making hazy clouds in the freezing air, she kept her head down, avoiding eye contact with passers-by. At the station, she pulled her thick wool cape around her and stamped her feet, willing the bus to hurry up. She'd take the long way to the airport. It was cheap and besides, she was already investing enough in this trip to Ireland where she would spend the week she was dreading in West Cork. It would be enough to honour the debt to her sister it had only taken thirty-five years to repay.

# Chapter Three

Although he wasn't sure why, Declan Byrne hadn't been able to get past the thought of a break in that guest-house. He might ask Colette Barry from downstairs for a few more details if he caught up with her in the car park as he sometimes did after work. But wasn't she only a flight of stairs away? He'd taken to using the lift of late, which wasn't doing his expanding paunch any good. As he swivelled now between his desk and a patient, holding an X-ray up to the light, it occurred to him that walking to and from his car was about the height of the fresh air he was getting these days. It hadn't always been that way. As a younger man he'd been a keen hillwalker, conquering Carrauntoohil – Ireland's highest mountain – countless times, even taking the kids up Ben Nevis on a holiday in Scotland one year. Might be just what he needed to get back on track. A get-away-from-it-all with a few rejuvenating walks in the bracing wintry weather thrown in.

'He'll need four extractions,' Declan announced to the mother of his thirteen-year-old patient.

The boy put his hands to his face and started to whimper.

'You're better to have them out now while you're still growing than to have a mouth full of heethers for the rest of your life.'

His attempt at humour didn't appear to be helping.

'It'll be all right, Jamie,' his mother soothed, but with a withering look added, 'I'm sure the dentist knows best.'

He left them to make the necessary appointments with Mags and wrote up his notes. But before checking the details of his next patient, he searched up the guesthouse he couldn't get out of his head. On the website, the place looked idyllic. It wasn't so much the comfortable interior – although Colette was obviously a pro – but the landscape that captivated him: the sea in all its splendour stretching out from the property, waves crashing against cliffs nearby, seabird colonies persisting on desolate edges of coastline. He'd forgotten how much he loved the great outdoors. And although he wouldn't say so out loud, he might well have forgotten his roots.

'Back in a mo,' he called to Mags before pushing open the main glass door of the practice and descending the curving mahogany staircase to the ground floor. Her office door ajar, he could see Colette was on a call. Annoyed at finding her occupied, he went to the hallway to check the stock of his own brochures. A good thing he had, as Fabulous Four Walls had strategically placed their propaganda so as to obscure his business cards and leaflets on oral health. Even the poster for Edwina and Prue's language school on the second floor was hardly visible for the generous bouquet of fresh flowers burgeoning out from an enormous vase Colette had no doubt deemed superior to any of her neighbours' attempts at advertising. He rearranged the display to his own advantage and went back to see if the interior designer was free.

'Declan Byrne, is that you skulking around our offices?'

The woman was nothing if not direct. Before he could reply by explaining his presence in his own building, she went on.

'No, I'm not available for a drink after work and actually, if you haven't heard, I'm in a relationship.'

*Lucky bastard*, he thought, still begrudging all the other knockbacks he'd received when he'd asked her out, assuming she was single after her divorce.

'I'm happy to hear it,' he said, swallowing the pang of envy he felt for whoever had managed to get the small but perfectly formed forty-something between the sheets. Standing in the doorway, he saw her eyebrows arch in surprise. 'I'm just down to ask about that place you renovated in West Cork.'

She eyed him for a moment, like one would assess an adversary, no doubt still questioning his motivation. 'Would you like to come in?' she asked, her tone softer.

'I don't have long . . . between patients,' he started.

She indicated one of a pair of cream leather chairs as he followed her into the spartan office. He hadn't seen much of what they'd made of it since Fabulous Four Walls had taken over what had been a dowdy seventies suite of insurance offices. They'd insisted on giving the outside a facelift and all. At the time, Declan had hardly been able to abide the constant drone of machinery from outside, but he had to admit that the months of mess and noise had paid dividends. Customers were always commenting on the building's modern look. The extra free parking spaces at the back were another bonus for all concerned. He'd never mentioned any of this to Colette or her boss, John Buckley, who occupied the larger front office. In fact, he barely saw either of them. After he'd parked his Lexus round the back in the mornings, it was upstairs, into his practice for the day and straight back out at night. Apart from the odd hopeful overture to Colette, there was no need for small talk with the neighbours and anyway, he had Mags to deal with any common business that cropped up from time to time.

Declan sat down, taking in the space as Colette walked over to the window from where he could see the River Lee rushing seaward in swirls of white against what must be a spring tide. He hardly noticed the Lee from his own rooms.

'It's a fantastic location,' Colette was saying. 'A bit of a trek from here, of course. You'd need a few days at least. Ellen is hoping people will stay for a week. She's running it with her partner, Gerry Clancy. Do you know The Stables down The Mall?'

Declan nodded. He had indeed frequented the city centre pub/restaurant, though more to drink than eat.

'Gerry is one of the sons. He helped myself and Ellen's brother with the renovation.' Colette paused for a moment, looking at him intently again. 'It's Ellen's brother I'm going out with.'

'Ah, very good,' he said, less to show interest than to assuage her obvious need to drive home the point that she was currently unavailable.

Assuming a professional tone, she carried on with details of the accommodation before asking, 'There's an opening week special, actually . . .'

She certainly had his attention now. It was a crazy time to be spending money on non-essential travel, but at a bargain price . . .

'Would you be going on your own or –'

'Alone,' he said, wishing she hadn't asked.

She began listing optional activities like mindfulness meditation and cooking demonstrations, but he'd lost interest. He just needed a break. They could keep their hippy entertainment package.

'I appreciate it, Colette,' he said rising from the chair. 'Best get back.'

'Good to see you,' she said a little hesitantly, but he was grateful. It was one of the few normal conversations he'd ever had with the woman. He could cross her off his list. No matter, there was always Plenty of Fish.

~

Taking the stairs for a change, Declan scrolled through his phone for Geoff White's number. That old codger was always after work to keep up his registration. If he was available at short notice . . . The dentist answered after two rings.

'Geoff, old bean!'

Their locum was available next week but not again until a couple of months time. It was now or never. Putting his phone back in his pocket, he took the last of the stairs before striding into his rooms to announce his decision.

'Mags, I'm taking a week off.'

He might as well have been any random who had walked in and said 'Freeze'. Mags's mouth opened as if to say something, but nothing came out.

'Geoff's happy to cover,' he told her. 'Malouf might squeeze in a few extras . . .'

'When would you be thinking of going?' she asked, her voice uncharacteristically croaky.

'Next week,' he said. 'And could you book that place you were promoting? A room with a sea view if at all possible.' He made to join Siobhan, but turned to clarify. 'Not some cramped back room. And try to avoid that over-the-top mezzanine thingy.'

In the treatment room, he pumped the hand sanitiser dispenser and took a seat beside his next patient.

'Mrs Twomey, sorry to keep you waiting.'

Siobhan looked at him like a stunned mullet.

'Sorry, Declan,' she said in a deviation from her usual quiet professionalism, 'but you know I go midweek?' He looked at her blankly. 'On maternity leave.'

'Oh yes, of course,' he said. 'But isn't your cover coming in tomorrow?' He smiled at the supine Mrs Twomey, who was taking it all in. 'I'm sure yourself and Mags can show her the ropes.'

He pulled on a pair of surgical gloves and fixed a fresh mask over his mouth and nose. He was going on holiday. The staff could deal with contingencies at the practice. God knew he paid enough in salaries. The Gortex gear would have to be pulled out of storage. Did those hill-walking boots he'd bought in Scotland survive the moves? He glanced at his watch. Mrs Twomey's filling, a couple of routine checks and polishes, and he'd be out of here. He'd start packing tonight.

'Where are you off to?' his patient asked.

'West Cork, Mrs Twomey,' he said as he prepared the anaesthetic to deaden her jaw.

'A bit cold this time of year.'

He smiled again but cut her off with an authoritative, 'Open wide', before inserting his needle and pressing firmly on the syringe whose contents would shut her up and bring the spur-of-the-moment holiday closer.

# Chapter Four

Lilian took off her flip-flops and set them near the breakwater that hugged the shoreline at Freers Beach. Natalie had been determined they walk to the tiny rocky outcrop of Penguin Island at low tide. Lilian was grateful they had set off early. At 9 a.m. it was already warm as they crossed the wide stretch of rippled sand, pockmarked with hundreds of holes, where an army of soldier crabs she was at pains to avoid scuttled about.

'Don't worry, Gran,' Natalie reassured her, 'they're not interested in biting you or anything. They're too busy filtering food from the sand.'

Lilian looked at her granddaughter in admiration. Under that head of fine sun-kissed hair was a brain for facts she and Jack had always loved hearing.

'When the tide comes in, they'll be safe in air pockets in their burrows.'

'That's amazing,' said Lilian, keeping one eye on where they were going and another on the tiny Trojans just in case of a nip.

With the tide still going out, they crossed a shallow pool where the sand dropped off into a gully just below the rise of rocks at the island's edge. Natalie led the way, finding the flattest surfaces for Lilian to plant her feet. At the top, they stood together, surveying the swathe of sparkling sea between them and Bakers Beach, where they could make out a couple heading in for a swim. Looking back the way they'd come, Lilian recognised the local surf club and took in the other two-storey buildings, beautiful well-kept houses with these views.

'It's no wonder your father doesn't want to leave here,' she said, thinking aloud.

Natalie frowned. 'It's far from Ireland, isn't it, Gran?' And without waiting for an answer, she added, 'I always wish you could stay longer. Would you ever think about living with us now that you don't work anymore?'

Lilian gave a wry laugh. 'And what would your cousins in Cork say to that?'

'But they're all grown up, Gran, and you minded them way more than us when they were younger.'

Twelve or no twelve, the child made a fair argument. Lilian and Jack had done their best to visit when circumstances and funds allowed, but she had indeed missed out on much of Natalie and Evan's childhoods. It was time she couldn't take back. How ironic now that time was something she had in surfeit. Her Irish grandchildren loved her for sure, as did their fathers and indeed the lovely partners her sons had been lucky enough to marry. No, everything on the family front at home was hunky dory, couldn't complain there. But they all had their own lives. She'd raised her four sons to be independent.

It was what she and Jack had worked hard to achieve. Work hard, set the kids up, enjoy retirement. He should have been here with her now, happily exploring with their youngest grandchild along the chain of golden beaches on Mick and Aisling's doorstep.

*Present moment*, she reminded herself, taking a deep breath of warm air and feeling her tummy expand. A month in the southern summer; a lot to be grateful for. No need to let in the dread of what the remaining months of the year would entail. She'd cope. She'd have to.

'Come on,' she said to Natalie. 'Let's enjoy the time we have right now.'

The girl looked at her thoughtfully. She was an old soul. Another child might have whinged and laboured the point, but for all her innocence, Natalie had a maturity beyond her years.

'Can we have those ice creams for morning tea when we get back?'

'Why not?' As Lilian knew only too well, life was far too unpredictable to miss an opportunity to eat ice cream on a searing hot day with someone you loved.

—

Under the pergola in the backyard, Lilian and Natalie stretched out on opposite ends of the corner lounge, licking ice creams in companionable silence. Charlie, the smoky kitten, looked at her through slits of eyes from where he was lying on the cool tiles and gave a low dreamy mew. As she began to meditate on the moment of intense pleasure, there was a crunching of footsteps over gravel. Straightening up on the sofa, she swung her legs round and turned to find Mick's neighbour coming round the side of the house.

'Heather! I was in another world.'

She was up on her feet and over with arms outstretched, the sleeves of her lemon linen shirt falling loosely round her freckled arms. As they hugged, she breathed in the smell of something sophisticated. The beauty therapist oozed the kind of poise Lilian had always admired.

'You're looking radiant as ever,' Heather told her. 'You have such beautiful skin.'

'And you're as kind as ever,' said Lilian, hoping the girl was sincere in her assessment that she didn't look like a complete wreck and might actually be ageing gracefully.

'I was so sorry to hear about Jack.' A frown gathered between the impeccably shaped eyebrows.

'Thank you, sweetheart. It's been very hard.'

Heather reached out a hand and rubbed her arm. She was a beautiful soul, always inviting them over for barbecues when she and Jack visited. Such a shame her husband had strayed.

'Hey Natalie,' said Heather, turning her attention to the child. 'How's Charlie doing?'

Natalie scooped the kitten up beside her, letting him lick from the remains on the lolly stick. 'He's a sweet boy,' she said, cuddling the pet in close and giving him several rubs with her cheek.

'Maybe *we* should get a cat,' said Heather. 'Might get my two off their phones.'

She laughed, but Lilian was in no doubt how challenging it could be for parents to get children away from screens.

A couple of her grandchildren in Ireland had tested their parents on that front. Natalie's quirky personality might drive her mother crazy at times, but Aisling couldn't complain about her daughter's preference for good old-fashioned play over technological entertainment. While so many young people were caught up in the minutiae of other people's lives, Natalie was content reading books and studying the natural world around her. When they'd presented the child with the longed-for kitten on her birthday, Mick reported that she'd taken to the mobile phone she was rarely seen with to make Charlie an Instagram account. Following it keenly to show support, Lilian had noticed the rush of cute kitty photos, falling off to only the odd post every couple of weeks. No harm, she'd thought, admiring the child's independence of social media.

'My dad is here for a few weeks,' Heather told them once the kitten had been duly acknowledged. 'I wondered if you'd join us for tea.'

'That's so lovely of you.' Lilian hadn't met Heather's father, but if he was anything like his daughter, he'd be great company. She wasn't sure she'd be up to the kind of scintillating conversation the man might be used to, but they all had to eat. At least she'd be spared preparing dinner for a night. 'What night were you thinking?'

'Would tonight be good?'

Lilian hesitated as she thought about the arrangements involved. There was her grandson to consider, not to mention making something to take along, and of course she would have to look respectable . . .

'Can we, Gran?' Natalie gave her one of her most beseeching looks.

'I'll have to see what Evan is doing –'

'He's working, remember?' Natalie didn't wait for a response. 'Come on, Gran. You'll even get to meet someone your own age.'

The two women burst out laughing.

'That settles it, then,' said Lilian.

'See you ladies, six-ish?' Heather gave Lilian a covert wink before leaving them to their afternoon tucked away in the garden.

# Chapter Five

Declan reached out from under his thick winter duvet and checked his phone. Oh Christ, he was supposed to be halfway to West Cork by now. Sitting on the edge of the bed, he let the spinning in his head subside before ambling over to the window and opening the curtains. The dull light of the foggy January morning washed in over the unkempt bedroom. Scratching at his overnight stubble, he padded down the corridor to the kitchen where he switched on the coffee machine, hoping the caffeine would counteract the effects of the two bottles of red he'd consumed the night before. He thought to put the empties and the takeout food containers in the recycling, but the cleaners would be in this morning. Wasn't that what he paid them for?

In the shower, he lathered soap over the flab of his belly, gasping at the onslaught of cold water on his skin as the shower took its time to warm up. Shampooing what hair he had left, he berated himself for not finishing the packing last night and being ready to go at the dawn – another of his good intentions. A shave would have to wait. This was a rare opportunity for a break from the humdrum. A week away from the demands of the practice, the patients, the staff. With any luck, it might even give him a chance to get back on track on the health front.

An hour later, he was motoring. The fog had lifted, but a low ceiling of cloud persisted as he travelled out of the city and into the winter landscape of bare trees and frosty fields, the breath of sheep and cattle visible in the air. He turned the seat's heat pad up a notch and settled in for the journey through the rural townships he'd been familiar with as a boy, but rarely visited as an adult. Thailand or somewhere in the Med might have been a better place to head in the middle of winter, but he was on his way now. He'd paid his money, he'd take his chances.

━

The Lexus got him to Crookhaven in under two hours. He may have broken the speed limit in the few places the road allowed, but he'd wanted to make up for the slow going through the plethora of congested one-horse towns with small-minded characters jaywalking aimlessly across their narrow main streets. There was a time when these places would have charmed him, but today he just wanted to get down the road without bringing up the sentimentality of his past. The village of Goleen, a stone's throw from Crookhaven itself, was his one stop, made only to check the address of the guesthouse. Goleen had hardly changed in forty years. If anything, it looked quieter than he remembered. In the time it took him to tell the navigation system where to take him, not a single soul appeared on the footpaths and only one car went past. *Getting away from it all,* he mused, setting course for Crookhaven and the final few kilometres.

As he rounded the last bend, the sea came into view, stirring in him something unexpected, akin to the surprise at bumping into an old friend you hadn't seen in years. The photo of his graduation day flashed across his mind, but he suppressed the image, concentrating on the voice of his in-car guide.

A prominent sign at the side of the road was enough to make Siri's directions unnecessary. The beachy pastels and cheery lettering stood out against the dull backdrop of grey clouds and shadowy fields. He took the turn-off and followed the road to an open farm gate with another sign directing him into a gravel driveway where he could finally see the old farmhouse he'd been so unexpectedly driven to visit. As he parked in one of the bays delineated by yellow-painted sleepers, a woman looked up from where she was gathering sticks into a wicker basket in the garden beyond.

'Hello,' he called, getting out of the car and taking in her smiling face and trim figure as she walked towards him.

*Forty-ish,* he thought. *Not bad for her age.* He took her outstretched hand and felt the softness of her skin. *Definitely not a farmer.*

'I'm Ellen,' she said, the smile broadening between wisps of fair hair that fell from a loose ponytail. 'Welcome to Lizzie O's. You must be Declan.'

After the warmth of the car, the wind from the Atlantic threatened to cut through him. He grabbed his gear from the boot and was grateful to follow her into the house where the traditional façade belied a modern interior. This was the work of Colette Barry. He wanted to let out a low whistle as he took in the whitened floorboards and sisal-clad staircase, but this Ellen was on to the welcome spiel about how they'd updated the old family home and called it after her grandmother.

'You can hang up your coat there, if you like,' she was saying, pointing to a vintage hallstand in that distressed style he'd seen in the magazines Mags brought in for the waiting room. There were already a couple of coats hanging there, but no sign of other guests as yet.

In the *parlour*, as the woman called it, a long cream sofa sat facing an inglenook fireplace where flames crackled around a pile of blackened logs. He noticed a chaise longue at the far end of the room and a couple of occasional tables with lamps and books placed invitingly between them. In truth, he could have thrown himself down there and then, but he wasn't going to give Colette too much credit until he'd seen where he was to sleep.

Before he could enquire about his room, Ellen was halfway down the hall, telling him about her optional home-cooked meals and the activities Colette had mentioned in which, at this point in time, he had little interest. Again, the modern kitchen surprised him, but it was the conservatory that impressed most. He took in the space that ran the length of one side of the house, a large dining table in the middle, other smaller tables set at the edges and a couple of easy chairs facing out to sea. A pair of binoculars rested on the extensive windowsill that hosted an array of pot plants without compromising the view out over the Atlantic. Memories of his grandfather came to mind unbidden, playing in his head like the Mirror dinghy they'd sailed together, darting through the chop down there in the small harbour.

'I'll show you to your room so, Declan.' Ellen interrupted his thoughts and he turned from the windows, not convinced this week could be devoid of nostalgia after all.

At the top of the stairs she crossed the landing and led him to a further staircase, spiralling up from what must have been a small bedroom but was now a cosy library. As they ascended, the smell of pine reminded him of a log cabin they'd rented on a family holiday in Norway. Karen had loved it there. Said she'd felt at peace. He dismissed the thought and concentrated instead on the grey door with the word 'Pebble' painted in white on what looked like a piece of driftwood. Inside, he set down his bag and surveyed the loft space that confirmed his earlier impressions regarding Colette's talent. *Beauty and brains*, he thought, smiling to himself.

'Your ensuite is in there.' Ellen pointed to where a sliding barn-style door stood open enough to see a white robe hanging on the wall and the reflection of a shower cabinet in a gleaming mirror.

Taking in the muted tones of the room and the shabby-chic furnishings, Declan thought it held a certain sophistication he suspected only Colette could pull off. He vowed to take more notice of his neighbour's business on his return. But going back was something he couldn't think about right now. He thanked Ellen, curtly agreed to her offer of tea and scones in the parlour, closed the door of the elevated sanctuary and went to the window, where he stood for a long time looking out to sea.

—

Behind the dusky pink door of the room named 'Coral', Aisling set to work unpacking the suitcases they'd been living out of for the past week. Four nights at her sister's, another three at Mick's eldest brother's. Too long to pack a weekend bag and not long enough to fully unload. She busied herself, transferring the various categories of clothing she'd packed into those handy zipper bags she'd bought in Tasmania into the upcycled wardrobe. Although she'd never have chosen such a piece of furniture for her own house, after closely inspecting it for any offending signs or smells she'd declared it worthy of their clothing and set about filling the wallpaper-lined shelves and hanging her 'good' outfits on scented fabric hangers. She'd read the place had been renovated by one of Ireland's top interior designers. 'Bespoke' was the buzz word in all the articles. The downstairs was amazing and yes, their boho room was growing on her. In keeping with the name, the pinks and oranges of lamps and different-sized vases added interest and brightness to the space, lifting the simple white of the linen and curtains. It was all the cleanliness you'd expect from a hotel room with a good dollop of cosy thrown in. When she'd finished unpacking, she turned to survey the room once again. Just as well there were a few pretty things to look at. She'd need all the distraction possible to survive the week ahead.

Mick was thrown on the solid armchair she suspected had been re-covered in the luxurious chenille with its pattern of books at varying angles. Instead of poring over a classic though, Mick was snoring his head off, feet still in his shoes, up on the comfy pouffe. She wasn't sorry. He could sleep all day if he liked. That way he'd be awake when she'd be asleep, and any awkward bedroom moments might be avoided altogether. Normally she would have zipped up the empty suitcases and tidied them away, but fearing Mick would wake, she left them open on the bed and slipped out of the room.

〜

'Everything okay for you?' Their host looked up from where she was bringing a tray of tea and scones to the parlour.

'Perfect,' said Aisling, breathing in the smell of fresh baking and immediately feeling her stomach growl. Although Mick had indulged in a massive plate of fish and chips in Schull on the way, she hadn't felt hungry until now.

In the parlour, a balding man, older than her, was sitting with a book on the large sofa in front of the fire. Unlike Mick, he'd heeded the invitation to leave his shoes in the hallway and, sporting a pair of thick woollen socks, looked like he was making himself at home. Instinctively, she paused in the doorway, pulled off her full-length boots and doubled back to deposit them beside the hallstand where they'd left their winter coats. When she returned, he was giving her that up and down scan she hated.

'Hi,' she said with a brief nod as she walked straight past him and left Ellen to serve him his scones. He might be contemplating her behind as she perused the bookshelves along the end wall, but at least she didn't have to look at him.

'Would you like tea or coffee, Aisling?'

'Coffee please,' she answered as she turned, eyeing the pottery plate heaped with well-risen scones and the matching bowls of thick cream and jams.

'I'll be right back.'

As Ellen swept out of the room, Aisling had to admire the unassuming yet capable air she had about her.

'Aisling, is it?' Without looking at her, the man eased his lump of a frame to the edge of the sofa and helped himself to the biggest scone, the steam rising off it as he sliced it in half. 'Means dream, doesn't it?'

'That's right,' she said, wishing Mick would join her now and talk to this eejit.

'You're welcome to dig in here,' he said, settling back into the sofa with a plate on his lap and mug of tea in that new pottery she'd seen in the shops in his hand.

Her stomach growled again. *Feck it*, she thought, walking over to the low table and taking him up on his offer. As she bent to take a scone, she was aware of him ogling her top half. She looked up to see crumbs falling on to his Ralph Lauren shirt as he took a massive bite.

Ignoring him, she spread blackberry jam on her scone, topped it with a dollop of cream and sat down at the opposite end of the sofa, grateful for its length.

'Are you here on your own?' she asked before tucking into the welcome treat.

'Yes. Declan,' he answered, setting the scone down on his plate and reaching out his hand. She shook it quickly. 'Just down from Cork for a break. And you?'

If the look on his face was one of hope, she delighted in shattering it. 'I'm here with my husband,' she told him. 'Celebrating our fifteenth anniversary.'

'First marriage?' he asked with a presumption that completely caught her off guard.

'Yes.' She didn't need to tell him about her failed relationship with the father of her first child or how Mick Fitzgerald had taken Evan on as his own from the moment they'd committed their futures to one another. But there she was, reminding herself again of the very commitment she'd betrayed.

Ellen arrived with perfect timing and a cafetière of freshly brewed coffee.

'Have you many in?' Aisling asked her, eager to talk to someone other than this Declan fella. She would remember to bring her phone next time she wanted to sit downstairs.

'We're fully booked for the week,' said Ellen. 'Some guests aren't arriving until tomorrow, so we'll have five for dinner this evening.'

'Are you running all this on your own, Ellen?' Declan asked with a familiarity that irked Aisling. Two minutes in the place and he was on first-name terms asking leading questions.

'Ah no.' Ellen gave a cheerful laugh. 'Gerry will be here soon. He's the domestic god around here.'

Aisling couldn't help but relax a little at the warmth in her voice. Some women were so comfortable in their own skin.

# Chapter Six

'Miss Daly!'

Katie opened her eyes and dragged herself up straight and out of her slumber in the back seat of the car where she must have nodded off soon after she'd been picked up at Cork Airport. With her eyes adjusting to the weak afternoon sunlight, she took in the farmhouse with the green door and mused over the old myth as to what secrets lay beyond. Her spine tingled. The house didn't need to have secrets. She had enough of her own.

As her driver got out, a woman appeared in the doorway, wrapping a loose-fitting sweater around her, holding it together with one hand while giving a friendly wave with the other. If she thought this was cold, Katie thought, she should try one of their winters in the States.

The smell hit her the moment the driver opened the door – a salty mix of freshness and the spoils washed up from the ocean. Her head spun at the assault on her senses. Between the naked branches of the tree-lined garden she glimpsed

the slate-grey sea. Tears smarted at the corners of her eyes.
Unexpected tears. Perhaps this was a mistake, coming here
after all these years, almost unravelling within the first thirty
seconds. No, she was stronger than that. Planting her feet on
the driveway, she took a deep breath and vowed to get through
this week unscathed by memories from a lifetime ago.

'You've got the best room of all,' the friendly woman in
wool was telling her. 'I'm Ellen.' Yes, they'd corresponded
by email. As they shook hands, the woman touched Katie's
elbow. 'You must be exhausted,' she said, looking at her as
if she were about to fall down. 'Come on and I'll show you
where you are.'

Katie smiled inwardly. She knew exactly where she was,
but Ellen O'Shea didn't need to know. She let her lead the
way, acknowledging a certain intrigue as to what had become
of the old O'Shea family home.

Hearing the car, Mick stirred from his sleep and looked
around the funky room he now remembered was to be his
home for a week. Setting his feet on the vibrant rug, he swiped
at the pouffe to remove the bit of grit from where his shoes
had rested. Aisling would not be happy with him if he dirtied
the place. At the window, he drew back the curtains and
looked down over the driveway to where a man in a suit was
holding open the rear door of a sleek black Mercedes. With
his jaw almost at his chest, he watched a woman emerge, a
black trilby hiding most of her cropped blonde hair. A pair
of dark jeans and shiny heeled boots were all he could see

from under a heavy cape-thing probably designed by someone Aisling followed on Instagram. Wait till he told his mother the kind of clientele this place was attracting. He wasn't sure how much herself and his brothers had paid for his anniversary/ birthday gift, but he hoped it wasn't as much as this woman looked like she could afford.

A phone pinged. He felt in the pocket of his hoodie. Nothing. *Must be Aisling's,* he thought, walking over to retrieve it from the bedside table. He'd go downstairs and find her. There'd been mention of afternoon tea. He hoped he hadn't missed it.

Grabbing the phone, he spotted the notification: *Brett Goodstone sent you a message. Hey babe hope you . . .* If someone had punched him in the guts, he mightn't have experienced as much pain. Holding the phone away, he took a step backwards. Was he seeing things? What should he do? Open the message? He threw the phone on the bed and brought his hands to his face. Surely to god, he was overreacting. What was going through his head couldn't be happening. It must be a message from work, or a friend he hadn't yet met. But a friend, at least the platonic variety, didn't say *Hey babe.*

Fighting the urge to look at the full message, he took a deep breath. She'd been prickly, distant these past few weeks, but wasn't she stressed out with the promotion, the buying trips, the responsibility of it all? And she'd been up to high doh planning their holiday and organising the kids. Fifteen years wasn't something to consider throwing away lightly on the basis of an odd, if arresting, text message. He'd join his wife in the bloody parlour and let her explain herself in her own good time. They had a week.

—

There was no denying the transformation the house had undergone. Katie had to stifle gasps of surprise as Ellen showed her through the downstairs before leading her from the beautiful conservatory across a small courtyard to Mussel Manor. Although Ellen joked about the grand title she'd given the tiny cottage, Katie couldn't help staring as they walked through the cheery yellow half-door and into the Scandi interior of what would have been nothing more than a byre when she was young. The parallels with her own transformation struck her as she surveyed the warm space while Ellen left to summon the driver to bring her suitcase. The place was hardly recognisable. With any luck, the same could be said of herself.

When she switched her phone from flight mode, a string of notifications appeared on screen. Bernadette had texted three times.

*Are you there yet?*

*How is Mammy?*

*Text me as soon as you arrive.*

So much for a break, Katie mused. Her sister had begged her for the week-long respite from caring for their mother and the girl hadn't even begun to relax. But that was Bernadette. The eldest, the responsible one of the four siblings. Even when Katie hadn't wanted anything to do with her past, Bernadette had been determined to keep in touch. She'd never been much for writing letters, but she'd made the long-distance phone calls that must have cost her a fortune. Latterly, they'd used apps, but it was Bernadette who always reached out. Their contact was like a loose thread Katie often wished she could sever, but it was a thread Bernadette insisted on maintaining.

Three years her senior, her sister had moved in different circles. At school, she excelled in all her subjects. The nuns had her earmarked for university. At home, her mother encouraged her to study while their father mocked and belittled her, calling her The Professor. She wasn't to get any notions, ideas above her station, he'd tell her. He piled on extra farm chores, making her work beyond dark and before school, but she did it all with a stoicism Katie couldn't comprehend.

Before she'd left for university, Katie asked why she put up with his jibes and putdowns. They were in their bedroom, enjoying a rare spare hour together listening to Radio Luxembourg while their father drank himself stupid at the pub. Tears pooled in her sister's eyes as she stood and slowly lifted her jumper to reveal the pummelled patches of skin that made Katie gasp. As she pulled up a sleeve, it was the same on her arm. 'Don't defy him,' she warned. 'Work hard. You'll get away too eventually.'

She'd asked Finbarr first to take care of their mother, but he'd said he was too busy at work and couldn't take the time off. Their brother worked in Cork, for God's sake. Most of his business was done online. He could have come down here for a week and his customers would have been none the wiser. But according to Bernadette, he'd obliged before. Katie was under no illusion he wasn't trying to make her do her share. He and Bernadette were entitled to think it was about time.

Those two had no idea. She sometimes wondered what Sean
Óg would have made of it all. Poor Sean Óg, the youngest
of the siblings. He'd have maybe been the best of the lot of
them if he'd been given a fair chance.

There was a soft knock on the door.

'Miss Daly.'

She showed the driver in and bid him leave her suitcase
near the door. There would be no gawping at the mezzanine
bedroom. Ellen had wanted to show her up, but she'd declined.
It wasn't the awesome interiors she'd booked this cottage for.
No, it was the distance from other guests. Bernadette had
offered her place in Schull, about twenty minutes away, but
the last thing Katie wanted was to be beholden to anyone.

'If you could just take me to that house I mentioned, I'd
be grateful.'

'No problem,' her driver responded, striding out the door
with a professionalism she had no doubt he'd had to muster
over curiosity.

She followed him out, shuddering at the sight of the
Mercedes Benz. Her intention in hiring a driver had been
merely to avoid the possibility of meeting anyone from her
past on the bus from Cork. A normal, nondescript car would
have done the job perfectly. But no, she'd been the *lucky* recip-
ient of an upgrade, her driver had informed her. Some luck,
she mused. The only thing she liked about the car were its
tinted windows that gave some hope of no one witnessing her
journey to her mother's house, where her ride for the week
awaited. The transition from this status symbol on wheels to

her sister's battered Datsun would be just another fall from grace to set the locals talking.

Obviously delighted to be behind the wheel of a Mercedes, William skilfully manoeuvred the vehicle round the front of the farmhouse and down the gravel driveway. As they neared the road, Katie's stomach began to constrict. She could have holed up in that cottage for the week and returned to her life in the States, but there was no avoiding the promise she'd made to Finbarr and Bernadette.

'She's your mother too,' her sister had railed when Katie argued against Bernadette's proposal that she come and help out. 'It might be your last chance . . .' she'd added, but Katie had stopped her in her tracks with that guilt trip. 'One week,' Bernadette changed tack. 'I'm begging you, Katie. This might be my only chance at happiness.'

Happiness! If ever there was an elusive commodity. Her sister, like most people Katie had ever encountered, was delusional on that front. A week in Alicante with some Spanish hot dog did not imply happiness. They'd met in the pub the summer before, Bernadette had told her. On one of her rare nights off from minding Mammy, Katie supposed. Bernadette could play the martyr all she liked, but if she expected her life to change in the course of a fleeting few days, she was in for a rude awakening. Her mother still wrote the odd letter, but there'd been no mention of any Spaniard.

Katie didn't write back but phoned Phyllis Daly twice a year, on her birthday and Christmas Day. Short, inconsequential connections made out of the same warped sense of duty that had brought her here. She might still call her Mammy, but Phyllis Daly had reneged on that role a long time ago. One week to mind her mother, give her sister the 'much needed break' she'd banged on about. Then she could go back to her own small life.

'Holy God!' William sat straighter at the steering wheel as they took the sharp bend towards the top of the hill behind Goleen.

She should have warned him, but she'd been lost in thought as she'd looked out over the drystone walls and sloping fields to where a broody sea melded with the grey forbidding sky. She'd travelled these roads countless times under far hairier conditions, but there was no abating the rise in adrenaline she felt at the prospect of navigating them herself, not to mind driving on the left, in what her sister described as a reliable old banger, the contradiction in terms obviously lost on Bernadette. But the car was the least of her worries.

'Here,' she called to William as the once-white pillars came into view.

She'd left it too late. He'd overshot. Without a word, he cautiously backed up the Merc before inching into the driveway. The thought of being liable for damage made Katie's eyes close tight, her fear compounded by images that had haunted her for her whole life, memories that might undo her. *One week*, she reminded herself.

When they came to a stop unscathed, she took a deep breath and opened her eyes again to see Phyllis Daly coming out of the house, a walking stick preceding her every shaky step. Reaching the car, she abandoned the stick and worked her way along, touching the vehicle with alternate hands,

leaning in, drawing closer to where Katie sat stunned in the
back seat.

'Mrs Daly.' William was out and coming round to open
the door. For a moment, Katie hesitated, watching her mother,
eagerness written all over her lined face, expectation bright-
ening the watery blue eyes under the shock of hair, now
completely white.

'Mammy.' She finally pushed herself out of the car, with
no choice but to let her mother fall into her.

'Katie!' It was like a cry from someone begging for help.
'You're so good to come.'

In her utter refusal to imagine this moment, Katie hadn't
prepared for her mother's tears, the clinging on to her arms,
the pity that welled up in her own heart she'd believed had
hardened against this woman, thirty-five years before.

While they'd quite literally reconnected, William had taken
her handbag from the back seat and was making his way
to the open front door. Looking after him, Katie's throat
tightened. Pinpricks of cold sweat covered her palms as her
eyes followed the ivy trail from above the doorway along the
upper level to her old bedroom window. How easy it was for
the driver to stride towards the house to which she'd never
wished to return.

'Will I offer him a cup a' tea?' Phyllis asked, still with a
tight hold of one of her arms.

'No, Mammy. I'll let him go now.'

William turned from where he'd dropped the bag in the
hallway. Noticing the walking stick, he picked it up and
handed it to Phyllis.

'Mrs Daly, Miss Daly,' he said with a bow of his head, 'I'll be off. Have a lovely time together.'

'Oh, we have a lot of catching up to do,' said Phyllis, giving Katie's near-numb arm another squeeze.

'Thank you, William,' said Katie. 'I'll see you next weekend.'

She stood there as he eased the car back out between the pillars, watching as the last obstacle between her and the house disappeared.

'Come in till I put on the kettle,' Phyllis was saying as she linked an arm through Katie's elbow and turned her head towards the sky. 'Looks like the heavens are going to open.'

———

Katie took another deep breath as she crossed the threshold of the house that was at once familiar and alien. The smell pricked at her nostrils, demanding attention, firing off memories; the kind of smell you notice in other people's houses but never your own, at least not until you've spent a lifetime away.

'It'll be much as you remember?' Phyllis said with an audible hint of hope.

*All too clearly*, Katie wanted to reply, but she managed a wan smile.

'The lino is new of course,' she continued as Katie followed her across the shiny diamond-patterned floor covering. In the kitchen, the pine units her father had cursed and sworn over installing remained unchanged, as unfashionable now as the multicoloured tiles around the faded work tops. Her mother shuffled between the sink and kettle-stand, filling her in on changes to the home, her tone apologetic, if Katie wasn't mistaken. At least she'd let go of her arm.

'Sit yourself down, girleen,' said Phyllis, beckoning towards the table with a crooked forefinger.

It was a long time since she'd been called *girleen*. Was she still a small girl in her mother's eyes, or was it just one of those Irish terms of endearment, the subtleties of which she'd forgotten with time? She sat on one of the wooden chairs at the rectangular table and watched her mother fill the teapot and cover it with a handmade tea cosy. She'd been a demon for the knitting.

'Will I get that for you?' asked Katie, rising from her seat, unable to watch the painful movements that required both hands.

'No, you're grand, sure. I have it,' Phyllis reassured, hefting the teapot on a tray that had been prepared with cups and the stainless-steel milk jug that never failed to spill. 'Are you still no sugar?'

'I am.' She wanted to tell her that she took everything black these days and tried to avoid sugar like the plague. Phyllis was no doubt too old for the anti-sugar conversation. She wouldn't understand.

'You'll have a biscuit?' she said, taking an unopened packet of Jacob's Chocolate Kimberleys from the cupboard.

A wave of exhaustion made Katie stifle a yawn. Jetlag or the energy it was taking to sit here, she wasn't sure.

'I'm fine.'

Phyllis may have bought in what was once her favourite biscuit specially, but if she thought that kind of sentimentality would somehow ameliorate the hurt Katie had endured in this household, and indeed for most of her adult life so far, she could think again.

'I won't stay long,' she told her. 'They're expecting me for dinner at the guesthouse.'

If her mother was disappointed, she didn't let on. Instead, she sat down opposite and quizzed her on what the O'Sheas had done to the old farmhouse. Katie filled her in, mostly parroting what Ellen had said when she'd shown her round. If nothing else, the stilted conversation provided some distraction from the empty chair at the head of the table. But even as she spoke, the sounds rose in her head, fists on wood, delft and cutlery quaking like the five of them, that invisible line down the middle of the table like the San Andreas fault they'd learnt about in school, chaos and destruction always possible yet unpredictable.

As rain began to spatter against the window, Katie muttered something about getting back. Phyllis walked her out to the hallway and took the car keys from one of the hooks beside the front door. Sean Óg had made the key holder in woodwork in secondary school. Simple things indeed remained unchanged.

'Will you be all right tonight?' said Katie, not allowing herself to be caught up in nostalgia.

Her mother's eyes glistened, but Katie held her resolve. Bernadette had told her she was usually in bed by six. There'd be no point worrying about her. She'd be back to take her to Mass tomorrow. She opened the door and felt the wind gust in, the rain now horizontal.

'God, you'll need to be careful driving the road in that,' Phyllis warned.

'I'll be fine,' she said, denying the dread she felt at getting into the Datsun and braving the winding road in any weather, not to mind this downpour.

'Sure you could have stayed here,' said Phyllis, with only a hint of disapproval.

Katie looked down at where drops of rain were hitting the mat that said *Fáilte*, the Irish word for welcome.

'I couldn't, Mammy.'

As she gave herself a quick lesson in how to operate the gears and switches in her sister's car, Katie was aware of Phyllis watching from the sitting room window. At least she'd had the sense to go inside. Katie lurched out of the driveway and headed for Crookhaven. She'd update Bernadette, let her know she'd been in and would do it all again tomorrow.

'Keep an eye on her,' Bernadette had said. It had sounded so easy, as if thirty-five years of not laying eyes on someone could be forgotten, the reasons somehow diminished. Taking the turn-off to the guesthouse, the tension in her shoulders began to ease. It was one week, but she couldn't focus on the enormity of how that felt. Right now, a nice meal and a bath in that mezzanine bedroom was all she wanted to think about.

# Chapter Seven

When Aisling announced she would go up to their room as she was about to fall into a food coma after the scones, Mick had thought to go with her and have this Brett Goodstone conversation over and done with straightaway. But he wasn't the kind to create a scene and if he upset his wife in their bedroom, she was likely to completely shatter the cosy vibe of the house and the warm contented atmosphere for which its guests, or their families, had paid good money. Instead, he'd taken Declan up on his offer of a stroll to the pub to show him the sights.

There was a comfort to be had in the men's no-strings-attached conversation as they tied up their jackets, headed off down the driveway and turned towards the village. His mother had reminded Mick of their trips to nearby Barleycove when they were small, but he could swear he'd never been to Crookhaven itself. When he said as much to Declan, his companion told him that as a child, he'd spent at least a fort-night here every summer. If Mick detected a note of regret in his voice, he wasn't about to pry. There was no need. They were strangers staying in the same guesthouse, killing an hour before dinner. They didn't have to share the stories of their lives.

Over a welcome pint of Murphy's stout, they talked about the trying times of the Irish rugby team and what Brexit was doing to cross-border relations. When they finished their pint, Mick shouted another round. Only fair to even things up, be able to leave later without obligation. Declan seemed delighted to have someone to talk to. Even the owner joined in the conversation in that easy way of a man who'd met all kinds of folks without ever having to leave his bar. When the phone beeped in his pocket, Mick couldn't believe it was quarter to six.

'Better drink up,' he told Declan. 'Isn't the dinner at six?'

'You're right.' Declan slid off his barstool and pulled on the red Gortex jacket he'd been sitting on. Through the door, they could see the rain that had been threatening, ricocheting off the road outside. Mick berated himself for listening to Aisling and wearing that short Crombie-style thing she'd insisted on buying him. 'It's one of our best sellers,' she'd assured him. He'd felt it disloyal not to support her. At least he'd had the sense to borrow his brother's waterproof. He'd dig it out of the suitcase tonight. God knows, if this weather kept up, he'd need it.

'Hold on,' he called to Declan who was about to head out into the dark and wet, 'I'll text Aisling.'

# Chapter Eight

That afternoon, with the rain hammering down outside, Mia Montgomery had spent a quiet hour in her room, drinking the blackberry tea she'd chosen from a little wooden chest she was sure had started its life as a jewellery box. Sitting at the cane dressing table admiring her newly applied nail polish, she took another sip from the delicate china teacup before replacing it on its matching saucer, relishing the endearing clink as the two pieces settled together. *Some things were made for each other*, she mused as she opened the notebook she'd purchased in that wonderful gift shop in Skibbereen. *Seashell*, she wrote, framing the title she'd taken from the name of the room in the shape of a bivalve.

Ellen had been so nice, welcoming her in from the freezing cold to the warmth of the house that she said had been her grandmother's home. If the place had lost some of its original features, Mia was sure it had lost none of its charm. As Ellen filled her in on arrangements, she'd taken in the modern but cosy feel, the easy uncluttered spaces, the red-orange glow from real fires in both the comfortable parlour and in the gorgeous conservatory where they would have dinner. She imagined herself relaxing in one of the armchairs there, looking out over the Atlantic in all its moody glory. Smiling to herself, she proceeded to record the details of the room where the bed reminded her of the puffy white clouds you'd see out of an aeroplane window and the sparse furniture induced a sense of calm. There were accents of colour in an oversized aqua cushion and soft throw, but it was the small details that impressed her most, like the crocheted flowers sewn on to twigs and set in vintage jars and vases. Ellen had been apologetic for not having fresh flowers due to the time of year, but these were beautiful.

Intention journaling, that's what she should really be doing. This week was her chance to think big, set some goals. Somehow find a way out of the holding pattern that had become her life. But she'd already kicked one mini goal. She'd spotted a poster for the guesthouse in the window of one of Skibbereen's cosy coffee shops and, despite spending a few sleepless nights alternately talking herself into and out of treating herself to the week away, she was finally here. This was about self-care in every sense of the term. She would keep a record of her thoughts and experiences and hopefully work out a few intentions for the future. Writing therapy, she'd call it. If she didn't have Harry to talk to, she could talk to herself on the page. At least there, she could be honest.

Not wanting to share her motivations, she hadn't mentioned her little holiday to Harry. He'd been as preoccupied with work as ever anyway, coming home, eating dinner and getting straight back on to his laptop to finalise preparations for his trip. He'd be away for a week, studying some breed of pelagic fish on Ireland's national research vessel. A child going to visit Santa at the North Pole wouldn't have been in more of a rush to get out the door. She'd offered to take him to meet the boat, but he'd ordered a taxi. Work were paying for it, he'd said without looking up from the screen. Yesterday morning, he'd given her a bare peck on the cheek and jumped in the taxi he'd been waiting on for a good twenty minutes before it was even supposed to arrive. Early in their relationship, he might have glanced back, made a love heart with his hands, given her a missing-you-already look. She would have spent the time apart nesting, making whatever home they occupied warm and inviting for his return. And regardless of what time he'd arrive back, they'd peel the clothes off each other with an urgency that guaranteed the intense feverish orgasms that had become a thing of the past.

Six weeks into their latest adventure, she'd grown tired of staring at the four walls of the ramshackle bungalow her husband's latest employer had rented for them. Since leaving Australia, they'd already lived in four countries, staying in houses of varying states of repair, not to mention décor. Her stomach churned as she remembered their house in Scotland with its calf-shit yellow walls. How she'd looked at them for two years, she couldn't say. The kind neighbours who'd tried to hide their incredulity in the beginning, but later told her it hadn't been touched since the former chain-smoking owner died in their bedroom. There was the gîte in France with the wind whistling through the brickwork; Harry, in his optimism, spent a weekend trying to shore up the walls with some plaster concoction he'd made after watching a YouTube video. She'd spent weeks vacuuming the crumbling waste of effort. It was a miracle they hadn't ended up with pneumonia. Their friends back home in Australia honestly believed they were on some amazing cultural life-enriching odyssey, but after eight years of renting around the edges of Europe, the gloss on their nomadic lifestyle was seriously starting to fade.

In all the previous moves she'd been able to secure work before they arrived. There were times when she wondered if she should have chosen a different degree than science, but then she'd never have met Harry. At universities and research stations, she'd put her laboratory skills to good use doing everything from cleaning microscopes to taking endless fish tissue samples. Fish diseases were Harry's specialty. They made his eyes light up. She wouldn't know how many hours she'd clocked up sitting at microtomes, winding the handle round and round as the machine cut through the waxy blocks of fish bits she'd meticulously prepare, tiny slivers sliding onto petri dishes she'd forensically examine, thinking of the money while her husband ogled over intracellular organisms, happy to carry out his research for the cause of science. Not that he'd always been lucky enough to land generous grants that kept them comfortable. He'd just never wanted to stay put long enough to actually invest in something practical like a home.

There was no sign of a job opening here as yet. It bothered her less than she thought it might. She was alone while Harry was at work, but she'd felt equally isolated in workplaces where everyone spoke to her in English but to each other in French or Spanish or whatever their vernacular. It hadn't been for the want of trying to learn new languages, but they were never in one spot long enough to get past the basics and were always among a mix of nationalities where English was the common tongue.

It had been fun in the beginning, she had to admit, but having had several weeks to mull it over, one thing was certain – she couldn't keep living this unstable life indefinitely. She needed a base, somewhere she might find a job she was passionate about, where she didn't just fill in time and supplement their bank account. If she was honest, she'd been living in denial for too long. It wasn't until she'd found herself rummaging around a charity shop in Skibbereen, searching for substitutes for the contents of her home that were sitting in a shipping container somewhere on the Irish Sea, that a sudden sense of deja vu had threatened to unravel her.

'Need any help?' the cheery assistant had asked at precisely the moment she'd realised her marriage might be over.

～

Aisling ignored the phone as she rolled over on her side under the soft duvet, promising herself another few minutes before she would get up and have a shower using those lush-sounding products. Fig and pear. Heaven! Between that and the smell of cooking wafting from downstairs, she was surrounded by luxury. Even the rain teeming down outside seemed to add to the atmosphere. If circumstances were different, it would be the most romantic place. Lily Fitz had, in fairness, chosen decent accommodation.

No, she was awake now. The thought of Mick and get-aways had brought her back to reality. She checked her phone.

*Can you collect us from the pub in the village?*

Driving to the pub in the lashing rain was the last thing she needed. What the hell was he doing down there anyway? They'd only just arrived and he'd gone out without her. Pulling on her jeans and checking the jumper she'd slept in for bed fluff, her thoughts panned to the last work trip to Melbourne and how she hadn't needed Mick's permission to go out and enjoy herself. But she wouldn't dwell on that now.

'Hmm,' she huffed as she grabbed the car keys and went downstairs to wrap up in her warm padded coat before braving the downpour.

'Thanks very much, Aisling,' said Declan as he plonked his generous behind into the passenger seat after her husband had shot into the back, no doubt using his new-found friend to avoid an earful.

'Time got away from us,' said Mick.

'Did it?' She sent him a smouldering look in the rear-view mirror.

Back in the house, Aisling let herself into the downstairs bathroom, admiring the sparkling surrounds of the floor-to-ceiling tiles and the bowl-shaped sink with its modern fittings and cool dispensers. As she dried her hands on a super-soft towel, she faced her own image in the mirror. Not so bright and shiny, she mused. The bags under her eyes were bad enough, but now the glossy shoulder-length hair she'd only straightened that morning had rain-frizz. Too late for a once-over with the straightener, she helped herself to some lime and coconut hand lotion and used her fingers to tame her hair. This week was supposed to be about chillaxing, not rushing around as her husband's taxi.

She took a deep breath. They were on holiday. Mick worked every bit as hard as she did. God knows, he deserved a break. It wasn't his fault she wasn't herself. She'd try to make more of an effort.

In the kitchen, Ellen was bent over a set of bowls, pouring cream in perfect swirls onto a thick soup.

'Smells fantastic!'

Ellen smiled.

'Carrot and cashew,' said the man who was draining a huge pot of potatoes at the Belfast sink behind her. A good-looking man, Aisling realised, as he turned to set the pot down on the island and flashed her a smile that reached a pair of blue eyes you could get lost in.

'Aisling, this is Gerry,' said Ellen. 'I'm about to serve this if you're ready.'

'Sorry I'm late,' Aisling started. 'The two lads found the pub . . .'

'No worries.' Ellen gave a small laugh. 'Sure, they're on their holidays.'

Aisling managed a smile before heading through to the conservatory.

⌁

When she'd found herself first down to dinner, Mia took in the conservatory that had looked so different in daylight when Ellen had shown her around Lizzie O's. On the long table, tea lights blinked in mason jars. Pinecones and winter foliage were crafted into a seasonal centrepiece. On each of five glazed pottery plates sat a knife, fork and spoon set wrapped in a linen napkin, all tied loosely with a piece of twine. Mia breathed in the smell of the rustic space and promised to take a few notes for a future Christmas gathering. If they went back to Australia, she could do Christmas in July one year.

But Mia didn't know what she was doing next week, not to mind any year soon. For a moment she thought of Harry slumming it somewhere out to sea. An urge to bolt back to her bedroom threatened to overwhelm her, but the volume of voices in the kitchen had gone up a notch. Other guests would come in and find her here, on holiday without her husband. But no one knew her from a bar of soap. She picked up a couple of the activities brochures from a beautiful old sideboard and took a seat at the table, willing her shoulders to relax.

When the door opened, the smell of dinner wafted in as a couple of windswept men came to join her. From their ruddy cheeks and damp hair, she reckoned they'd got caught in the downpour. They took turns to shake hands and introduce themselves. Despite cold hands, their smiles were warm, especially the younger one who must have been in his forties. Irish, living in Tasmania, he told her in an accent that left her in no doubt of his origins. The older one, Declan, who'd felt it necessary to tell her he was a dentist, had taken the seat between them at the head of the table and was doing that roving eye thing she hated. She'd look out for him. Harry sometimes looked at women that way and she always called him out on it. He said it was human nature. She had her doubts.

At least this man hadn't quizzed her. When she'd mentioned she was from Melbourne, it was enough to set him off on a tangent about the Melbourne Cup. What a spectacle it was, the winners often Irish horses of course. Had she been to the national stud in Kildare? Well worth a visit. He could mansplain away; the less he knew about her the better. Mick had sat patiently listening. He seemed like the kind of person you could actually have a conversation with, if given the chance. But conversations with strangers often led to life stories. Mia didn't want or need to share her reasons for being here with these people she would never see again.

'Here's Aisling now,' Mick was saying as he got up and pulled out a chair for the woman she presumed was his wife.

'Hello, I'm Aisling.' The woman sat opposite her, replacing an uncomfortable look with a broad smile and reaching out a manicured hand.

'This young lady is from Melbourne, Ash,' said Mick.

'I'm Mia.' Taking the soft hand, Mia noticed the thick cranberry acrylic on the squared-off nails and the quality wool of Aisling's charcoal jumper. She too must have been out in the rain if her hair was anything to go by. Mia doubted the frizz was deliberate.

'Lovely to meet you, Mia,' she was saying. 'Isn't the weather shocking?'

*Safe territory*, thought Mia. The Irish could talk about the weather all night if they wanted. As she peered out the conservatory windows into the darkness, a light went on across the courtyard. Mia watched as a woman appeared from one of the cottages, opening up an umbrella and making a run for the mudroom entrance at the other end of the house. Apart from a low hissing from the wood heater, the room went quiet with anticipation until Ellen broke the silence, appearing with a trolley bearing the starter, the woman right behind her.

'Have a seat anywhere, Katie,' said Ellen as she kept her eyes on the job in hand and served the welcome soup. Mia couldn't think of anything better to eat on the wintry night. She helped herself to a round of crusty bread and passed the basket along. This was like being at a family dinner, only with a bunch of strangers.

They were all tucking into the meal before anyone introduced themselves to the stern-faced woman who had joined them. First to finish, Declan made a production of setting his spoon down, wiping his mouth with his napkin and doing some weird sucking thing to clear his teeth.

He cut into the sound of rain battering against glass with, 'Does anyone object to me doing the introductions to this lovely lady at the end?'

They murmured 'no's and 'not at all's between mouthfuls.

'I'm Declan, *all* the way from Cork,' he began, his comment met with polite laughter. 'On my right, we have another pair of Corkonians, Mick and Aisling, who have come *all* the way from Tasmania to celebrate an anniversary, I believe.'

Mia noticed the sausage fingers and wondered how he managed the delicate work required of dentistry.

'And on my left,' he continued, smiling broadly at her, 'we have young Mia from Melbourne . . .' He paused and raised his eyebrows at her expectantly, but she deflected the attention with a glance down the table towards Katie.

They waited as the woman barely looked up from where she continued to eat. Something in her expression scared Mia. The cropped bleached blonde hair with the kick-ass fringe reminded her of a female politician. The black kohl eyeliner didn't help, nor had her choice of seat. At the table for eight, there were three perfectly good chairs she could have taken closer to either herself or Aisling but had instead chosen the one opposite Declan at the far end.

With what looked like the slapping on of a fake smile, the woman cast her eye around the group. 'I'm Katie,' she said finally. 'I live in New York. I have some business here in Ireland which I would rather not discuss. So if you had any plans to make friends with your fellow guests here, please leave me out of it.'

They were still looking at her after she'd finished, perhaps like Mia, stunned into silence at the cutting speech and the American accent. Mia thought to say something friendly like 'Are you staying for the week?' or weather-related, like, 'It's lucky you had an umbrella,' but changed her mind. This Katie wasn't the only one who needed some privacy, but there were ways and means of being discreet.

'God, whatever's coming next smells fantastic.' Mick broke into the collective incredulity as he began to stack his and Aisling's bowls, setting the spoons on top. Mia and Declan passed theirs to him, seeming equally grateful for the distraction.

'Ah Mick, you'll be looking for a cut.' It was Gerry coming in now with a tea towel over his shoulder and bearing a tray to collect their dishes. Mia had been introduced to him earlier. A cheery forty-something you couldn't dislike. Mick laughed in response. Only Gerry seemed oblivious to the sting in the air.

Over a main course of asparagus and grilled Atlantic salmon in a Hollandaise sauce worthy of Manu Feildel, Mia took it upon herself to lighten the atmosphere. Referring to her brochures, she took them through the activities she'd been perusing.

'That upcycling workshop sounds good,' said Mick, if only to encourage her. 'That's all the rage with the war on waste and climate change.'

'I'm here more for the fresh air and walks,' said Declan, 'but I'd be interested in your seashore foraging session. I used to spend hours mucking around in rockpools here at low tide.'

'Are you from here?' Mia asked.

'No, my mother was. Spent loads of summers down here as a boy.'

The balding dentist didn't look like he'd ever been a boy, but the flush in his cheeks at the mention of his youth gave Mia a glimpse of what might be a whole other side to the mansplainer. She'd be kind. He hadn't said why he was here either.

# Chapter Nine

Lilian stood at the mirror in Aisling and Mick's guest bedroom fluffing her short greying hair into what she'd hoped would give her ageing face a little Judi Dench sophistication. The last time she'd been out here, Aisling hadn't hesitated to tell her she'd needed to do something with the hair that was then chopped into a triangular bob. It was no small step to keeping her daughter-in-law happy, but if there was one thing Aisling knew about, it was fashion. She'd been a humble shop assistant when Mick met her. Now she was state manager for one of Australia's biggest retail chains, tripping off to conferences and shows on top of the regular meetings and nights away in Hobart. Lilian was exhausted even thinking about it. *Mick must hardly see her*, she mused. Another excellent reason to gift them a week in West Cork. Jack would have been delighted.

'Are you right, Natalie?' she called to where her granddaughter was changing in the front bedroom.

'Almost, Gran.'

In the kitchen, she went to the fridge and took out the platter she'd put together earlier in the afternoon, securing the cling film around the edges. At least they weren't going empty-handed. Natalie appeared in a pair of denim shorts and a white singlet, the outline of what might be the child's first bra visible underneath. God, she was growing up fast.

'You're onto it, Gran.' Natalie ran her eye over the selection of cold meats, cheeses, olives and dried fruit and nuts they'd picked up earlier at the supermarket. 'Have you seen these beeswax covers I bought Mum for Christmas?' She opened a drawer and took out a selection of oily looking fabrics. 'We use these now,' Natalie explained, handing one of them to her to feel. 'But don't worry, we recycle the soft plastic too.'

Lilian felt the waxy fabric, promising to invest in a set before she went home, although she did prefer clear wrap to show off the platters she liked to call her signature dish. She'd spent the last week trying to keep her grandchildren nourished, enlisting their help with dinners as much to cover her own culinary shortcomings as to include them in the decision-making. Of all the domestic chores, cooking was her least favourite. She'd always loved to come home after a long day's work at the bank to find Jack fossicking in the cupboards, inventing their main meal. These days, she usually grazed on the cold smallgoods she collected on her regular trips to the Old English Market in Cork's city centre. Visitors were always impressed when she'd throw together a mouth-watering array on the good wooden chopping board they'd picked up on one of their visits to Tasmania. The piece, with its lacquered lines of sassafras, myrtle and Huon pine, was often a talking point over the food. Most nights, on her own, she dispensed with the board and threw a few items she kept in plastic containers onto a side plate. On a Friday or Saturday night, a glass of bubbles or a gin and tonic washed it all down well, but she kept it to one glass. She'd never enjoyed drinking alone.

Flip-flops and sandy wetsuits lay abandoned on the front step of Heather's, a couple of doors down. Straightening her light shift dress, Lilian checked her reflection in the glass panel of the door and rang the bell.

'They'll be round the back,' said Natalie when there was no response.

Just as she thought to ring again, a shout went up from within and one of Heather's daughters appeared in the hallway and opened the door.

'Mum's in the kitchen,' she told them before disappearing into a bedroom.

Lilian and Natalie shared a *that's so rude* look and proceeded to the kitchen, where Heather was standing over the sink peeling a carrot.

'Welcome,' she said, turning and eyeing the platter. 'That looks amazing.'

Lilian set her contribution on the bench, chuffed at Heather's reaction.

'Can I help at all?'

'I'm just going to finish this coleslaw,' said Heather. 'Dad's supposed to be firing up the barbecue . . .' She looked towards the backyard and shouted, 'Dad!'

A tall, slightly stooped man shuffled in from outside. Lilian couldn't believe her eyes.

'Lilian, this is Doug . . .'

The grumpy boatman stood in the doorway and nodded, not even a hint of recognition on his pursed lips, let alone in his grey-blue eyes. Lilian stretched out her hand and smiled despite wishing she didn't have to endure an evening with this dour individual. Perhaps he'd just been having a bad day when she'd met him in the garage, but this could potentially be torture. After the briefest handshake, he turned to gather up some utensils from a drawer and returned to the garden. Normally, she'd have blurted out, 'Oh, I met you in the garage', but something about his manner made her hold her tongue. Anyway, it was Heather who'd invited her. Lilian would be grateful for her hospitality even if her father was going to be hard work.

In the garden, the outdoor table was set with a stripy cotton runner and pink serviettes. Natalie had been happy to help Heather with last-minute preparations and, with the daughters of the household nowhere to be seen, Lilian found herself alone with their grandfather who was standing with his back to her, fiddling with a Weber. She only knew the name of the device because her son owned one, but in her limited experience of Australia, any barbecue worth its salt was supposed to be an instrument of social connection, not an excuse to ignore someone.

'Can I help?' she asked.

He turned round and waved the tongs about. 'Take a seat,' he told her. 'Heather won't be long.'

Without so much as the offer of a drink, she helped herself to a glass of iced water from a gorgeous carafe with floating pieces of mint and lemon. Leaving Doug to his aluminium foil and potatoes, Lilian took a walk around the garden. By the time the girls came out, she had taken in every flowering plant, tree and succulent. If someone had asked her to sketch the place with her eyes closed, she'd have probably done it to near perfection.

'Dad looking after you?' said Heather, setting the platter and a bowl of chips in the centre of the table. Natalie followed with a couple of dips.

'Oh, they look fabulous,' said Lilian, ignoring the question and accepting Heather's gestured invitation to tuck in.

'You'll remember my girls, Ruby and Darwin.'

Lilian smiled. 'You two have certainly grown since I was here last.'

There was a self-conscious nod of agreement from one of the teenagers, while the other, who had come to the door, plonked herself down at one end of the table and focused her full attention on her phone.

'Ruby!' The exasperation in Heather's voice was audible.

'I'm just watching the end of this.' The girl slipped an earbud out of one ear and twiddled it between her fingers without taking her eyes off the screen.

'That can wait,' said Heather. 'Or you can give me your phone for a week.'

Lilian stifled an urge to laugh.

'Those phones are so addictive,' she said instead. There was no response, but she kept going. 'Do you know, sometimes I waste hours on mine, looking at my socials.'

Ruby looked up from her phone, her face turning from defiance to doubt. 'Do you have Instagram?'

Lilian finished off a cracker with a good helping of the creamy corn relish.

'Instagram's my favourite,' she said. 'But I've tried everything.'

As Heather gathered glasses and cutlery from a smaller table and began to set them out, Lilian wished the girls would move their butts and help, but she had their attention now.

'Gran's an addict,' said Natalie with a giggle.

The girls looked impressed as Lilian explained how her children and grandchildren in Ireland insisted she keep up with the times and download all manner of apps to keep in touch.

'I don't know,' she said, aware they were weighing up whether or not to take her seriously, 'I think social media is great and all, but I wish it were simpler.'

'How do you mean?' Ruby asked, phone still in hand but eyes firmly on Lilian.

'I'll give you an example.'

As they tucked into her platter and sat back to listen to her story, Doug joined them at the table.

'The other day, a friend of mine sent me a message,' Lilian began. 'I was busy out shopping at the time and saw the message but thought I'd look at it properly later. Anyway, when I was on the bus home, I took out my phone and do you know, I looked through WhatsApp, Messenger, texts, emails, Facebook, Viber . . . and for the life of me I couldn't find the damn thing.'

A snigger went up from the two teenagers.

'Oh, Gran,' said Natalie, her face full of concern. 'What did you do?'

'Phoned her up of course. 'Cos that's what we did back in the Stone Age.'

A burst of laughter erupted around the table. Even Heather's dad gave a bemused smile.

'Your grandfather would have done the same, wouldn't you, Doug?'

Oh God, she'd put him on the spot.

'Aye,' he said and slowly got up to see to the barbecue.

*Life and soul of a party, that one*, Lilian thought, but no one else seemed surprised in the slightest that the grandfather had so little to say.

—

In the guest studio at the back of Mick and Aisling's, Lilian lay in bed in a state of happy exhaustion. Despite the elephant in the room that was Heather's father, herself and Natalie had had a lovely night. Heather was such a breath of fresh air. Must take after her mother, Lilian thought, mulling over the evening and piecing together the snippets Mick had told her about their neighbour over the years. She'd been unlucky, losing her mother to a stroke five years before. The day after, her then-husband told her he no longer loved her. Heartless bastard. But she had to hand it to Heather; the daughters who hadn't always been the easiest children to raise, by all accounts, had done her proud tonight. Once they'd managed to detach themselves from their phones, Ruby and Darwin were great company. They'd given Natalie the lowdown on the high school they attended where she too would start in a few weeks. Lilian did her best to keep up as they waxed positively lyrical about subjects like coding and catering and the personalities of the teachers who delivered them. It was good to see Natalie show some enthusiasm for the big step Mick said she'd been dreading. Although he hadn't contributed an awful lot to the conversation, even Heather's father had seemed mesmerised. By the time he quietly excused himself and retired to bed, Lilian was sure he'd relaxed a smidgen.

Settling into a comfortable position, she brought her attention to her breath, sending thoughts of her son's neighbours and their visitor floating away on soft clouds as she drifted off to sleep.

# Chapter Ten

Conor Fox couldn't believe the nerve of the driver who nearly creamed him as they rounded the tight bend and he only minding his own business on his regular Sunday morning ride. With the skin on his bare legs smarting from grazes, he pulled himself up out of the gorse bush he'd fallen into when the car had whizzed past. *Could have been a lot worse*, he told himself as he straightened the bike and pushed it on up the hill, brushing the leaves and prickles off the reinforced backside of his cycling shorts.

At the top of the hill, he stopped the bike and took in the blue Datsun that had come to an abrupt halt at the end of the Dalys' driveway. The driver emerged, a frown drawing in the once familiar face under a dark trilby.

'Are you all right?' she shouted, pulling a black wool cape around her.

He nodded, his brain unable to produce words as he took in the much-changed Katie Daly. When her sister had mentioned she was coming home, he'd tried to imagine what she might look like after all these years, but the serious woman in front of him wasn't what he'd expected. Her mother, Phyllis, looked to be the only one unperturbed as she shuffled towards the car, oblivious to the fact that her daughter had nearly killed him.

'Morning, Mrs Daly,' he said, trying to sound cheery.

'Ah, Conor, isn't it grand to see Katie after all this time?'

''Tis indeed,' he managed for the woman's benefit. Poor Phyllis. She was like the father of the prodigal son, delighted to have the errant daughter home.

'Mammy, will you get into the car, we'll be late for Mass.' Without another word to him, Katie was back at the wheel, engine running with her reverse lights on. Berating himself for not shifting out of his stupor and opening the door for the old lady, Conor watched as Phyllis took what looked like a painful minute to position herself in the front seat.

'Take it a bit slower on the roads,' he called out, but Katie wasn't listening. The passenger door had barely closed, and she was gunning Bernadette's Datsun back down towards the church.

—

Conor had long dispensed with going to Mass. This cycle around the back roads of West Cork was his prayer, his penance, all rolled into one. As he wended his way home, he considered the change in Katie Daly. They'd both grown up here in this place that had remained relatively unchanged; both as much a part of it as the wild gorse and the blackthorn bushes that leaned over the drystone walls, like locals at the village bar, drinking in the salt-laden air. He never tired of the view; the steep hillside sloping towards the sea and the time-sculpted cliffs beyond where tides ebbed and flowed from far out in the Atlantic. Other people he grew up with had left and come back but were still their old selves. Like Ellen O'Shea, who used to come down from the city in their childhood summers. There she was, back running her dead grandmother's house as a business after years in Australia. He'd heard she'd had her own troubles, but any time he'd run into her, she'd been as warm and friendly as he'd remembered. No airs, no notions, just herself. He'd like to have chatted so easily to Katie, heard snippets of what her life had held in the intervening years, but if this morning's encounter with her curt commentary and minimal eye contact was anything to go by, there'd be no 'It's like yesterday when we last met' conversations.

He tried to remember the last time he'd seen her. It was towards the end of Leaving Cert. She'd got a job in Cork and left school. Their friends thought it must have been a great job altogether not to stay on and do the exams. Some of them envied her. At Christmas and in the following summer, they'd asked after her. The older sister, Bernadette, only said she was busy, working away; she was grand. As time went on, they asked less and less often. Apart from the monotony of getting the same response, he noted a weariness in Phyllis's face when he'd ask, a resignation in Bernadette's.

The year came to him. It was 1985, their last year of school. They were both a bit on the fringes of their peer group, quieter than the popular kids who wore the right clothes and listened to the cool bands, but they kind of suited each other.

When the gang would meet down at the beach or in one of their houses, their friends would be all loud talk about music and fashion, smoking and stealing from their parents' whiskey bottles, topping them up with tea. He and Katie would be off to one side, talking books and films. The most risqué thing they did was listen to a banned copy of *The Life of Brian* LP on the record player in his cousin's bedroom.

As the graduation ball got closer, he knew she was the only girl he wanted to go with, but he'd never had a girlfriend. It took him ages to work up the courage to ask her. He was so twisted with angst, he could manage nothing but furtive glances and nods in the passing for weeks. Until the hurling club disco, when it took him until the last slow set to ask her to dance. Despite the hot stuffy hall, he was shaking like a leaf as he took her hand and led her to the dancefloor. But instead of the ugly weedy teenager he'd seen himself as, he grew a foot taller as she put her arms around his waist and let her head rest against his chest. 'In the Air Tonight' would always bring back special memories; it was that night he'd asked her to the grads.

The weeks in between were some of the most intense of his life. His mother had him driven mad with shopping trips and clothes fittings. Always looking for an excuse to act the big man, his brother slagged him constantly about his 'new girlfriend'. Martin had done it all two years before and considered himself a babe magnet now that he was working and owned his own car. Their mother, God rest her, kept talking about how good he looked in a tuxedo, how proud she was of him. Their father let it all wash over his head, offering a minimum of lighthearted advice about not overdoing the drink and pushing a tenner into the pocket of his tux before he left. They'd even offered to let him bring a few friends back after the dance.

Sometimes he looked back and imagined that graduation ball as the best night of his life. Only one thing was certain – nothing was ever the same after it. Not only had he lost his brother in the crash, but he and Katie Daly were never the same. He'd asked his friends and family why she'd become so distant with him, but no one claimed to know. Water under the bridge, he told himself as he free-wheeled down the hill. He'd put Katie out of his head, take his coffee and have a read of the Sunday papers just as he did every week, in peace.

In The Coffee Pot, Katie gave a quick glance around the empty space, relieved to have it to herself. A young woman, younger than her anyway, pushed through a beaded curtain, smiling like she'd won the lottery.

'Have a seat and I'll take the order.'

Katie opted for a spot at the far corner, out of sight of the doorway. Plonking herself down, she placed her hat on the table and reworked the gel to smooth her hair behind her ears. She'd managed to pull in at the church just as one of the neighbours was parking. In less than two sentences, she'd communicated the fact that it was only her mother who'd be attending Mass. Rita Kelly helped the older woman out of the car and into the church, sparing Katie the ordeal of meeting anybody.

'A cappuccino,' she told the waitress.

The smile didn't abate.

'Sure I can't tempt you to one of the cakes?' She went to point at the display cabinet, but Katie cut her off.

'Coffee's fine,' she said, dismissing the woman and reaching across to a nearby table to pick up a newspaper.

At the tinkle of the bell over the door, she looked up to see Conor Fox enter in his lycra. She flicked open the broadsheet, ready to hide behind it if necessary.

'Good morning, Marit,' he was saying to where the girl had disappeared behind a red coffee machine. 'The usual, please, when you're ready.' As the machine hissed and sputtered, he took a couple of steps towards a table. 'Katie,' he said, halting awkwardly, hand poised ready to set down his cycling sunglasses.

'Hi again.' She barely looked up. Giving the paper a shake, she feigned interest in its contents. He turned back to the counter.

'I'll take that to go if you don't mind, Marit.'

'In a hurry this morning?' she asked as she swept past him with the cappuccino and set it down in front of Katie.

He kept his back to her, but she could see his shoulders shrug.

'Just a bit short-staffed at the shop,' he said. 'Have to cover for the after-Mass rush.'

Katie imagined the apologetic smile she knew of old.

As he stood waiting for his coffee, she wished the woman would hurry up, but couldn't help sneaking a couple of covert looks over the paper. She studied the wiry flecks of grey that dotted his once dark hair, the sweat patches on his fluorescent lycra. She might have asked if he wasn't too badly hurt after the near miss, but memories bubbled up from a place she'd spent years and thousands of dollars trying not to revisit. The feel of sweat on his white shirt that night, the taste of it on her tongue, her first French kiss . . .

'There you go.'

The sound of the woman's voice broke into her memories. She felt him glance round once more before he left, but she kept her eyes on the black print that may as well have been hieroglyphics. What did he expect? A warm hug? One of those air-kisses-to-both-cheeks greetings like two country hicks gone all continental? She didn't think so. It wasn't as if she could have said, 'Hey Conor, see that night we went to the grads all those years ago? It ruined my life.' She sucked in her anger and blew out the deep breath on her coffee. One week. She didn't have to play long-lost buddies with anyone.

# Chapter Eleven

Mia had decided to relish every moment of the week in the guesthouse. Not a huge eater, she'd savoured each mouthful of main course the night before, but only managed half of the rich bread and butter pudding Gerry had served with homemade vanilla-bean ice cream and the whipped cream he told them came from the cows on next door's farm. There was a platter of local cheeses for those favouring savoury, or like Declan, had room for both. She'd surely put on a couple of kilos here, but she didn't care. It wasn't like Harry would notice.

After a full night's sleep, she'd been up early, grateful to see the first rays of sunlight streaming in through the frosted bathroom window as she'd jumped into the hot shower. Her plan was to go for a long walk and find that coffee shop she'd heard about. With any luck, they'd have wi-fi and she could line up a few real estate agents to call on Monday. There was no point wallowing in self-pity. This week was about working out some kind of exit strategy. She'd been far too easygoing, tripping around the world after a semi-committed husband, like a supporting actress in what was clearly The Harry Show. There'd been enough tears, always shed in his absence. If he'd failed to notice her unhappiness, she was partly to blame. She'd been Mia the Willing, Mia the Accommodating, Mia the Downright Martyr. But no more. As scary as this was, she needed to regain her independence and indeed her self-belief. When the prospect of what she was considering threatened to overwhelm her, she'd written it down, broken it in to doable tasks. First on her list was somewhere to live. Australia was too far. She wouldn't abandon Harry altogether. His family were her only family. It would be good if they could remain friends. She would find a place in the area before the week ran away from her and go from there.

Downstairs in the conservatory, there was a buffet arrangement where she helped herself to a bowl of yoghurt and muesli, topping the lot with a generous spoon of warm rhubarb compote. If Harry were here, he'd have bored her about the ingredients down to the last sunflower seed. She used to be in awe of his knowledge and intelligence, hanging on his every word as he enthused about projects and species of fish and their parasites, but lately she was more likely to think he sounded like a broken record. Sure, he was passionate about how things worked, how living systems regulated, proliferated, but the world wouldn't be less of a place if he toned it down a bit. It wasn't intentional, she knew, but she'd grown tired of how Harry managed to both outshine and overshadow her. She gave herself a mental shake. *Get a hold of your self-esteem, Mia. It's all in your head.*

She settled into one of the green velour armchairs and enjoyed her meal. In the stillness, a log shifted in the wood burner that kept the place toasty warm. Looking out onto the garden, she knew it would be quite possible to remain in this chair all day, feet curled under her, watching birdlife or writing in her journal. But that could be saved for a rainy day. This morning, she would forgo the rich-smelling coffee and get out into the fresh air.

'Morning,' she said as Mick carried a plate of decadent pastries to a table for two near the window. 'Isn't this food amazing?' Without waiting for an answer, she made her way out through the kitchen.

'Have you had enough to eat?' Ellen asked, a concerned look on her face.

'Plenty, thanks,' said Mia. 'I'm still full after last night.'

'Okay.' She smiled. 'But you know to help yourself if you're hungry during the day.'

Fridge-raiding was encouraged at Lizzie O's. Gerry and Ellen had given them the spiel when they'd served dessert the night before – they were to indulge their inner Nigella if the couple weren't around to serve. Mia couldn't imagine leaving her warm fluffy bed in the middle of the night, but it was another reason to love this place and justify her decision to come here.

~

Grateful for the crisp, clear day, Mia rugged up with scarf, gloves and a beanie she'd made to pass the hours in their rented bungalow, and set off to walk the seven kilometres to Goleen. Staying fit was another of her goals. In the early weeks, it was lovely to just amble around Skibbereen, discovering the quaint shops and coffee spots, but as the weeks went on, she'd found herself falling into the abyss of social media and net surfing more and more. She'd read about wonderful coastal walks like the Sheep's Head Way, but between the near incessant rain and Harry's focus on his new job, their spare time had been mostly spent indoors. There was no shortage of stunning scenery and wild places to explore, but that required two things: good company and good weather. Right now, neither was guaranteed.

Crossing the road to walk along the beach at Galley Cove, her spirits lifted at the sight of a collection of dogs paying varying degrees of attention to a lone man who was hurling sticks into the surf. She smiled at their antics: a young border collie and a golden retriever bounding in after every stick, a Bernese mountain dog dithering at the water's edge, a pug and a couple of bitzers sniffing and marking territories around the low dunes that bordered the beach. God, she missed Banjo. Her dog would have been such a comfort in all this isolation had he lived a bit longer.

He'd been a birthday gift from Harry when they'd first moved overseas, long before she'd realised her husband was a rolling stone. She'd broached the subject of starting a family a couple of times in the lead-up to her twenty-fifth birthday and he'd arrived home with the dog. No choice, no discussion, just a poor whimpering adorable pup placed in her outstretched arms when he'd told her to close her eyes. The most romantic gesture, she'd thought at the time. Coming up for seven years later, she wasn't so sure. Whatever her husband's motivation for the gift, she'd welcomed Banjo into her life like she would have a child, wholeheartedly. He'd been a constant in amongst all the moves and change, asking nothing but a few basics and her companionship. For Banjo, at least, she'd been enough.

Closer now, she took in the tall lean man in a pair of skinny jeans and an open parka jacket, a head of fair hair pulled back in a man-bun. Must be nice, she mused, having a pack of dogs and idyllic surroundings to walk them.

'G'day.' The dog man turned and smiled at her. 'Better weather today, eh?'

'I like your dogs,' she said, stopping to pat the collie, who had sidled up for a sniff.

'Oh, they're not all mine,' he said. 'A couple of them are actually looking for a home.'

She registered the tight vowels of the New Zealand accent, intrigued at how someone's life could take them to a remote corner of Ireland to live with a pack of canine companions like a Kiwi Cesar Millan.

'I'm just on holiday,' she began.

'I'm sorry,' he said, his cheeks reddening above the angular jaw. 'I run a kennel that doubles as a dogs' home. Always on the hustle . . .'

When the retriever dropped the stick at his feet, he picked it up and deftly flung it far out into the water. She watched as the dog rose to the challenge and bounded in until he was out of his depth and swimming hard against the waves.

'I'm staying at the new guesthouse . . .' She wasn't sure why she added that detail, but she gestured in the direction of Lizzie O's.

'The O'Sheas' old place?' he asked

She nodded, hoping he wouldn't pry.

'Some place,' he said, sucking in a breath. 'I've heard they've done an excellent job.'

'It's beautiful,' she agreed. With a last look around at the dogs, she took a step back. 'I'd better let you go.'

'No worries,' he said, raising a hand in a quick wave that made a woven leather band bob at his wrist. She continued her walk along the otherwise empty beach, breathing in the sea air and all its promise.

―

There'd been no small talk with the locals after Mass. No, Katie got back in her car before they spilled out onto the church steps, ready to take her mother straight home. She'd passed that overenthusiastic young woman from the guesthouse as she'd left the cafe.

'Hi, I'm Mia, from the –' she'd started when Katie tried to get past without engaging in what that girl probably thought would be a long conversation, comparing notes about their accommodation and swapping life stories.

Katie had given her short shrift. 'See you back there,' she'd said with a nod and a smile she could barely muster. 'Twas well for that young one, smiling like a half head. She was on holiday, not an estranged-mother-minding mission.

At the house, Katie pushed in the front door and headed for the kitchen. The sitting room that had been closed the day before was open now. Glancing in, she saw the assemblage of blankets strewn across the sixties settee that looked like an unmade bed. *Exactly what it must be*, she thought, holding the idea as she trudged into the kitchen, setting down her handbag before filling the kettle.

'I'll do that, love,' Phyllis was saying from where she was making her slow way down the hallway. If the laboured breathing was anything to go by, she was too worn out after her excursion to do anything of the sort.

'Sit down, Mammy,' Katie ordered. 'I'll make you a cup of tea and then you can tell me about your sleeping arrangements.'

Her mother took another audible breath. Katie thought she might have fallen on to the kitchen chair as she sat slumped at the table, arms crossed in front of her.

'It's just the odd night,' she began. 'Old age, I suppose.' She gave a small self-deprecating laugh, but Katie wasn't amused.

'Are you not able to get up the stairs at all, Mammy?' The last thing she needed was for her to fall down the staircase and kill herself on her watch. For God's sake, why didn't Bernadette tell her things were this bad?

'Does Bernadette know?' she asked, anxious to cover herself and not be the only one with this uncomfortable knowledge as to the state of their mother's health.

'I didn't want to tell her in case she wouldn't go.' Katie's gaze fell to the gnarled hands that pinched at where her navy cardigan covered what was left of her biceps. 'I have the blankets and things tidied away before she comes. I meant to close the door so you wouldn't –'

'Jesus Christ, Mammy! You can't be living like that.'

A trembling in her bottom lip made Katie tone down the inquisition.

'Will I make you a toasted sandwich with the tea?'

Her face brightened. 'You were always the practical one.' She made to get up from the chair. 'If you don't mind, I'll take myself to the bathroom while you're making it.'

'Will you manage?'

'I will.'

Katie watched her rise slowly from the chair, grasp her walking stick from the back of it and make her unsteady way to the downstairs toilet. As she went to the bread bin, Katie began to wonder just how her mother managed to do basic things for herself and if Bernadette was indeed giving her the amount of care she obviously needed.

By the time Phyllis returned, Katie had poked out a toasted sandwich machine that had to be doused in boiling water before she dared use it. The brown bread she found in the bread bin was almost at the end of its edible life. Just as well she was heating it. A few slices of easy cheese, a couple of pieces of ham and a half-used tub of butter were all that was available in the fridge her sister had promised to stock. She'd only picked up a carton of milk from that woman in the cafe after remembering they'd drained the milk jug the day before. This was an awful state of affairs. Her mother's bed would have to be brought downstairs, but there was no way Katie could manhandle that on her own.

'Do we still have that camp bed, Mammy?' she asked as her mother eased herself back into one of the kitchen chairs. 'I could set that up for you. It's wider than the settee at least.'

'That's a lot of trouble to put you to, love.'

*Trouble!* she wanted to shout. *That sister of mine will be in trouble when I talk to her.* But she sucked in her anger.

'Do you remember where it is?'

''Tis folded away down the back of your wardrobe.'

She said the last two words as though Katie was in and out of the piece of furniture every day of the week. She'd have liked to avoid the house altogether, but she'd definitely hoped never to have cause to enter her old bedroom again. As she took the stairs, Katie's heart pounded in her chest. The damp clammy feeling she'd experienced in her hands on first seeing the house again returned. You've got this, she told herself. You are just going in there to retrieve a camp bed to make an old woman comfortable – an old woman you never have to lay eyes on again after this week, once your sister has got Antonio Banderas out of her system.

At the top of the stairs, the floorboards creaked under the worn carpet. The sound, the familiar pattern, all conspired to make her want to vomit. Taking a breath, she pressed on towards the closed door of the bedroom she'd shared until Bernadette moved out to go to college. As a teenager, Katie had never imagined missing her sister, only what she'd do to the room when she had it all to herself. Turning the door handle now took all her courage. Diversion, distraction, breathing, any strategies she'd learnt in therapy would be useful if only she could calm the hell down enough to let them override the revulsion she felt at entering the room she wished her sister had never left.

# Chapter Twelve

Aisling and Mick had spent the day as tourists. Mick groaned when she'd suggested they take advantage of the dry day and get up out of the big comfortable sex-worthy bed. But there was no way she could have stayed there with that night in Melbourne and its consequences playing on repeat in her head any time she lay down next to him.

'Are you all right?' he asked for the umpteenth time as they took the turn-off at Goleen and headed out along the Mizen Peninsula.

'Grand,' she lied again. 'Just a bit tired.'

*Sore tummy, change in the water*, more of the lame excuses she'd been giving the man for weeks. They'd been through thick and thin with fifteen years of marriage and a couple of years dating behind them. He'd even taken on a child that wasn't his own. This was not how it was supposed to be, but what was she going to say? 'I cheated on you and have been struck down with a most vengeful punishment.' The sooner the day was over and she could find a clinic open tomorrow, the better.

'I haven't been here since I was small,' she said, mustering a smile as they parked the car and made their way into the visitors' centre. The walk to and from the lighthouse at Ireland's most south-westerly point would kill a couple of hours, she told herself. With any luck, they'd meet a few fellow tourists. Anything to distract them from the conversation she was so desperate to put off having with her husband.

—

At the guesthouse, they went into dinner in silence. Mizen Head had been its majestic spectacular self with all the drama of wild Atlantic waves crashing below the iconic bridge and cliffs dropping off the southern edges of Ireland. They'd made their way along the zig-zag path and scaled the hundreds of steps, meeting a few hardy travellers who'd braved the wintry gusts, stopping here and there to capture the breathtaking vistas with fancy cameras and the latest smartphones. At one of the viewing points, she and Mick stood as much in awe as any of them. He'd slipped his arms around her waist and cuddled in close behind her. They could have taken a selfie and saved what should have been a special moment, something to look back on. She'd wanted to reach a hand up to his face and turn to kiss him, but instead, she'd pulled away with a comment about getting in out of the cold.

She was doing the same now, ignoring the hand that reached for hers under the table. Grateful his attention was diverted by Declan and his excited talk about the weekend's rugby fixtures, she turned to that nice young Australian woman she imagined must be travelling on her own. They were just discussing the local beauty spots when the conservatory door opened and two women in their late fifties or early sixties appeared.

'Declan! Is it yourself?' the taller woman rumbled in a voice that would rival Vesuvius. 'I had no idea you'd be here.'

Declan's face was a picture. With his back to the kitchen, he hadn't seen them walk in. For a second, Aisling thought Mick might have to engage his paramedic skills, but Declan recovered from what looked like shock and, regaining his oversized ego, explained to his new-found friends, Mick and Mia at least, the nature of their connection.

'Prue here, and Edwina,' he said, waving a hand in the direction of the lady standing beside her, 'they run a language school above my dental practice.'

'It's a wonder we even recognised you for all we see of each other,' the smaller woman remarked with a laugh that made her whole ample frame jiggle with enthusiasm.

Mick, being Mick, got up to shake hands with them and make the remaining introductions while Declan sat looking like he wanted a refund.

'I suppose you booked last minute like me . . .' he ventured as they took their places at the table.

'Oh no,' Prue replied with gusto. 'Colette told us about this project ages ago. We'd always planned to support her, and the O'Sheas of course.'

Aisling detected a heightening in the colour of Declan's pasty cheeks and wondered if he was getting enough vitamin D at all. Prue and Edwina exchanged a coy look before Prue addressed the group.

'Do you all know Colette Barry, the interior designer on the renovations of this house?' She asked the question as if she were trying to assess prior knowledge from a group of students before delivering a lesson.

Her interest in this Colette, Aisling noted, was obviously very different from that of Declan, who was still blushing at the topic of conversation.

'I had a google,' said Aisling, keen to sound knowledgeable and rescue poor Mia, who looked as though she was hearing about a party in her apartment after the event. 'She's some talent. The best in Ireland, I read.'

'You only need to look around you,' said Prue, panning the conservatory. 'She works out of a boutique agency on the bottom floor under ourselves and Declan.'

'Imagine,' Edwina added, eyes wide under a layer of brow definer you could seal a road with.

Declan, who'd obviously had enough of this Colette, quickly changed the subject. 'So, what are you two loose women doing down here in the middle of the academic year?'

The ladies exchanged another one of their looks before Prue, setting an elbow on the table and a hand under her chin, fixed her eyes on him.

'Didn't you know, Declan?' she said in a voice less volcanic and more molten chocolate. 'Ed and I are on honeymoon.'

Aisling thought she might pee herself as Declan's jaw shot towards his chest. This might have been the best laugh she'd had since she left Tasmania, but given the company, she kept her amusement to a wide smile. At least she and Mick would have something to talk about later.

'Congratulations,' Mick was saying, beaming at the pair of them.

'That's awesome,' Aisling chimed in. 'We wish you both every happiness for the future.'

It sounded trite. How many of her and Mick's wedding and anniversary cards had said that very thing?

'Champers aperitif, anyone?' Gerry appeared pushing a trolley with a bottle of champagne in an ice bucket. What a man! Good looking *and* useful. But there she went again, eyeing up other people's property like greener grass.

—

Declan didn't have the energy for another trip to the pub after dinner. He'd had enough challenges for one day and went straight to his room after the 'wedding cake'. Their hosts had laid on a three-tier death-by-chocolate affair in honour of Prue and Edwina's nuptials. True to form, he'd tried all three flavours. Ellen assured them they wouldn't be getting this every night, but he needed to calm down. His cholesterol was already through the roof. Tomorrow he'd go for a proper walk, not like today where the furthest he'd got was a short trip down memory lane followed by a couple of hours in the pub watching rugby.

Lying on top of the duvet, still in his clothes, images of his grandfather's house played in his mind. It had been sold after both grandparents passed away, none of their offspring having the foresight to realise what an investment it would be. Certainly not his own mother. But then, his father would hardly have supported the idea.

Standing in front of the two-storey this morning, Declan had been relieved to see it well looked after. There was no car parked as his granddad's used to be, impossibly close to the downstairs sitting room window so that traffic, summer traffic at least, could squeeze past. Declan thought it was probably an Airbnb, snuggled in amongst the other mostly silent houses on the narrow street behind the pub. Not that any of the few current residents would have recognised him as he'd wandered along that morning to see if the place had changed. The half-door was still intact, but it was now shielded from the weather by a porch extension that made for a cosy appealing frontage. A couple of white cane chairs with yellow cushions were set either side of a wooden table, a miniature sailboat as its centrepiece. Whatever happened to the clipper ship he and his grandfather had painstakingly assembled over a stretch of rainy days on one of his summer visits? Such easy times they'd been. Messing about in boats or building them in that house where his grandmother made only two demands of her grandchildren: no trailing sandy feet through the house and be home by dark. Wonderful freedoms he and his brother had relished.

His mother had a similar nature, deep down, somewhere their father couldn't access and tarnish. But she mostly toed the line, upholding the strict standards he set for them all. They'd met at University College Cork, although her degree in archaeology was another subject for belittlement. Woe betide either of his children would do a lowly Arts degree. Declan and his brother excelled at school, at sport, were always well turned out; 'a credit to her', people remarked.

'Best-looking woman to ever come out of West Cork,' his father used to tell them on the rare occasions he was in a jovial mood. 'I saved her from all those culchies who had their sights on her.'

She'd blush and laugh it off. 'Would you go way outta that.'

Then he'd mock the West Cork accent she tried so hard to subdue and take the good out of the compliment. His brother was braver than him, asking, in his father's absence, why she put up with it.

'It's just his way,' she'd say. She was always immaculate, the surgeon's wife, denying any dreams of her own. How cruel now she lingered in a home, too far down the dark road of dementia to even recognise the man who'd put her there. Declan saw him once a month out of a sense of duty. He saw her less. Too ashamed, too busy?

As he lay in the warmth of the room, awash with soft light from the lamp at his bedside, he had an uneasy feeling that he might have become far too like his father. Had he treated Karen just as his mother had been treated? The dentist's wife. A trophy to bear his children and continue the Byrne line. She'd been working as a dental hygienist for George Powell when he'd met her. Took time off when the kids were born, but unlike his mother, returned to work in both his and other practices around the city. Hadn't he been a good enough husband, letting her have her independence? And what of his own boys? Surely he could take some credit for bringing them up and giving them a good education. But he'd left Karen to do most of the parenting. Play dates, parent–teacher meetings . . . she'd even taught them to drive. And where were they now on the evenings and weekends he spent mostly by himself? Robert working all hours in a Dublin law firm and Luke on what must by now be his fifth gap year, skippering boats somewhere off the coast of South America.

For a moment he considered retrieving the phone he hadn't bothered to recharge. But what was the point? Karen and the boys had their own lives, lives they had carved out while he'd focused on building the business. He covered his eyes with his hands and for the first time in as long as he could remember, he wept rivulets of pure honest tears.

—

Katie Daly couldn't sleep either. She'd set up the camp bed in the sitting room, made sure her mother had everything she needed and got out of there without the vomiting, fainting or falling apart she'd feared might occur on entering her old room. Unable to face the crowd at dinner, she'd opted instead to dine alone in an overpriced restaurant run by incomers who thankfully valued their customers' privacy and left her in peace.

It didn't matter whether she closed or opened her eyes, the same images plagued her. The room was unchanged – her Duran Duran posters, Simon Le Bon and the lads with their mad head scarves and mullets, faded now like the primrose patterned wallpaper she'd chosen with Bernadette. The flowers were no longer yellow, but she remembered how vibrant they'd been when she was ten and Bernadette thirteen. How they'd agonised over the different styles and textures of the rolls piled high in the decorating shop. They'd hurried home, eager to help their mother assemble the paste and brushes, watching as she painstakingly measured the lengths she'd line up with precision, stems and petals merging into a near-seamless picture as she ran the cloth over the drop, smoothing out errant folds. The parallel beds had looked so innocuous, made up as they always had been since they'd changed from sheets and blankets to continental quilts. They should have been safe in those beds.

The bulk and smell of him came at her again like a wild animal disturbed in bushland, thundering out of the scrub, hooves trampling, nostrils flaring. She felt for her own breath, inhaling deeply, letting the sensation override the image, the hammering of her heart in her chest, the cool sweat on her palms. *Breathe out*; long slow air moving up from her abdomen, out over the tiny hairs on her skin. Thank God he was dead. It had happened years before. She hadn't attended the funeral. Bernadette had sent her a message. She hadn't replied. He'd been dead to her since he'd made her leave home at seventeen.

Had her mother actually expected her to return all those years ago? Unable to rationalise or even bear the thought for another second, she swung her legs over the edge of the bed and rubbed her eyes. Yawning, she pulled on her jeans and wool cape. It was a dry night, but cold. She put on her hat and boots and strode across the courtyard. Ellen had said they could raid the fridge. The portions at the gourmet restaurant had left her stomach half empty. She wouldn't deny herself a bit of comfort food. Wasn't she after paying for it?

Aisling slid out of bed, put the complimentary fluffy white robe on over her passion-killer pyjamas and crept out of the room. She'd abstained from dessert earlier, unable to enjoy the food, such was her preoccupation with the karma she'd convinced herself would be meted out on her for having slept with Brett Goodstone. They hadn't even used a condom. How stupid she'd been. God knows what she could have contracted from the man. At least she was taking the pill.

Downstairs was bathed in soft light from lamps left on throughout the house. A standard lamp in the hallway lit her way while one of those classic green desk lamps gave out a comforting glow from near the bookshelves in the empty parlour. Only the light above the cooker was on in the kitchen but moonlight filtered through the French doors from the conservatory, giving a silvery sheen to the tiles and worktops. A laminated note on the fridge read 'Leftovers. Help yourself!'.

Not without a modicum of guilt, she opened the door. The cakes had been sliced into decent but not over-generous portions and the beef and mushroom stroganoffs placed in takeaway containers. At least she could report to Lilian and the family that the food here was excellent and there was plenty of it. She was putting the kettle on to boil when there was a noise from the mudroom. Looking up, she saw the gruff Yankee woman shedding her hat and hanging it on a hook together with that big cape Aisling coveted.

'Kettle's on,' she half-whispered as the kitchen door opened.

The woman took a moment to adjust to the dim light and take in who was speaking.

'Just me . . . Aisling . . . catching up on dessert.'

There was a small laugh in response that sounded like relief. Relief at not encountering a burglar, or at running into a guest she could actually tolerate, Aisling couldn't be sure.

'I didn't think anyone would be up,' she said.

Aisling smiled and took her cup of chamomile tea to have with the cake at the island. Taking the midnight snack upstairs wasn't an option. She'd wake Mick. He'd quit with the are-you-all-rights and softly-softly approach and had gone to bed in a huff. She could read him like a book. Fifteen years of marriage would do that, she supposed.

'Spoiled for choice on the tea front,' the woman was saying in that dodgy American accent.

It wasn't her taste in tea that interested Aisling. She eyed her as she went between fridge and microwave to warm up a portion of dinner. She'd come in a Merc for God's sake. She must be loaded. Even in this light, Aisling could tell that sweater was cashmere. And those jeans were definitely designer, something exclusive, Armani maybe. For a fairly average-looking woman, she certainly knew how to dress. She probably had her hair done by John Frieda. Even that master couldn't tame a cow's lick like hers, but he certainly made the most of it with that short style, cropped in tight on the one side and that swish of a fringe falling down the other. Aisling tucked a length of her own shoulder-length bed hair behind her ear and shifted on the stool, busting to quiz the mystery woman. But with a cup in one hand and the container under an arm, she was making for the door.

'Before you go, Katie,' Aisling began, hoping to dissuade her from leaving and engage her in a chat about America's top retail outlets and the up-and-coming designers she would later follow on Instagram. The woman turned but kept her hand on the door handle. Talking faster, Aisling went on. 'I hope you don't mind, but I'm a buyer for a department store in Australia and I have to ask, where do you buy your clothes?' She held her breath.

'Goodwill stores mostly.'

'Oh,' was all Aisling could manage as the woman left with what looked like a smug smile.

She took her phone out of the dressing gown pocket. Maybe Heather was around. She needed to vent.

*Jesus Christ, Heather,* she messaged, *this is shaping up to be the longest week of my life. How are things with you?*

She took a forkful of cake but hardly tasted it as she waited for a response.

*Good Ash! I've adopted your mother-in-law. Hope you don't mind. Got a client. Better go. Hang in there and do everything. You'll be home before you know it. Miss you x*

*Christ!* Aisling thought. Talk about adding insult to injury.

# Chapter Thirteen

A trio of rosellas picked at a lilac bush as Lilian washed up the breakfast dishes. It was Monday morning, which meant there was another whole week before she would have to share this utopian corner of the world with her son and his wife. Resting her wrists on the sink, she watched out the window as the parrots pecked in the dry earth for a few moments before taking off again and perching in the gum trees above the hammock. This was exactly what that mindfulness course was about. Being in the moment. Paying attention. The instructor's words played in her mind as they had done so many times over the past year since she'd spent eight Thursdays learning how to be present in an effort to get past the overwhelming grief that came with losing Jack and never seemed to leave.

A knock on the door interrupted her stillness.

'I'll get it, Gran.' She heard Natalie chatting to someone on the front steps. The door closed and her granddaughter appeared holding the white serving plate they'd taken to Heather's.

'They want us to go fishing,' she said, opening a cupboard and setting the plate inside.

*Her mother has her well trained*, Lilian thought as she took in the idea of spending hours in a boat. With Doug, no doubt.

'Who's all going?' she asked, not wanting to give a flat no before she had the facts.

'Ruby, Darwin and their pop.'

'Ah, Mr Bundle of Laughs himself.' Lilian smiled.

'Please, Gran. Darwin said they'll only go if we go.'

Lilian would have liked to spend the glorious day in the hammock. She only had a couple of chapters of her book to finish, but she was here to mind Natalie and if that meant putting aside her reservations about boats and a particular boatman, that's what she'd have to do.

'What'll we bring in the way of food?' she asked, the practicalities of the excursion starting to register.

'I'll get the esky. We'll take a picnic.'

'What about Evan?' She'd hardly spoken to the boy since her arrival.

'He sleeps all day, Gran. Don't worry about him.' Natalie went off to find the esky in the garage, leaving Lilian to her mental to-do list. There was shopping to be done for the picnic. The beds weren't even made. Clothes needed to be washed.

'Feed the cat as you're at it, love,' she called to Natalie as she proceeded to gather the dirty washing from the bathroom and bedrooms. Evan's door was closed. He'd be fast asleep no doubt after a late shift in the resort where he was working for the summer. Lilian pushed the door in gently and tiptoed into the room, still dark thanks to the blackout curtains Aisling had hung everywhere. There was a groan from the bed.

'Sorry, love,' she whispered. 'I'm just putting some washing on. We're heading off fishing with the neighbours. You can come if you like.' As she spoke, she began to pick up the clothes that were strewn across the carpet, a black lacy bra stopping her in her tracks.

'What's your mother's bra doing in here?' She had it out before giving the idea a second thought. Looking up, she saw Evan's arm curve around the shape of what could only be another human body.

'It's not Mum's,' he mumbled without opening his eyes.

'Oh!' She backed out of the room. 'I'll talk to you later.'

Closing the door behind her, Lilian didn't know whether to be amused or mortified. No one had mentioned a girlfriend. *Does your mother know?* She hummed the ABBA song as she loaded the washing machine in the laundry, knowing both the song and the scene would play in her head all day.

—

Armed with a full esky, sunhats and sunscreen, Lilian and Natalie set off for the neighbours'. Lilian had thought it best not to mention her encounter to Natalie and left Evan and his visitor to the privacy of the house. He was seventeen. She'd prefer he'd waited, but he wasn't her son. He wasn't even really her grandson. God knows what age the girl was; hopefully not under whatever was the legal age in Australia.

Lilian had come here for a rest, but this was Aisling's family after all. She should have expected some drama.

Doug and his granddaughters were loading up the back of his dual cab ute on the grassy parking strip across from the clutch of houses that made up the street. The solid-looking boat sat proud on the trailer, its white hull gleaming in the sunshine, glass panelling and a blue canopy sheltering the controls. Through the she-oaks, Lilian could see the calm waters at Hawley Beach where the midmorning sunshine dried the dark rocks that sported a thriving growth of bright orange lichen. Natalie had informed her it was a sign of good air quality. As she took a couple of deep breaths, Lilian didn't doubt the child was right.

'Glorious day,' she said to Doug, who gave her a bare nod from where he was bent over the coupling between ute and trailer. A flutter stirred in Lilian's tummy. Torn between fear and a sense of adventure, she said a silent prayer she'd survive the day.

'Hop in,' Doug told them.

When the three girls piled into the back seat, Lilian was impressed by the respect they were showing their elder, until she tried to sit in the front. It took about three goes to scale the height of the doorway with the girls giving all sorts of advice about holding inside handles and pulling herself up. In the end, she lunged towards the handbrake and nearly fell in before straightening in the seat and gathering what was left of her dignity.

'Buckle up,' said Doug, who hadn't offered any assistance, but had stared straight ahead during the whole embarrassing series of manoeuvres.

Lilian was grateful for the slow drive through Hawley that gave her a chance to do a surreptitious mindfulness exercise as their driver navigated the speed bumps and tight corners, keeping an eye on the boat in his side mirror. The sandy beaches were busy with locals and holiday-makers, but not in the kind of numbers you'd get in popular resorts. Mick had told her about the families from Sydney and Melbourne who came every summer, their holiday houses lying empty for the rest of the year. Aisling had wished his job had brought them to somewhere a bit more lively, but Mick loved it here, acutely aware of how lucky they were to have this as their front yard.

As they drove, Lilian was amazed at how many new houses had gone up since her last visit three years before. The suburb of Shearwater had expanded to become a seamless link between the more established hamlets of Hawley and Port Sorell. She might have pointed this out to Doug and asked if he'd noticed, but the prospect of a monosyllabic answer put her off.

At the boat ramp, he got them all to get out before backing the trailer down to the water. Lilian held on to the door for dear life as she slid to the edge of her seat and did an ungainly hop out of the vehicle. The girls were already pulling on life jackets when she joined them. She was relieved to find there was one for her too.

With a little help from her granddaughter, Lilian made it safely onboard. Standing at the wheel, Doug checked they were all in and clear to get underway. Lilian was grateful for the gentle pace and the pleasant thrum of the engine as they pulled away from shore, but still held on to Natalie's hand.

'You'll be fine, Gran,' she assured her.

Lilian squeezed her hand and pulled the strap of her life jacket tighter all the same. She couldn't remember the last time she'd been in a boat. Many moons ago, that was for sure, but Natalie didn't need to know that. As they made their way out into the estuary, Lilian eyed Doug from the cover of her sunglasses and sunhat. Must have been a good-looking man in his day, she thought, taking in the tall lean frame and the thinning grey-blond hair. As for personality, she couldn't say. Perhaps he'd always been a man of few words, destined to be an old grump, but there was a sadness about him. She'd seen it in some of the residents where she visited a relative in a care home. Once vibrant, with a vitality that got sucked out of them with the insidious senescence of ageing. It was hard to put an age on him. She'd thought mid seventies at the house, but here out on the water, there was more of an energy about him, a glimpse perhaps into a younger, happier version of himself.

Natalie took it upon herself to point out the local land-marks as they motored out to where the Rubicon Estuary flowed into Bass Strait. Lilian had seen it all on maps and from the air, but there was something magical about being out on the water, part of it, as if she were right there in the map, navigating the channels from the inside as opposed to referring to a picture to get her bearings. She took a deep breath of the sea air. As long as the life jacket remained secure, Doug's heart held up and his faculties could be relied upon, they'd survive. But she had no reason to question their skipper's health, mental or otherwise. What a cheek she had to be ageist. Only the fear talking, she decided. Another deep breath, concentrating on the passage of salty air down into her lungs, and her misgivings subsided.

At the end of Hawley where the land curved round towards Devonport, Doug instructed the girls to drop anchor. Eager to assist, Natalie shot up and went to the front of the boat. Ruby and Darwin looked up from their phones and watched their neighbour and grandfather feed the rope over the side. Yawning, Darwin eventually moved and took one of the fishing rods perched in holders at the back of the boat, absently casting into the navy-blue depths.

'Have you put the bait on?' her grandfather asked.

'Oops!' With a tinge of red in her cheeks, she wound the line back in and opened the tackle box. 'Ew!'

Lilian felt her pain as she spotted the plastic carton inside the box, literally crawling with her friends the soldier crabs. She tried not to squirm at the sight of them but looked away, pretending to admire the sparkling waters while the girls impaled the creatures on hooks and threw them over the side. It wasn't long before Natalie had a bite.

'Help!' she called out, waving the rod about as she struggled to keep the tension on the line and not let her prize get away.

'Pull it in,' Lilian shouted, more to encourage the girl than offer any useful advice.

Doug, who'd been helping Darwin at the other side of the boat, came to the rescue, saying nothing but placing his weather-beaten hands around Natalie's and showing her what to do.

'Like this?' she was saying while reeling the line back in.

'That's the way,' said Doug. As a sizeable fish broke the surface, Lilian felt her chest swell. Natalie kept her excitement in check long enough to land the shiny specimen into the boat.

'Let's put him out of his misery,' Doug told her before grabbing a mallet and delivering a swift blow to the gulping head.

For a second, Lilian feared Natalie would regret her catch, but she was back into the tackle box, organising her bait and casting off for another go. The girls, meanwhile, were only half-fishing, rods in one hand, mobile phones in the other, at least until Ruby got a bite and the phone was shoved inside the pocket of her shorts in just enough time before her catch got away.

Darwin, who wasn't catching anything, soon lost interest and offered her rod to Lilian.

'Thanks, love, but I'm happy to watch,' she said. 'Don't want to be pulled in by anything.'

The girl took a seat beside her. 'Did you used to fish when you were younger?'

'I have cousins who were great anglers,' Lilian told her. 'They lived in a beautiful part of Ireland called Crosshaven.' The girl actually looked interested, so she went on. 'Won angling competitions every weekend. I'd go along to meet boys at the weigh-in.' She winked, receiving a conspiratorial smile in return. 'But do you know what? All I remember now are the Conger eels.' Darwin frowned. 'Big black dirty-looking fish that would thrash about making everyone stand aside.'

'Ew!'

Lilian laughed.

'Are you ready for a sandwich?'

The pair of them set to preparing lunch while the others landed a few more fish. Whiting and trevally, Doug called them, but to Lilian and Darwin they were all slimy sea-dwellers, better on a plate with chips than writhing around on the floor of a boat.

After they'd eaten, Lilian was grateful for Darwin's help in packing the lunch things back in the esky. Doug had eaten in silence but thanked her for the sandwich and the cup of coffee she'd decanted from a thermos she'd found at the back of Aisling and Mick's pantry.

'Onward to Bakers Beach,' Natalie announced.

Lilian held her life jacket to her stomach as Doug gunned the craft into the chop where the tide worked against them, feeding the river towards open sea. They crossed the mouth to Griffiths Point and followed the pristine shoreline where golden beach backed on to bushland. A few curious seagulls came to check out their catch, an extra-opportunistic one resting on the bow as they neared the shallower water and dropped anchor once again.

Lilian took the sunscreen from her bag, reminding them all to reapply. More relaxed now that they'd come to a stop again, she lay down along the cushioned seating, hoping to improve on her nicely developing tan. She always felt healthier with a bit of colour. Arriving back to midwinter Ireland, she could use all the feel-good factor she could get. It would be back to the 'long-short days' as she'd come to call them since retiring. At least after losing Jack, she'd had work to fill the daylight hours. Now she had to look for ways to pass the time.

She didn't realise she'd drifted off until she heard a great splash to one side of the boat. Sitting up, she saw Ruby in the water, life jacket up around her chin, hair clinging to her head, looking like she could kill someone.

'Arrgh!' Ruby pounded on the surface with both fists.

As Lilian took in what was happening, Doug divested himself of his T-shirt and Crocs and was leaping from the side in a kind of pike that sent him into the water like a heron after its prey. The other girls looked on agog as he searched the sandy bottom before resurfacing, holding the pink phone aloft and swiping seawater off his face.

'It's wrecked . . . all my contacts . . .' Ruby wailed.

'We'll put it in rice,' said Darwin, reaching for the phone.

A well-practised technique, Lilian mused as she stifled a belly laugh.

'Anyone fancy a swim as we're here?' Doug was treading water near the boat.

Lilian would have loved the wherewithal to fling herself into the cool shallows beside him, but shook her head.

'Let's do it, Gran.' Natalie was oblivious to her shortcomings when it came to aquatic pursuits.

'Off you go, love. I'll sit tight here. Someone has to mind the boat.'

It was a pleasure to watch the four of them. Once Ruby had thrown her life jacket onboard and recovered from her shock, the three girls raced each other to shore while Doug swam off in parallel to the beach with an impressive overarm. Jack had been a fine swimmer, taught all four boys, but Lilian had never been much for the water. Too busy carrying the supplies and tidying up after her rambunctious brood.

Doug returned and pulled himself up the small ladder at the back of the boat. Lilian made to look away and rummage in a bag for fear of being caught ogling at anything lower than the hairy chest and strong shoulders of the man dripping onto the seat beside her. She handed him a towel.

'I bet that felt good,' she said, smiling at him but not expecting much of a response.

'I'll tell you what would feel good,' he began. Her heart skipped at the prospect of what he might say. 'A cup of that coffee you brought.'

'Coming right up,' she said, grateful to have to turn away to the esky for fear she might giggle at her own silly fantasy. What would Jack say if he knew she was letting her imagination run away with her over another man? He'd be in no danger, she smiled to herself. This Doug character might be well preserved, but unless he was hiding a personality under those hirsute pectorals, there was no chance of anything her imagination might conjure.

～

Relieved to be back on dry land, Lilian thanked Doug and the girls for a wonderful day out and shooed Natalie round the side of the house to the outdoor shower. Charlie seemed happy to see them return, but quickly backed away, shaking out his paws when he'd ventured too close to the running water where Lilian left Natalie to shampoo her hair and get off all the sand.

Inside, she put the wet towels on to wash and went to hang out the load she'd put on that morning. There was no sign of Evan or his love interest. She'd send a text in a minute to check if he was okay. He was another one shaping up to be the strong silent type. My God, she was surrounded.

The next-door neighbours were enjoying the good weather. She could hear chatter from their beautiful front veranda that was raised high enough to give them a million-dollar view right onto the beach. A couple of campervans had parked on the green area opposite. Visitors of the neighbours no doubt. She marvelled again at the lifestyle her son and his family were lucky enough to enjoy. *Worked hard for, more like*, she reminded herself. Both Mick and Aisling were grafters. Just a shame they were all so far away. She would have gladly pitched in if it made their lives easier.

Charlie was winding his way round her ankles when she heard sobs from the side of the house. After nearly face-planting on the lawn over him, she rushed round to find Natalie leaning against the end wall, head resting on crossed arms, sobbing to herself.

'What is it, sweetheart?'

'Oh, Gran, Gran . . .' She could hardly get the words out.

Looking down, Lilian saw the cause of her distress. A patch of bloodied water pooled between the paving stones. Lilian grabbed a fresh towel from inside the laundry door and went back to her.

'Come here, love.' She turned the shower off and wrapped the towel around the quaking child. 'Is this your first time?' she asked.

Natalie nodded. 'Oh, Gran, it's horrible.' The sobbing started up again.

'Don't you worry, sweetheart. Let's get you dried off and into some fresh clothes.'

Lilian had no idea whether the house was stocked with sanitary essentials, but she left Natalie to dry off in the laundry and went to search the bathroom drawers. Not a thing. She tried Mick and Aisling's ensuite. In behind four hundred bottles of nail varnish in every hue known to man, she found a box of tampons. Not her first choice, but there were no pads. Expensive perfume, yes, extra bottles of salon hair products, yes, but no sign of contingency plans for her only daughter. Lilian sucked in her frustration. How the heck would she explain to Natalie how to insert one of those things? Raising four boys never prepared her for this. She'd got her first period when they were still using belts and bandages. Stick-on pads were such a luxury, she'd never bothered with tampons. Of course, at that time in Holy Catholic Ireland, exploring one's nether regions was completely frowned upon. She'd hardly known what was down there let alone poke something inside.

'Do you know what to do . . .' she began when she found Natalie in her room pulling on a clean T-shirt, the towel tucked around her like a pair of shorts.

'Yes, Gran.' She took the packet from Lilian and ran off to the bathroom.

Lilian said a silent prayer the girl wouldn't do herself a damage with those things and went to empty the esky. Her phone beeped on the bench. It was Evan.

*Working. Home for tea.*

Well, at least the boy had the sense to let her know where he was. When her granddaughter emerged, Lilian had an urge to fill a hot water bottle and make her curl up on the couch under a blanket, but it was twenty-five degrees. Instead, they opted for a cool drink and spent the rest of the afternoon reading books in the garden, Charlie lying across Natalie's tummy as if he knew it was just what she needed.

It was after six when Evan appeared from his shift at the resort.

'Busy day?' Lilian asked as he set his keys and sunglasses on the kitchen bench and helped himself to a glass of the iced tea she'd made in an effort to combat the heat.

'Yeah, what's for tea?' he asked before sculling the drink.

'I thought we'd get pizza from that nice place by the campsite.' As well as feeding them, it would give her an excuse to get the boy on his own. 'I'll give them a ring and we can pick it up in a bit.'

Happy with the prospect of takeaway anything, Evan agreed, even phoning in the order for them.

In the car, she willed herself to speak calmly. He wasn't her son, not even really her grandson. She'd loved this shy dark-haired boy since he'd first come to visit her and Jack as a toddler. How he'd blossomed in Australia with the sunshine of his parents' loving care, much of the hands-on parenting from Mick, she knew, given his mother's crazy schedule. That father of his hadn't even put up a fight to have him stay in Ireland. Aisling was well shot of him by all accounts. But Lilian and Jack had never pried. Aisling could be hard work, but Mick loved her and their children and that was all that mattered in the end.

She waited as Evan negotiated the bends and speed bumps of Hawley, saying nothing until they were on a straight strip of road.

'Was that your girlfriend?' she asked finally, glad to have the words out there.

Out of the corner of her eye, she could see the colour in his cheeks and the bobbing in his throat where an Adam's apple had moved in since she was here last. Along his jawline, a patch of pimples took her back to when her own boys were teenagers. She'd tread carefully.

'Yeah, nah,' he said, which of course was of no help.

She laughed. 'That sounds a bit like when you ask an Irish person to do something and they say, "I will in a minute," leaving you with no idea whether it will ever be done.'

He smiled then, the signature shy smile.

'I know I'm old, but I was young once, you know.'

He took a hand off the steering wheel and rubbed it along the other arm.

'Two hands,' she cautioned, the warning out before she could retract it.

'I know what I'm doing, Gran.' He put his hand back on the wheel nonetheless.

'That's good, son.'

They pulled up outside the takeaway and went in together.

Sitting back in the car with the warm pizza boxes on her lap, she considered the confidence of the seventeen-year-old as he went through the steps of mirror, indicate, manoeuvre that would make any driving instructor proud. Apart from the one-handed steering, Mick had taught him well.

'Does your mother know?' She had to ask; she'd been singing that song all day.

His face flamed again. 'Not really.'

'Ah Jesus, Evan, you're killing me here.'

'You weren't supposed to find out,' he said, his voice up an octave. 'We were trying to be . . .'

'Discreet?'

'Yeah, that word.'

She tried her best not to laugh. 'It's okay to have a girl-friend, you know.'

'Mum wouldn't agree with you.' He relaxed for a second, but tensed again as he said, 'Please don't tell, Gran.'

'Dear God, are you serious?'

He shrugged. 'She wants me to get through Year Twelve . . . without . . . distractions.'

'Oh for God's sake.' Lilian had worried about her sons at that age, but she'd never denied them a social life. She'd got that from her own mother. Never one for 'spare the rod and spoil the child' thinking, she'd always been relaxed when it came to their youthful shenanigans.

'I could bribe you,' she said, letting out a burst of laughter.

'I'll vacuum . . . clean the showers . . .'

She put a hand on his arm. 'Don't get in a tizzy. It's up to you. I'm not judging.' She thought for a minute. 'Can you just promise me you'll be safe?'

'Oh, Gran,' he groaned. 'They teach us all that in school.'

'Well, don't hide her away. Invite her for tea.'

He shook his head. 'I'll see.'

It might be beans on toast, but at least she'd meet the girl fully clothed.

# Chapter Fourteen

Mick strolled into breakfast, all clean-shaven and freshly showered. New day, he'd told himself, trying to shake off the nagging thoughts that were threatening to spoil his holiday. Aisling was taking that long to get ready, he'd thought to come down on his own. They'd never used the lock on an ensuite before this trip. Whatever she was trying to hide, locking herself into bathrooms wasn't going to help.

'Morning,' said Mia, giving him a warm smile as he brought a bowl of muesli to the table and sat opposite her.

'I'm branching out today,' he said, looking into the bowl to double-check the contents before eating. 'What do they put in this stuff?'

'Try it,' she said. 'If you don't like it, you can have something else.'

He gave a warm laugh. 'You're right. I'll embrace the modern and I can always have bacon and eggs afterwards.'

They ate in companionable silence.

'Do you know it isn't that bad,' said Mick after a couple of mouthfuls.

'Good on you for giving it a go.'

'A red hot go, as we'd say Down Under.' He laughed as he spooned up the last of the milky mush. 'All set for our excursion?'

'I sure am,' she said, finishing her meal and gathering up her ware and cutlery. 'Can't wait for a good fossick on the beach.' She got up to leave. 'See you soon.'

Her enthusiasm was infectious. Maybe a busy day on the beach with the crew here was just what Aisling needed to 'blow out the cobwebs' as his father always said. She'd been distant again yesterday. He was starting to get a bit that way himself. But it was a new day. He'd hope for the best.

As Mia left, Prue arrived, her voice filling the quiet room. When the door opened, he'd hoped it would be Aisling. She'd be down soon, he told himself.

'What a spread!' Prue was holding her upturned palms to the breakfast buffet. 'What to have!'

'How're ya, Prue?' he asked as she plonked herself in Declan's spot at the head of the table and made a production of freeing herself from a paisley-patterned pashmina.

'Enjoying the top nosh here,' she said before tucking into a colourful selection of fruit and pastries. 'In some places it's continental or cooked breakfast,' she went on, washing down a mouthful with a gulp of orange juice. 'Here you get both.'

He smiled at both the comment and her appetite, which he suspected might extend as much to life as to food.

'Your wife not an early riser?' Prue asked, but before he could answer, she continued, 'Just like Ed. Had to nearly pull her out of the bath last night and make her get some sleep. Avid reader, you see. Keeps her up half the night.' With a conspiratorial smile, she added, 'Wish I could say it was me.'

Mick burst out laughing. 'I'm sure you have your moments, Prue.'

'I like to think so, Mick.'

The French doors opened again.

'And speak of the divils.' He got up and pulled a chair out for Aisling who avoided his attention and headed straight to the buffet.

'Good morning, Mick isn't it?' Edwina came towards the table, eyeing him through a set of spectacular eyelashes and laying a hand on Prue's shoulder.

'It is,' said Mick. 'Nice day out there now.'

He left them talking about breakfast and joined Aisling.

'You want to go to that seaweed thing today?' he asked.

He thought the glass of apple juice she was holding might break, such was the grip she had on it. There was a pause as she went to speak, but nothing came out. When she finally looked him in the eye, he thought he saw worry.

'Do you mind if I have an hour or so to myself?'

He knew she was decoding his frown and tried to look normal, or at least as normal as one can possibly look when standing in front of the spouse you think is cheating on you and you have to be on your best behaviour as you are, after all, in a goddamn guesthouse.

'I'll need the car,' she said, returning her attention to the buffet.

God, she looked desperate. Tired, drained. Surely the jet lag had subsided by now. Maybe she was coming down with something. His hand shot to her forehead.

'What are you doing?' she said, swaying a little away from him.

He put his hand in his pocket. 'Sorry, Ash. I thought you might have a temperature . . . that you're getting something.'

'No, I'm fine,' she said. 'Just have an errand to run before the big day.'

He gave a shrug. 'You don't need to spend anything on me. Sure, isn't this our present?'

'From your family,' she corrected.

He thought to push the point, but Gerry appeared all smiles asking what they'd like from the kitchen where he was obviously after cooking up another culinary storm. The smell of bacon set off a low growl in Mick's stomach despite the bowl of muesli he'd just consumed.

'Go on so,' he told her. 'I'll take my time here.'

She folded a serviette round a couple of pastries and left him wondering what the heck she was up to.

—

The health centre didn't open until 9 a.m., but Aisling wasn't taking any chances at being turned away. She watched as the door was unlocked by a lady inside and legged it out of the car.

'Hello,' she said to the woman before she'd even got behind the reception desk. 'I don't have an appointment, I'm on holiday . . .'

'You'll have to fill this out.' She thrust a clipboard at her. 'We're quiet this morning, so we might squeeze you in.'

Aisling gave her a grateful smile and took a seat in the waiting room where she filled out the form as directed while trying to reassure herself. These people dealt with tourists all the time. Okay, maybe not ones that had unprotected sex while cheating on their husbands, but they were qualified to deal with the consequences. She suppressed an urge to chew on one of her acrylic nails, instead smoothing them out, even though they were like ganache. The receptionist came to retrieve her form.

'I'll take that from you,' she said. 'Help yourself to a magazine.'

Hardly able to sit still with the worry, Aisling got up and took a copy of *Red* from the pile on a glass coffee table. Colourful pages with everything from handbags to nappy bags favoured by celebrities flashed in front of her as she flicked through, unable to focus for fear of what might be ahead of her. It was an article in a magazine just like this one that had made her wonder if she might have something seriously wrong with her in the first place. Not only could she no longer keep the whole sorry affair from Mick, but she might have passed something on to him.

She was trying to concentrate on an article on how long it takes for people to move in together when her name was called.

'Aisling,' the receptionist was brisk. 'Doctor Morrison will see you in Room Two.'

*Aisling Fitzgerald, dirty little cheat,* was how it sounded in her head, but she gathered herself and her Kate Spade clutch and strode down the carpeted corridor.

Doctor Morrison was perched at the edge of an office chair, thin legs crossed at the knee under a flowing skirt, a set of exquisite cheekbones framed by a bright hijab.

'Come in, Aisling,' she said with a friendly smile that was enough for Aisling to let the door close behind her and commit her problems to the thirty-something stranger.

'I see you're from Tasmania,' the doctor said with an enthusiasm Aisling hadn't expected.

'I'm originally from Cork,' she heard herself respond, almost apologising for fear of disappointing the beautiful exotic young woman who smelled as good as she looked. She made a mental note to check out this year's fragrances in the airports on the way home. 'We live in Tassie.'

'Hobart is my favourite place,' the doctor went on. 'That's where I met my husband. We studied there.' The dewy-eyed look made Aisling almost forget why she was here, but Doctor Haute Hijab was on the job, with a friendly but firm, 'So what can I do for you, Aisling?'

At the prospect of verbalising her infidelity for the first time, Aisling felt tears smart at the corners of her eyes. The woman before her looked like someone who would never dream of cheating on that husband of hers, let alone go through with it, and why in all fairness had she done that very thing with the good husband she had in Mick?

'I'm afraid I might *have* something,' she began, the doctor listening as she went on to explain how she'd been feeling for weeks now; the tiredness, poor sleep and frequent trips to the bathroom that had all conspired to convince her she had some kind of sexually transmitted disease.

Without letting the sympathetic smile slip, the woman turned to her computer and went through a list of questions about symptoms, some of a most painful nature that Aisling was grateful to have avoided. There were questions about sexual partners, standard information-gathering she knew, but mortifying nonetheless.

'I'll examine you,' the doctor said, inviting Aisling to hop up on the bed while she went to a wall dispenser and put on a pair of surgical gloves.

After what felt like a thorough examination, the gloves were pulled off.

'Everything seems normal . . .'

Aisling went to suggest she might be mistaken but pulled on her jeans and underwear and sat back in the chair without a word.

'I'll give you a form for a blood test just in case.' The printer whirred on the desk beside the doctor. 'Have you been experiencing a bit of stress lately?'

'You could say that.'

'Your symptoms could definitely be stress-related.' She took the form from the printer and set it on the desk between them. 'Have you talked to your husband at all?'

Aisling looked down at her lap and shook her head.

'I'm not a psychologist,' she went on, 'but maybe you're feeling guilty about what happened and the stress is causing these symptoms.' There was a softness to her voice. 'He's a reasonable man, I assume?'

Aisling bit her lip. The woman was right. Of course she was. The god-awful imaginings of the fallout of her night with Brett Goodstone were just that – a distraction from where she really needed to focus her energy. Tears leaked onto her cheeks as she looked up, desperate to reassure this woman that Mick was nothing other than a decent person.

'Oh he is . . . a good man . . . the best, really.'

The doctor passed her a tissue box.

'You're right.' Aisling sniffed. 'I'm sorry to have wasted your time, but I'm glad I came in.'

'Not at all,' she said, handing her the form. 'Peace of mind is more important than all the pills I prescribe here.'

At reception, the woman checked her computer and quoted some arrangement about reciprocal agreements. Aisling handed over her card and let her take the necessary details. As she turned to leave, a tall gruff-looking man appeared in the doorway.

'Mrs Daly,' he called out.

To Aisling's amazement, Katie from the guesthouse began helping an old woman to her unsteady feet and handed her a walking stick. With her full attention on guiding the frail creature, she didn't see Aisling stare. Was there no end to the enigma of the American?

In The Coffee Pot, Aisling cradled a mug of hot tea after devouring a piece of carrot cake that had gone some way to alleviating, at least temporarily, the emotional pain of what she'd just undertaken. To think she'd gone in there and poured out her sorry story to a complete stranger while having been unable to tell another soul what she'd done.

She checked her phone for messages. There was a reassuring note from Heather to say the kids were fine and the house was still standing, followed by several laughing emojis. Such a dependable friend. Lilian had posted in Mick's family's WhatsApp group – a selfie of herself and Natalie on Penguin Island and a picture of them out in a boat with Heather's father and daughters. Looked like her mother-in-law was having a better holiday than she was. *Typical!*

She still hadn't responded to Brett. He'd said he missed her. Could they hook up again when she was next in Melbourne, or maybe he could come to Tasmania? They could find a quiet getaway, pretend they were working. The thought of him made her feel sick. She'd have to face him soon enough at the next interstate meeting. God knows how many other married women he might be stringing along. It had been all fun on the night – a stupid one-night stand – but here he was, pushing for more. A colleague from Queensland she'd shared a room with had caught her sneaking back in the early hours when shame and a pounding headache had brought her to her senses. At breakfast the following morning, she'd taken Aisling aside and warned her to be careful if she wanted to keep her job. Brett had a reputation for swapping sex for promotions and salary increases. He wasn't even that good-looking, but somehow, she'd gone along with him, stayed for kick-ons in his room when everyone else had had the sense to call it a night. Wine in, wit out; she could say it was that simple. The tailored suit, the four-hundred-dollar aftershave, copious amounts of Christmas punch and cocktails compromising her judgement. But how could she have been so shallow, shagging the senior manager when she had a perfectly good partner of her own? The doctor was right. She had to tell Mick. Regardless of what the blood test showed up, the guilt would haunt her for the rest of her life.

Scrolling through her photo gallery, she stopped at a selfie Natalie had insisted on taking at Devonport Airport. Her beautiful family all smiles for the camera, hers belying the devastation her secret could unleash. How had she lost sight of what was important? Behaved so recklessly? Contrary to his mother's opinion, Mick Fitzgerald wasn't a saint, but he'd never cheat on her. He put up with her working long hours and always picked up the slack, encouraged her in her career. She'd been desperate company, irritable and withdrawn. They used to have fun, make each other laugh. She had to be honest with him. But the anniversary . . . his birthday . . . The timing couldn't be more lousy.

Not knowing what to do with herself, she left the coffee shop and hopped in her car. It wasn't a bad day. With zero traffic and spectacular scenery, she could drive around for hours putting off the inevitable. At a bend in some back road, she spotted the ruins of a small church overlooking the sea. She wasn't the church-going type, but something made her pull over and drew her up the path where clumps of soft moss pushed up between battered paving stones.

Zipping up her jacket, she began to walk around the ruins where time-weathered gravestones rose like rotten teeth from the overgrown plot beside the one church wall that remained intact. The salty wind whipped about her legs, cutting through the exposed stretch of jeans between where her jacket ended and the leather boots shielded her calves. She wished she'd taken her longer coat and gloves, but then she hadn't bargained on a tramp around a graveyard in the bogs of Ireland. A traipse around the shops in Skib to find a special gift for her husband might have been a better use of time, but she was here now. She could say a prayer for the dead. They might say one for her in return.

'A fellow ghost hunter?'

At the sound of the male voice, she put a hand to her chest. But her fears were allayed when she saw Declan Byrne making his way towards her from where she'd been unable to see him behind the church wall. *Of all people to run into in this godforsaken neck of the woods.*

'My forebears are buried here,' he said with a melancholic smile, completely unaware of having startled her.

'Is that right?' said Aisling, at a loss as to how to explain her own presence on the hallowed ground. 'I love old graveyards.' The lie that had come from nowhere seemed to satisfy him.

'Great history here, you know. Come and I'll show you the wart well.'

Before she could make her excuses and get away from him, he was off striding through the bracken, hands shoved into his Helly Hansen jacket. There was nothing for it but to follow him over the uneven ground to where he stopped and pointed to something invisible in the knee-deep vegetation.

*Lonesome old bugger*, she thought, peering down to where she could make out a stone mound like a super-sized doughnut, a dark pool of water at its centre, still despite the stiff breeze.

'Found it again after years,' he was saying. 'When we were kids, we'd cycle up here and dip our hands in, thinking we'd be cured.'

'We used to rub bits of potato on them,' she said, remembering primary school friends and their innocent antics. If only all hurts could be so easily cured.

'Piseogs, we called them,' he said, breaking into her musing.

'Oh, we had lots of them.' Hearing the word for those crazy superstitions from childhood made her smile. Life was so much simpler then. She thought of her own Natalie happily trawling the beach for cowries, still inventing stories about sea creatures and fantasy worlds like those in her beloved books. On the cusp of adolescence, she was hardly ready for the deep dive that would be her teenage years and the loss of all that beautiful innocence.

Anxious to be alone, and fearing Declan was about to launch into one of his monologues, Aisling began stepping past him.

'Sorry, Declan, but 'tis bitter cold. I'd better keep moving.'

'Rightio,' he said. 'Are you going to the seaweed session?'

'No. I have a few things to get . . . in Skib.'

For a split second, she thought she caught a look of scepticism in his eye, but he gave a nod and went on his way.

'I'll see you for another sumptuous meal tonight, *gan dabht.*'

'*Gan dabht*,' she heard herself repeating the Irish 'no doubt'.

Watching him make his way out, lifting his knees to navigate through the neglected field, she had a maternal urge to call out and tell him take his hands out of his pockets. But she had enough to think about. He was a grown man. If he took a tumble it would be his own fault.

# Chapter Fifteen

When Katie had arrived at her mother's and got no answer, she'd let herself in.

'I'll be out in a minute,' Phyllis had called from where she remained holed up in the bathroom for another forty minutes.

Katie had felt like cursing her until she finally emerged in a smart blue skirt and twin set, the pearl necklace that had been her own mother's around her scrawny neck and she smelling of hairspray and the powder she'd applied to her lined face. The energy it must have taken wasn't lost on Katie. She'd sucked in her impatience and retrieved the good coat hanging on the hallstand, holding it out while the old woman slowly manoeuvred her skeletal arms into its heavy sleeves.

'Doctor Healy's a gentleman,' she'd said on the way.

The disappointment on her face when that Doctor Smit had shown her into his room was painful. Sitting in the spare chair beside her now, Katie cringed at what felt like the Spanish Inquisition.

'How often are your bowels moving?' 'What did you eat for breakfast?' 'Do you know what day it is?' the doctor quizzed flatly in between measuring her blood pressure, checking her pulse, listening to her chest. 'You missed your last two appointments,' he noted, consulting his computer screen. 'Why is that?'

'My daughter gets a bit busy,' Phyllis answered.

He glared at Katie then.

'Not me,' she said, quickly coming to her own defence.

'My other daughter,' her mother corrected. 'Doctor Healy knows her.'

'Doctor Healy's on holiday,' he said, dismissing her comment and turning a cool gaze on Katie. 'And where do you fit in?'

Katie found herself explaining somewhat pathetically that she was only here for a week after travelling from America.

'Do you always make such short trips?' he asked, smiling now as if the prospect of tripping back and forth from America amused him.

She shook her head. *Not since 1985*, she might have said, but he could no doubt get the lowdown on how long she'd been away if he'd asked any local.

'Your other daughter,' he went on, looking back at Phyllis, 'she lives with you?'

Her mother patted the pearls at her neck before answering in a small voice, 'She's in Schull, but she comes out when she can.'

'How often?' Katie couldn't stop herself.

The doctor began typing and when her mother failed to answer, he prompted, 'Would that be every day, every week?'

'She does her best, doctor. She calls out to me on her lunchbreak some days and always takes me to Mass on a Sunday . . .'

Katie rolled her eyes. Her sister might be blissfully unaware of their mother's sleeping arrangements, but of course she went to Mass.

Turning again to them, he asked, 'Is anyone else looking in on you, Phyllis? A neighbour?'

'Rita down the road is very good,' she said, but Katie could see she was trying to give him answers that would reassure him she was being better looked after.

'How often do you see Rita?' he persisted.

Katie interjected before she could answer. 'Would she do the shopping for you?'

'I'm sure she would if I asked her,' Phyllis answered with a positivity Katie suspected was put on. 'But sure doesn't Bernadette make all my meals for the week on a Sunday after Mass?' She said it as if this was a piece of information Katie should have known. Had Bernadette honestly expected her to be cooking up meals in that kitchen she could barely set foot in?

Both she and the doctor looked on as Phyllis pulled her walking stick closer and shrugged. As angry as she was with Bernadette for not giving her the full story on their mother's living arrangements, Katie was determined to keep her cool. This was not her responsibility, but she was damned if anything untoward should happen on her watch, letting Bernadette off scot-free. It was a case of speak now or forever hold your peace.

'Mammy, I think we should tell the doctor about your sleeping on the settee.'

Phyllis shifted uneasily in the chair as the doctor waited for her to elaborate. 'It's just the arthritis,' she said, patting her left knee. 'Can't really do the stairs anymore.'

'Have you had a fall?' he asked.

'Just a tumble or two.' She gave a small self-deprecating laugh. 'Stupidity really. I need to be more careful.'

'When was this?'

She thought for a minute. 'Before Katie came.'

*Thank God*, thought Katie.

'Did you notice anything?' He was asking Katie now.

'I hadn't seen her for ages,' she began. 'I thought she looked very stiff all right.'

It was a feeble explanation for the difference thirty-five years had made, but that was not her fault.

'Are you sore anywhere else beside the knee?'

Phyllis hesitated before placing a hand on her right hip and giving it a rub. The doctor didn't need to hear anymore. He was up on his feet.

'Let me examine you.'

Katie helped her out of the chair but turned away to give her privacy as she lifted her skirt and pulled down her tights.

'Come and see,' the doctor told her.

When she turned back, Katie winced as she saw the purple and yellow of the bruised skin.

'You're lucky you didn't break your hip.'

He returned to his desk and began typing.

'We'll have to do a formal assessment,' he announced. 'Make an appointment for Thursday.' He glared at her as she stood up to leave. 'And don't miss this one.'

'I'll get her here, don't worry,' said Katie, scuttling out the door like a scolded child.

Back at the house, Katie helped her mother off with the good coat, put the kettle on and sat down at the kitchen table to ask a few questions of her own. No, she didn't get out much. No, she didn't see many people. Weren't her friends all gone or too sick themselves? Yes, she had enough to eat. A boiled egg in the morning and whatever Bernadette brought was plenty. Holy God! If she didn't step up, the woman might starve. Why in God's name hadn't Bernadette been more clear? But Katie hadn't even replied to her sister's texts. In all honesty, she'd been that focused on the enormity of making the trip back to Goleen, she hadn't put much scrutiny into the details of her sister's or her mother's lives. 'Keep an eye on her,' Bernadette had said. 'She's in bed by five thirty, six. You won't have to do much.' *Understatement of the year!*

One week and she'd have paid her dues. She'd do as the doctor asked and bring her back on Thursday. But she didn't need an official assessment to tell her the woman needed help. If Bernadette was working all the hours God sent and their mother couldn't look after herself, there was only one thing for it. Phyllis Daly should be in a home.

Katie thought about calling Bernadette but imagined her cosying up with her lover on the Costa Del something or other. Her brother was closer. Maybe he could come down and discuss arrangements, find out what Phyllis wanted to do. After all, it was her life. She could do what she liked. Besides, Katie wasn't about to get involved in sending her off to a home even if it did seem like poetic justice.

—

At Lizzie O's, the group met in the conservatory where Gerry invited them to fill keep cups with tea or coffee and to take packages of fresh scones and pastries he'd made. Ellen had already kitted out the less prepared with gum boots she'd procured from a charity shop and brand-new woollen hats and gloves she said they could keep as she was getting them cheap from a local.

*This place is the best.* Mia smiled to herself, depositing her snacks into her backpack. As the minibus arrived, they filed out into the sunshine. All set in her beanie and gumboots, she was reminded of her university days and the annual field trips where the whole class would take a bus up the coast and spend a week studying different habitats. She felt the same excitement now, eager to find out what their guide had in store.

'Good morning, everyone!' A short stocky woman alighted from the bus and smiled a big beam of a smile that spread across her weather-beaten face framed by a set of wiry greying curls. 'I'm Lindsey O'Leary. Hope you're all nice and warm. A bit windy today, but I'll keep you moving.'

'God help us all,' said Mick as they climbed on board.

If Mia wondered as to the absence of his wife, she didn't enquire. Maybe the outdoors wasn't her thing.

Half an hour later, they were tramping over rocks and wet sand on what she suspected might be a desolate beach irrespective of season. Lindsey led the way, encouraging them to forage for the brown, green and red seaweeds growing in abundance along the coastline. Mia did her best to keep abreast of the characteristics and virtues of the different species as extolled by the quirky woman who made the seashore sound like her own veggie patch. Strolling around the soft sand and sloshing in shallow pools, Mia delighted as much in the feel of these plants as in the sounds of their names. *Fucus vesiculosus* or bladder wrack, the guide told them, was used in alternative medicine. She squeezed on the bladders now, the salty ooze sputtering out, surprising her. Another brown, *Ascophyllum nodosum*, with bladders like strings of beads, swayed in the splash zone where a gentle surf played around the rocks that were teeming with life. Other seaweeds – like green sea lettuce, nori and the red dulse they were encouraged to taste right there – covered the jagged surfaces where barnacles, limpets, dog whelks, mussels and tiny periwinkles all coexisted, equally dependent on the ebb and flow of the tide.

Mia felt a shiver of something that had nothing to do with the temperature. For the first time in a long while, she felt happy. All the stress of packing, organising, moving, house hunting, job hunting, fell away in that glorious moment as the water lapped around her gumboots. Looking across the beach, she couldn't help but smile. Prue and Edwina were bent over a swathe of sea spaghetti while Declan held court, telling the guide about kelp forests in Canada as Mick listened, trying to look interested.

Harry would never have done this with her. For all his scientific knowledge and dealings with fish, she'd never seen him catch one, never known him to walk mindfully on a beach at low tide, foraging, blissfully unaware of the passing of time apart from the movement of clouds and the slow inching of the tide. A single tear trickled at the corner of her eye. She had been oblivious to the ebb and flow of her own life, going with the whims and opportunities arising for someone else. Turning to look out to sea, she wondered what her life would have been like if she'd never met Harry. Perhaps there were times when he thought the same.

'Look, Mia,' someone was calling.

Putting a hand to her forehead to block out the sun and hide her tears, she saw Mick pointing to a spot some way up the shore. She could see it now. A lone seal hauling itself on to the rocks. She watched as it groomed its snout with the claws of a flipper, pausing between strokes to have a good look around. Fate or coincidence, she couldn't be sure, but she took the seal's appearance as an affirmation that it was indeed time to haul herself out of the relentless wash that had become her life and find a base of her own choosing.

$-$

'Well, that was a revelation,' said Declan as they settled back on board the bus after depositing the treasures from their foraging in the back. 'Shame your lovely wife missed it.'

'Had a few errands to run in Skib,' said Mick, looking out the window to where the bus pootled its way around the narrow byroads towards the Seaweed Visitor Centre.

'Yes, she said as much,' said Declan, unwinding a thick woollen scarf from around his neck. 'Ran into her in the graveyard over there by Barleycove. My mother was another one who loved wandering around old graves.'

He let out a guffaw as if it was funny. Mick wasn't sure whether to laugh along or quiz him about their meeting.

'To each his own,' he said, keeping his eyes trained on the road which had run out of tarmac and was now a narrow boreen, a strip of low grass running down the middle.

'Indeed,' said Declan. 'But I for one am very glad I chose the seaweed tour. Absolutely marvellous.'

Mick was none the wiser about what exactly Aisling was doing with her day, but at least he'd avoided any awkwardness with Declan. It was most unlike her to go round graveyards. For a second, he wondered if she was quite herself in terms of her mental health, but then he remembered the message from Brett Goodstone that made his stomach churn all over again.

For someone who prided himself on quick thinking and problem-solving, he wasn't getting anywhere with figuring out what was going on in his marriage right now. Already, it was feeling like a lonesome station – on holiday with his wife, a holiday gifted to them by his family to celebrate the very relationship whose future was less certain this week than ever before. Sure, they'd had their falling-outs, what he considered normal, run-of-the-mill disagreements like any two people in a relationship might experience. They could both be pig-headed, even blowing their stacks at times in heated arguments, like when she'd suggested they remortgage the house to fund the boutique she thought she could run on the side, or when he'd suggested she go part time when she complained about not seeing enough of the kids. Aisling was a strong woman, her ideas not always in keeping with his own, but he'd never known her to be deceitful. In fact, the opposite was usually the case; she could be honest at an ear-piercing volume that would enable the neighbours to testify as witnesses if any of their differences of opinion were ever tested in a court of law.

*Are you okay?* he texted now, lagging behind the others as they headed into the centre.

'*Tá fáilte romhaibh,*' their guide welcomed them in Irish. 'Come in out of the cold. Seamus here has a few delights for ye to taste and as I'm the driver, we might be able to persuade ye to try a couple of our seaweed-infused beverages.'

There were murmurs of enthusiasm, but Mick was less interested in what could be concocted from swathes of slippery slime than getting a response from his wife. A nudge from Declan made him tuck his phone back into his pocket.

'Sounds like we're in for a treat,' he was saying as the group began to shake off their outer layers and sat down at a long table decked out in beautiful ceramic ware. Not wanting to draw attention to himself, Mick joined them and tried to put thoughts of Aisling to one side. At least he'd have something to share with her later, if she was still even speaking to him.

# Chapter Sixteen

Ten courses later, the group were back on the bus and returning to the guesthouse, chatting companionably about the array of seaweed-filled foods they'd just sampled. Mia would have been happy with the first course, a kind of brittle made with nuts and seeds and the red dillisk they'd tried on the shore. But that had only been a taster to get them started. She couldn't even remember everything they'd eaten, but the stand-outs had to be the salad based on the green sea lettuce that had looked so unworthy on the beach. And the hearty sea spaghetti dish with sauces seasoned with the black sea salt they were told was made from kelp ashes. She could hardly believe the revelation that was the last three hours. Hugging her open backpack to her chest, she put her nose down and deeply inhaled the pungent smell from the seaweed bag she'd purchased at the gift shop.

'Wasn't it amazing?' said Edwina who was sitting beside her. 'I told Prue, I'm going straight upstairs when I get back and running a bath for that seaweed.'

'Me too,' said Mia. A pang of disloyalty threatened to thwart her plans. She had bought the item with Harry in mind, but this week was about self-care. She'd soak in the iodine and other mineral goodies while contemplating the day. In fact, she'd ask Ellen for a suitable glass and crack open a bottle of the seaweed beer they'd been gifted that she'd also thought to save for her husband. *What he doesn't know won't hurt him*, she decided.

With her wet hair tucked into her terylene turban, Mia pulled on her jeans and jumper and padded down the stairs in the slipper socks Harry's mother had sent her for Christmas. She'd send a photo later and let her know they were coming in handy in the Irish winter. She didn't need to say exactly where.

In the parlour, Declan was poring over a coffee table book on Ireland's coast.

'Great minds,' she said, smiling as she walked past and began to browse the bookshelves at the end wall of the room.

'Ah, Mia,' he said, looking up at her through a pair of trendy purple-rimmed glasses she hadn't seen him wear before. 'I'm fascinated by all this seaweed stuff.' He sat up straighter on the couch and gestured to one of the shelves. 'There's a field guide or two that looked good.'

She found the books and took a seat beside him, noticing the blue of his eyes, magnified through the lenses of his glasses. *What was his story?* she wondered. Here on his own, his crisp shirt and expensive jumper at odds with the denims that still bore a few damp patches from their trip to the shore. He was less formidable up close, or maybe he was just worn out after the active day and incapable of the leering or lecturing she'd expected. But experience had taught her to assume nothing. She'd spent most of her adult life trying to live up to assumptions and expectations she was only now starting to question.

'Do you have a family?' she heard herself asking.

He set the book on his lap and turned to her. 'Two sons.' And as though he was taking a deeper look, he added, 'One is probably your age.'

'As old as me?' She laughed, lightening what felt like a lead weight between them.

'He's thirty.' There was a softening in his voice as his smile reached the lines that crinkled around his eyes. 'And you are?'

'Thirty-two.' *Old enough to be your daughter*, she thought. But this was too familiar territory. For every question she asked, he could well demand an answer to one of his own. She opened the *Complete Guide to Irish Wildlife* and searched for her seal.

―

'Would you two join me in a dram?'

As they'd sat reading and swapping notes, neither Mia nor Declan heard Prue come in.

'Prue,' he said, pulling off his glasses and taking in the miniature vodkas she must have purchased at the centre.

'Ooh!' Mia eyed the bottles with interest. 'I'll see if Ellen's around. We might have a Russian coffee.'

Setting her book on the table, she jumped up with an alacrity Declan envied and tripped off to the kitchen.

'Don't you want to save some of that for Edwina?' he asked, not wanting to take from the couple's enjoyment of the rare drink.

Prue gave a loud laugh and came to join him on the sofa. It was hard to believe they'd worked in the same building for years and never once had he considered herself and Edwina to be lesbian, let alone partners. Colette's boss, John Buckley, was a different story, camp as anything, fitting with the whole 'Fabulous Four Walls' business, he imagined. One Christmas his sons had got him to watch an episode of *Queer Eye*, but he'd abandoned it after ten minutes saying it was the most ridiculous show he'd ever watched. They hadn't been too impressed. In fact, homosexuality wasn't something he'd bothered about until the referendum on gay marriage. Luke had begged him to vote Yes as he couldn't vote from abroad. He'd done what his son had asked, but that didn't mean he had to live with them. *Twenty-first century*, he reminded himself, conscious of the warmth rising in his cheeks as he breathed in the wafting woody scent of Prue as she took off her jacket and threw it over the back of the sofa beside him.

By the time Mia returned with Ellen and a tray of cups, glasses, cream and coffee, Mick had joined them, his wife conspicuous by her absence.

'There'll be a recipe in here somewhere,' Ellen was saying as she went to the bookshelves.

'No recipe required, my girl,' was Prue's response, as if Ellen was seven.

'It's got to taste good,' said Mia. But Prue wasn't having any talk of proportions.

'Just lash it in.'

Declan looked over at Mick, who seemed a bit quiet in himself, standing with his back to the fire.

'Seaweed vodka, Mick. What do you make of that?'

Mick shook his head. 'Don't knock it till you've tried it, I suppose.'

'Exactly,' said Prue, striding over to him with the first glass.

'And you, Declan?' she said, holding up another of the indulgent mix with its generous dollop of whipped cream.

'No need to ask me twice.' He laughed, accepting the glass and taking a tentative sip. He wasn't a vodka drinker at the best of times, but he wasn't above having a taste. Like him, Mia sipped from her glass and screwed up her face.

Prue was having none of it. 'Oh, get it into you, girl,' she said, raising her own glass to her lips and downing a good mouthful. 'God bless the Russians,' she said, ignoring the exchange of sceptical glances between the others.

By the time Ellen came back to let them know dinner wouldn't be far away, they were all in markedly good form with Mick much relaxed compared to earlier in the afternoon. Mia had transformed from the quiet young woman he'd met the night they'd arrived. The trip to the seashore seemed to have acted like some kind of stimulant. She'd been a revelation, asking questions of their guide and speaking knowledgeably about Australian seaweeds. The willingness of the group to pool together the vials of vodka they'd acquired after their forage had them all loosening up a bit. So much for souvenirs!

In the company of these strangers, Declan realised he didn't need a lot of drink. A couple of pints with Mick, a taste here to be sociable. Maybe he was beginning to make a few changes to help curb the senseless habits he'd fallen into of late. Calming down on the food mightn't be so easy, he mused as he followed the others and the mouth-watering smells emanating from the kitchen.

Aisling entered the conservatory to find her fellow guests, except for Katie, engaged in jovial conversation and drinking beer. Mick was so much a part of it, he hadn't noticed her come in. When she took the seat at the far corner of the table, he gave her a sheepish look. He really had no clue as to who should be feeling guilty here. Turning to Katie, she tried to put the thought of telling him out of her mind for now.

'Everything okay?' Katie asked in a low voice.

'Yes . . . thanks,' said Aisling, taken aback at her interest. 'Just had a run in to Skibbereen.'

Katie nodded. 'I spotted you earlier. Just a bit too busy to say hello.'

Aisling wasn't sure which surprised her most – the fact that Katie had seen her or the unnecessary explanation.

'Looks like we both missed out on an eventful day,' she said with a nod to the rest of them, who were now involved in an animated discussion about the brewing of seaweed beer.

As Ellen set bowls of mussels dripping in parsley butter at either end of the table, Gerry offered them a sample of the beverage the others were raving about.

'Wouldn't want you ladies to miss out,' he said with a wink. Aisling took a sip and asked him to fill her glass.

'Go on,' she told Katie, who was hesitant to try. 'It's only seaweed.'

At the sight of a small movement of the woman's lips that could almost qualify for a smile, Aisling felt the beginnings of a thaw in whatever was holding Katie to that ice queen image she portrayed.

'*Slainte*,' said Aisling, raising her glass and gaining the attention of the others.

'*Slainte mhaith*,' the natives replied, Mia doing her best at repeating the Irish toast to their good health, and Mick glancing at Aisling again with a host of questions in his eyes.

As he followed her upstairs to their room after dinner, Aisling could hear his feet drag.

'Everything okay, love?' he asked, catching her hand as he closed the door behind him.

She stopped but couldn't meet his eyes. Reaching down, he took her other hand and standing in front of her, rubbed his thumbs gently over her skin. There was a smell of drink off him. Enough to put him to sleep soon, she hoped.

'Declan said he met you at some graveyard,' he said with a hiccup.

'Ah, you can't go anywhere around here, can you?'

Bringing her hands towards his face, he looked at her intently. 'I missed you today, love.' He gave another hiccup and swayed a little, pulling on her to steady himself.

She looked away. 'Go to bed. We'll have a talk in the morning.'

Letting go of her, he put his hands on his hips.

'Jesus, Ash, what is wrong with us?'

Tears welled in her eyes. She had an urge to blurt it all out then and there, but instead she bolted to the bathroom.

'Can we at least talk about it?' he said leaning on the locked door.

'You're pissed. We'll talk about it tomorrow. Go to bed, Mick.'

There was silence, before he finally said, 'Promise?'

It was a thing they had, never to argue when drink had been consumed. She could blow up sober and frequently did, but they'd made a pact early in their relationship to keep alcohol for fun and winding down. Her relationship with Evan's father had given her enough experience of alcohol-fuelled aggression to know she'd never risk arguing with a man with a drink in him.

'Promise,' she said and listened as he walked away from the door and slumped on the bed.

In tears, she ran the bath and spotted one of the seaweed bags Mia and Edwina had been raving about at dinner. A small gift card attached read, *To my lovely wife, Mick xo.* Stifling a sob, she berated herself again for betraying her husband. She loved Mick. How thoughtful he was, thinking of her while he was on that foraging tour. She should have been with him instead of wandering around graveyards in the depths of winter.

She emptied the contents of the bag into the bath and stepped in. Surely with the vitamins and minerals they'd all enthused about, it might do her some good. Lying back and letting the textured fronds swirl and wrap themselves around her, Aisling closed her eyes. When Mick found out, he might hate her, leave her, demand a divorce. But she owed him the truth. If it was dry in the morning, she'd suggest a long walk on Barleycove Beach. That way, at least she wouldn't have to look at him.

Katie had returned to her private cottage, pleased she'd eaten at the guesthouse and enjoyed the mussels and outstanding chowder that would rival anything she'd tasted in the States. She was grateful for Aisling's discretion as to the circumstances of their encounter at the doctor's surgery. They'd talked a little over dinner, Aisling seeming as disinterested in being involved with the main group as she was. If her husband's wasted efforts to catch her eye were anything to go by, Aisling was probably equally grateful to have someone she could talk to and not feel like a fish out of water. They spoke about fashion, a topic that allowed Aisling to do most of the talking and both of them to avoid the quagmire of any personal dramas.

Turning on her laptop now, Katie began to research what her mother's future might look like. The GP visit had left her in shock, if she was honest. It had been bad enough that they were almost an hour late, but that Doctor Smit character had made her feel like an elder abuser. She might have told him about the reserves of patience it had taken to get Phyllis out the door, not to mind the huge effort she'd made in coming back in the first place, but she was counting down the days. Three down, four to go. Saturday couldn't come quick enough.

# Chapter Seventeen

Lilian was fixing some lunch for herself and Natalie when Heather came to the front door looking all professional in her work uniform, a bunch of beautiful fresh cut flowers in her arms.

'These are for you,' she said, proffering the bouquet.

'That's very kind,' said Lilian, 'but I'm not sure –'

'It's just a thankyou,' said Heather.

Lilian stood in the doorway somewhat bemused as Heather explained.

'I don't know how you did it, Lilian, but I came home exhausted after my shift yesterday expecting the usual sullen atmosphere and I was actually met with three animated human beings.'

Lilian laughed. 'I'm not sure that any of the credit for that is mine.'

'Oh you wouldn't believe it,' Heather went on. 'Darwin met me in the hallway before I even had my shoes off, telling me all about the drama of Ruby's phone going in the ocean.'

She looked round as if to check her daughters weren't within earshot and went on. 'To be honest, my day was that full on, all I wanted to do was sit down, but Ruby insisted I hear her side of the story too. Normally the girls are holed up in their bedrooms.' She shook her head, the loosely upstyled hair bobbing in her enthusiasm. 'And Dad – I thought he'd been replaced by Rick Stein. The smell of frying fish that met me when I opened the door ... mmm. He was in the kitchen, at the actual cooker, plating fillets of fish on beds of mashed potato, buttery green beans ready to go ...'

All Lilian could do was smile. She thought to ask her in, she was so keen to share the story, but Heather was interrupted by the chiming of her phone. Her bright smile turned to a frown as she checked the screen.

'The mother-in-law,' she said, her voice terse. 'I'd better take it.'

As Lilian went back inside and searched for a vase, she considered the change in Doug his daughter had talked about. Maybe he wasn't the curmudgeon she'd pegged him as after all. As to 'the mother-in-law' – she'd never met the woman, but sincerely hoped Aisling never referred to *her* with the moniker and its negative connotations. Glancing out the front windows, she saw Heather jump into her car where she'd pulled in right outside. On her way back to work, Lilian thought. About to look away, she saw her rifle in the glove compartment and take out a packet of tissues, realising the girl had just burst into tears.

In the afternoon, Lilian took a walk along Hawley Beach, delighting in the warmth of the sand underfoot. She marvelled at children diving off rocks and steering different kinds of watercraft, all drenched in the summer sunshine that made this place idyllic. Her chest swelled at the thought of Mick and the good life he'd made here with his family. Sending a mental message of gratitude to the universe, she prayed for the health to let her continue these visits to Tasmania.

Finding her flip-flops where she'd cast them off beside the little pathway from the road to the beach, she steadied herself against the wooden handrail and shook off the excess sand from her feet. At the roadside, she stopped to wait for a string of summer traffic to pass on its way, she presumed, to the small car park where a long bush track meandered its way to the city of Devonport. Mick had taken her some way along the trail there, but she'd been happy to sit on the occasional bench and soak up the views.

She was about to cross when the sight of someone on a ladder at the side of Heather's house caught her eye. It was Doug. She thought to get in home and avoid an awkward exchange with the man, but he'd spotted her. With a stiff wave, he made his way down the ladder.

'Doing a spot of DIY?' she called, not wanting to appear unfriendly.

He looked at her for a moment, his face serious.

'I wonder if you have a minute, Lilian?'

'Heather's very upset,' he began as he led her into the kitchen, striding ahead and grizzling to himself as he switched on the coffee machine. 'Cheryl – her ex's mother – just put the house on the market.'

Grateful he had his back turned, Lilian climbed inelegantly onto one of the stools at the breakfast bar and listened.

'Heather's rented it from her since her husband walked out,' he explained as he wrangled with the machine. 'Horrible woman. Charges over the odds, pops in when she feels like it . . . more concerned with her property than her grandchildren . . .'

Although concerned for Heather, Lilian was at a loss as to why Doug had chosen to share this with her. Setting a mug of milky coffee in front of her, he read as much in her face.

'I'm sorry, Lilian.' He shook his head and leaned both hands on the bench. Looking squarely at her, he spoke in a calmer voice. 'I have a bit of savings,' he began. 'Heather mentioned you were a banker.'

'A bank manager, yes,' she said, a little taken aback by the whole scenario, not least by the title he'd used, one she would normally associate with men in pin-striped suits or indeed Monopoly. But yes, before the great gaping hole that was retirement, she had managed the small local branch of an Irish bank.

'How can I help?' she asked, aware now that this was no 'getting to know you' coffee date. She pushed the niggling disappointment aside and channelled her old professionalism.

'Back in a mo,' he said, disappearing into the sitting room.

Lilian let her eyes roam around the space. She wasn't interested in the casual mess, although she had to smile inwardly
at the clothes piles and breakfast plates left to tidy themselves
that would have given her daughter-in-law a conniption. It
was the state of repair she was trying to assess. The windows
looked single-glazed, their frames in need of a coat of paint,
some maybe needing to be replaced. There were cracks in
the walls that could do with being seen to. Mick had told
her how cold these beachside bungalows could be in winter.
Must cost a bit to heat, she thought. Maybe Doug had found
some issues with the roof.

He was back, bearing a laptop, looking relieved to have
found an ally. He sat next to her, positioning the device so
they could both see the screen.

'I want to have my homework done before I say anything,'
he began, typing in a web address, 'but I'd love to buy it for
them. Give them a bit of security, you know?'

'That's so generous . . . and kind of you,' she said, hoping
not to have sounded too surprised. He gave a shrug, but his
cheeks were tinged with embarrassment at the remark.

It was good to see that underneath the gruff exterior, the
man had a heart. But while trying to provide a permanent
home for his daughter and granddaughters was an honourable
intention, whether he could afford it was another matter. It
might be somewhat run-down, but the location would attract
wealthy buyers and inflate the price. In any case, it wasn't
sentiment that had made him invite her in, it was hard facts.
She pulled up the sleeves of her linen shirt and set to work.

Two cups of coffee later, Lilian's face was flushed from the mix of caffeine and the kind of number-crunching she hadn't done in what felt the longest time. There were pens and pads of paper where she'd made calculations and drawn tables to explain to Doug the different options. In the end, she'd recommended he use an international online bank to avoid excessive fees. Although he was fronting up the deposit, Heather would be paying the mortgage. They would have to appeal to Cheryl's compassionate side – if indeed she had one – to convince her to sell it to them in the first place, and at the minimum asking price at that. If it worked, Heather would still need to be ultra-careful, putting everything on her credit card and ensuring it was paid off at the end of every month.

Seeing her to the door, Doug stopped in the hallway.

'I can't tell you how grateful I am for your time and energy on this,' he said.

'No problem at all. I'm only too happy to help you . . . and your family in any way I can.'

He held the door open for her, looking pleased but drained.

'I'll say nothing,' she told him, mustering a bright smile as she left.

She would spend the rest of the day thrown on the lounge in the garden, but she didn't need to tell him that. *Not just a pretty face*, she told herself, smiling with satisfaction at having had the opportunity to show the enigmatic man a little more of what she was made of.

Conor Fox was sweeping up wet leaves from around the door of the supermarket when Orla arrived.

'Morning, Conor.' As he held the door open for her, she breezed in past him and headed for the dairy aisle. 'I'm only in for a few extra milk for the place below.'

At the counter, she set down her basket and took out her card.

'No Ava today?' he enquired.

'No, I'm on below in the guesthouse.'

He should have known by the speed with which she'd zipped around the shop.

'How is it all going down there?' He shook out her shopping bag and set it neatly beside him.

'Oh, 'tis mad,' she said. 'The place is full all week and the next couple of weeks are the same.'

Conor smiled. 'Who'd have imagined we'd have so many tourists in winter?'

'I know,' she agreed. 'Ellen tells me they're from all over.'

'All except one maybe.'

Orla looked at him, not understanding.

'Katie Daly,' he said, doing his best to suppress an unexpected warmth gathering at his cheeks.

'Katie Daly from the back of Goleen?' Orla gestured with her thumb over her shoulder.

'The very one.'

She leaned an elbow on the counter. '*She* must be away over thirty years.'

Conor wanted to give his forehead a slap. Orla could have found out for herself. He didn't have to be the one who told her, but she was off now and he only had himself to blame.

'The Dalys . . . now let me think,' she was saying. 'I went to school with Finbarr. He married and moved to Cork City years back of course.' When Conor didn't respond, she went on. 'There were four of them, weren't there?' She didn't wait for an answer. 'The other brother died abroad years ago, but the sister is in Schull all the time.'

'Oh, she is,' he said, bringing the handles of the shopping bag together and moving it towards her.

Absently, Orla grasped at the bag. 'My mother, God rest her, was friends with Phyllis Daly. She used to say she was a pity. Odd thing for Mammy to say, but she always refused to elaborate on what she meant.'

*Just as well*, thought Conor.

Orla hefted the bag off the counter but didn't make to leave. Conor could see the cogs whirring in her brain. He took a clipboard with a stocktaking list from beside the till and made to look busy, but she still hadn't moved.

'Why in God's name would anyone travel that distance to see their family and not stay under the same roof?' she asked. 'If any of mine did that to me, I'd be devastated.'

He was in no doubt that Orla would have the whole country told about the washing, bed-changing and all that went with an invasion of her children and grandchildren, but that she'd be delighted to do it for them.

'Why do you think she's home at all?'

He shrugged. Torn between being disloyal and getting her out the door, he told her as much as he knew. 'Bernadette was in last week saying she was going to Spain and asking if I'd run a few things up to her mother if she needed anything. Said Katie would be home to mind her.'

'And when did *you* see her?' asked Orla, finally moving towards the door where a few leaves he'd missed were edging their way into the shop.

'I've seen her around a couple of times, but she hardly spoke to me.' Having already given Orla too much information, he decided not to mention being run off the road by their visitor. 'Don't expect to get her life story if you see her,' he said. 'Probably wants to get the week over with and go back to America.'

As Orla left the shop, Conor registered the uncharacteristic coolness in his voice. After all these years, why did it matter what Katie Daly did or didn't say to him? She could do what she liked. It was none of his business what she did with her life.

—

In the conservatory, Mia curled up on one of the armchairs, her notebook open at the list of pros and cons of leaving her husband. Behind her, Ellen tidied away the breakfast things, her mundane movements and the clinking of dishes a soothing backdrop to the major life decision Mia was trying to navigate. She hadn't slept well. Even the cloud of cotton softness that was her bed for the week couldn't help her drift off. Conflicting images kept coming into her head. Her with

Harry, her without him. Feelings bubbling up – guilt, resentment, ingratitude . . . It wasn't only about her either. Harry might be positive, career-minded on the face of it, but what if all the while, he'd been soldiering on, doing the right thing by her? Trying to give her an out at every move but putting up with her misplaced loyalty. Or was she being too kind?

'Are you all right there, Mia?' Ellen asked. 'Can I get you a coffee or anything?'

Mia turned to where her host was finishing up at the buffet table. Ellen would surely be a good source of local knowledge.

'Do you have time for a quick chat, Ellen?'

The lovely woman came and sat at the edge of the other armchair.

Mia sat up straighter. 'Sorry to interrupt,' she began.

'Not at all. What can I do for you?'

'I was wondering if you could help me find a job, actually.'

'Here, in Crookhaven?' Ellen's surprise made Mia realise how little she'd told anyone in the guesthouse about herself.

'We moved to Ireland recently . . . my husband and I . . .' She paused, not sure about sharing the complicated details of her situation with this woman who no doubt had a lot to do. But she would stick to the programme. She'd asked Ellen for help in her job hunt, not to listen to the gory details of her personal life. She flicked the pages of her notebook to where she'd drawn a spider diagram, 'Career Change' circled in the middle, short deliberate lines coming out at angles with notes scribbled at their ends.

'First of all, I have to tell you,' she said, shooting out a hand for emphasis, 'that foraging session was the bomb.'

Ellen smiled. She deserved to. This place and everything associated with it was a credit to her and Gerry.

'I think I had an epiphany,' she began. 'You know, when you see something or even feel something that really stops you short, makes you reassess?'

Ellen nodded, encouraging her to go on.

'I studied zoology in Melbourne, but I've always worked inside, in labs.'

She found herself smiling with excitement as she thought back to the excursion the day before and the smell of sea air, so much stronger than at home in Australia. You only had to walk out the door of this place, open a window, and there it was filling your lungs. Such a contrast to the sterile environments where she'd spent most of her working hours.

'Yesterday, on the shore, there was this seal,' she went on, 'hauling itself out on a rock, doing its thing . . . I suppose I admired its independence . . . wanting some of that for myself.'

She looked towards the window where she could see the ocean stretching out to a foggy horizon. Fog or no fog, it was beautiful in a way she hadn't appreciated in any of the coastal places she'd lived before. Magical almost. She gave herself a mental shake and looked back at Ellen.

'I hope you don't think I'm losing it,' she said. 'I've been going around hating Ireland for weeks . . . but this place, this week . . .'

Ellen smiled, and when Mia failed to find words to express herself, she asked, 'So, if you don't mind me asking, Mia . . . why did you come *here*, to the guesthouse?'

'Ah!' Just when she'd started to feel all warm and fuzzy, but it was a fair question. 'The house we moved in to, six weeks ago . . . it's a shithole, to be honest.'

Ellen pursed her lips in sympathy. Mia gave a brief account of their lives thus far in terms of Harry's work and the moves; eight years condensed into a few short sentences.

'I suppose with Harry away, I just wanted to treat myself to a bit of comfort. Give myself a break from the latest episode in the story of our lives.'

There was no getting away from the toll marrying Harry had taken. Saying she wasn't happy out loud just brought it into sharper focus. She couldn't help the tears pooling at the corners of her eyes or the pinching in her nostrils that made her sneeze. Ellen reached for a box of tissues on the window-sill. Mia took one, squeezing it in her hands.

'Sorry, Ellen. I must sound so ungrateful.' Aware of her shaking her head, Mia went on. 'Some people would give their right arm for the opportunities life with Harry has given me.'

'It's okay, Mia,' Ellen reassured her. 'Your life is your own, nobody else's. No one's judging you here.'

'I just want to get off the hamster wheel,' she said, head bent, talking to her hands. 'I want my own life . . .' She started to cry, sniffing back the sobs she'd wanted to avoid.

'Apart from the seal,' said Ellen, her voice gentle, 'was there something particular about the foraging that sparked your imagination?'

'Yes,' she said, regaining her enthusiasm and grateful for Ellen's understanding. 'I know it might sound crazy, but I'd love to do something like Lindsey O'Leary and her husband, getting out and about. I used to love fieldwork.'

Those field trips of her uni days came to her again. Easy times, taking samples on the shore by day and downing shots in the pub by night. As she'd dug deeper into these memories over the past twenty-four hours, it was the physical act of being outside, collecting life with her own hands and bringing wondrous specimens of the natural world back to the lab to examine that was the highlight. She wanted more than to sit at microscopes collecting data for other people's research. Maybe it was too much to ask, but she wanted to own her job in a way she had never done before. In truth, she wanted and needed to *own* her life.

'I see you're a mind-mapper like myself.' Ellen smiled, nodding to the notebook. 'Why don't we both do a bit of research and find out what's about? I'm sure Lindsey would be happy to help too.'

Overcome by the kindness of this woman she hardly knew, Mia gulped down a fresh wave of tears. Ellen touched her arm as she got up.

'Have no fear, Mia,' she said, 'I'm a firm believer in "a problem shared is a problem halved".'

# Chapter Eighteen

On Barleycove Beach, Mick and Aisling took the boardwalk path through clumps of marram grass growing like heads of unkempt hair blowing in the onshore wind. A lone surfer paddled out past the shallows. They stopped for a minute, watching as the brave soul bobbed patiently waiting for a decent wave. Aisling envied him what must be the freedom he felt out there, thinking only about the motion of the sea and how to move with it for the biggest thrill. Mick had gone to hold her hand when they'd begun their walk, but she'd kept going. He was standing a little away from her on the white sand, hands in his pockets. She'd left her gloves at the guesthouse. Under normal circumstances she would have shoved one hand into his pocket and interlocked fingers with his, curling the other hand around his arm and leaning into him. But these were far from normal circumstances.

'Will we walk down a bit?' he said, pointing towards the sea. She followed as he trudged through the soft sand to the tideline where it was more compact under foot, catching up with him as he swerved off to walk parallel to the shore.

'So do you want to tell me what's been going on?' he asked.

A loud ugly squawking erupted as a gannet searched for prey. Aisling's story had its own ugliness, but tell it she must. Fifteen years of marriage were on the line. She owed it to Mick to be honest. There'd been enough ducking and diving already. But she couldn't look him in the eye. Instead, she focused on the dark diminishing shape of a small boat heading out to sea.

'I'm not sure how to tell you this,' she began, her shame and anger at herself twisting like a knife inside. 'I should never have done what I did . . .' She hesitated. 'But it's done now, and I can't live with myself without telling you.'

Hot tears streaked down her freezing cheeks. Mick reached out a hand and touched her arm, but she shrugged it off and stepped away towards the water's edge. It hurt to think she might never feel his touch again once she told him, but it would be a punishment she'd brought only on herself.

'Is this about Brett Goodstone?' he called from where she'd left him standing behind her.

As the white foamy surf swirled near her feet, she dropped her head in a shameful nod. It came back to her now, the stern look on his face when he'd come into the parlour of the guest-house the first afternoon and handed over her phone. That look that always meant she'd gone too far. Had he read the message from Brett, she wondered. He could have challenged her there and then, but he'd held his cool.

'Yes,' she shouted, raising her head but no longer seeing the seascape through the blur of tears. 'It was the office Christmas party in Melbourne. Trashy, right?'

'You must have been unhappy?' he ventured, his voice even.

She turned and faced him, taking in the pained look on his face. 'Mick! I was stupid. Very drunk, yes, but monumentally stupid.'

Digging her hands deeper in her pockets, she wished he'd shout out, call her something horrible, curse her to the high heavens and swear he never wanted any more to do with her. But as the clouds took on a darker hue and the first drops of rain heralded a downpour, he spoke gently.

'Come on till we go up to the hotel.'

Without waiting for a response, he turned and began to trudge back over the sand, hunched against the spitting rain in that lovely warm jacket she'd bought him, snug around the broad shoulders she wished she could cry on.

⌐

In the hotel, Mick sat cradling a hot port as he waited for Aisling to come back from the ladies. There was, in part, an incredulity to what she'd told him. But it hadn't been a major surprise after seeing that message on her phone the day they'd arrived. In fairness, he'd showed a good deal of calm. Another man might have roared and bawled right there on the beach, giving the crashing waves a run for their money. Some men might have cried, utterly devastated at the news of their wife's infidelity. Despite having days to think about the possibility, there was still an element of shock. It was the context that floored him most. Friday would see them married fifteen years. They'd come from the other side of the world and instead of kicking back and enjoying each other, they were discussing the flouting of their marital vows. He took a fortifying sip of his port and steeled himself for what might be the most important conversation of his life.

In the restroom, Aisling splashed cold water on her red-rimmed eyes. They'd walked back in silence, making it impossible to read Mick's reaction. She was the drama queen of their household, saying it loud or at least emitting the strongest vibes when something upset or annoyed her. Meek wasn't in her makeup, but that was exactly how the consequences of her irresponsible actions had made her feel. She needed to own it, sure, but so much of her just wanted to snuggle up beside her husband and be held. Their marriage had never been the easygoing synchronised ride some couples experienced, but she had worked hard to keep this beautiful man, the father of her children, regardless of biology, the man who would risk life and limb for them. Mick always went the extra mile. He was going the extra mile now. She didn't deserve him.

Afraid she would cry all over again, she took a deep breath and checked her phone to distract her. Natalie had sent a photo of Charlie. She'd started to miss that bundle of cuteness who drove her mad with his meowing and claw-sharpening on her new lounge suite. Her sister wanted to know what time they'd be back in Cork on Saturday. For once, Aisling didn't respond. Her sister could wait. They were hardly here, and although she'd come hoping to get the week over asap,

Saturday was approaching like a high-speed train she wished she could stop in its tracks.

*Hope you're having a ball, Aisling,* Heather had messaged. *Smiley face. Love heart.*

She didn't respond. *A ball is right,* Aisling huffed as she turned to the mirror and tamed her weather-blown hair. But at least she had Heather. She would need her friend for some serious support and debriefing when she got home.

Mick pushed the other hot port and its coaster along the glass coffee table, closer to where Aisling had sat down in a comfortable armchair matching his own. He would like to have been having this conversation in the privacy of their own home, but at least they were inside in the warmth, where the deteriorating weather could be safely witnessed through triple-glazed windows. She'd been honest – of that he was one hundred per cent certain. To say he was gutted would have been an understatement, but as much as he was hurting, she was the one who had spent the last month living with the secret she obviously regretted. He remembered early in their relationship counselling her not to bottle things up, to be open with him. But it was easy to give advice and not heed it yourself. His particular indiscretion had remained unsaid for almost five years.

He glanced at her now as she sipped the hot drink, fingers clasped around the neatly tied serviette, absorbing the heat. His kick-ass, all-businesswoman wife looked vulnerable. To stay quiet would be to take advantage of her wrongdoing, and that just wasn't fair.

'Aisling, there's something I want to tell you,' he began. She looked at him over the steaming glass, her eyes red-rimmed. 'Remember when the Watsons moved in and I helped tidy the garden up a bit and –'

'Yes, you were a great help . . . very neighbourly.'

She really had no idea what he was about to say. The trust he'd betrayed was still written in her eyes. He hoped it wouldn't disappear forever once this confession was spoken into the warm fireside air.

'You'll remember Heather was at a low point after her husband . . .'

She nodded.

'Well, there was one afternoon . . .' Her head leaned to one side like a dog hearing the rustling of something in its owner's pocket. 'I was nearly finished in the garden. She offered me a beer.'

This was even harder than he'd imagined every time he'd thought to tell her. There was none of her usual butting in, finishing his sentences. She sat, waiting.

He cleared his throat. 'So we sat and had a beer. She wanted to talk . . . about Nathan . . . started crying . . .' His hands made slow back and forth movements, as if showing his open palms and withdrawing them again made for a more forgivable defence.

She was staring at him, suspicion beginning to register.

'I went to give her a hug. God love her, she was very upset . . .'

'And?'

He hung his head. 'We kissed.'

Although he couldn't look at her, he knew she was drilling into his head with those big brown eyes that had captivated him from the day they'd met. But they were a long way from those days where friends' weddings and nights out ended in Saw Doctors and Van Morrison singalongs. His brown-eyed girl was stunned into silence. She put a hand to her mouth and pressed hard, glancing round. They were alone in the lounge where a late morning sun was making only a token appearance to light the path of the rain that had turned from spattering to torrential.

'Jesus, Mick,' she said finally, setting the drink down and dropping her hands in her lap. 'Heather's my best friend.'

'In fairness,' he countered, 'she was hardly your best friend at the time.'

'But in five years, did you not think to tell me?'

She bit down on her lip as though to contain the pain she must have felt at what was dawning on her.

'Ash!' He scooted to the edge of his chair and went to touch her knee, but she swivelled her legs to one side. 'I'm sorry, babe. We regretted our mistake immediately, apologised to each other. It was nobody's fault.' He sighed now and looked down at the floor. 'It happened and I wish it never had.'

A young man in a white tunic and chequered pants emerged from the swinging doors of the kitchen bearing a rectangular plate on the palm of one hand, smiling like a sunbeam. Oblivious to the gravity of their conversation, he bent down, cutting the atmosphere between them with a collection of confectionery that would normally have both him and Aisling swooning in delight.

'Compliments of our head chef,' the lad announced in a voice that was definitely not the one he used at home.

Mick glanced at the spot on the chest where his name was embroidered, ready to politely respond, but Aisling stood up with a speed that almost sent the tray flying and this Benjy with it. He must have played Gaelic football in another persona, such was the deftness with which he saved the tray and its contents from tumbling to the floor.

'Sorry, not for me,' said Aisling, her lips trembling as she gathered her jacket from the chair behind her and pulled it on.

Mick waited for the boy to recover before standing himself. It wasn't the poor bugger's fault the only customers were having a domestic. He followed Aisling out. In the foyer, he went to call to her to wait up, but they were accosted by an immaculately turned-out receptionist. *A slow day in all departments*, Mick thought as she slapped on a smile worthy of a prize from Fáilte Ireland.

'Just to let you know, it's two for one at the spa today.'

Aisling blanked her but he managed a muted acknowledgement. She was only doing her job.

'Aisling!' They were outside on the slate steps, horizontal rain slicing through them.

'I've got to get out of here, Mick,' she shouted over the wind. 'Just give me some space to process this.'

And she was off down the steps, holding her hood over her head, boots tripping through puddles. He stepped back under the eaves of the hotel entrance, torn between running after her and letting her go. *What a fucking day*, he thought, watching their hire car pull out onto the main road, wipers going like the clappers, disappearing round the sharp bend towards Crookhaven.

—

In the lounge, he ordered a coffee and sat back down, wishing she hadn't run off. 'Space to process this!' he railed to himself. She'd slept with another man and *she* needed space? Sure, he'd made a mistake of his own, but what happened between him and Heather was nothing compared to what Aisling had done. With the slow burn of anger building inside, he went to retrieve his jacket and go after her. But she'd taken the car.

Reining in the emotion and trying to think straight, he thought to call the guesthouse and ask for a lift. They would no doubt oblige. But then what? Mope about all day, shut out of his own room while Aisling 'processed' their predicament?

Maybe Declan was free. He might at least help to distract him.

'Lizzie O's. This is Gerry.'

'Eh, hi Gerry, Mick here.' He decided to drop the small talk. 'Is Declan around, I wonder?'

'Oh hello, Mick. Give me a sec and I'll check for you.'

Mick listened as Gerry walked through the house, hearing footsteps and then a knocking sound.

'Mick on the phone for you, Declan.'

He heard the door open.

'Mick! What can I do you for?'

He imagined the look exchanged between the men. There was a whisper before the door closed.

'Sorry to bother you, mate.' He took a deep breath. What exactly was he doing, asking a bloke he hardly knew on some kind of play date?

'No bother, Mick.' The cogs in Declan's brain were almost audible as he was no doubt trying to compute the reason for the call. It would be rude to back out now. He may as well be up-front.

'I'm on my tod again, I'm afraid . . .' There was a soft sigh from the other end of the phone, but Declan let him go on. 'I know this might sound like a weird request, but it's two for one here at the hotel spa . . . Would you be interested in helping me pass a few hours? Miserable day.'

There was a pause at the other end of the line. He imagined Declan checking the Rolex at the cuff of his Pringle sweater as he considered the prospect of spending the afternoon with him.

'Oh, right, yes . . . Be with you in, say, twenty minutes?'

Mick sat back and let the warm drink pervade his body. Aisling would take a few hours to cool off, but she wasn't the only one who needed time out. It had taken all the calm he could muster to sound normal on the phone just then. Brett Fucking Goodstone. If he had him, he'd strangle him. What the fuck had Aisling been thinking?

Seething with anger, he wondered how the hell they could come back from this. At some point they would have to have an adult conversation about it all, but any moving on would take some serious soul-searching. No, he didn't want his marriage to end, but what Aisling had done hurt. Man, it hurt!

# Chapter Nineteen

Aisling gunned the hire car up the driveway of Lizzie O's and made a dash for the house. Hoping not to run into anyone, she shook off her jacket and hung it on the hallstand. Sitting on the cushioned bench, she pulled off her boots. Sand fell onto the whitened floorboards, but she didn't care. All she wanted was to plonk down on her bed and cry her eyes out.

She didn't see Gerry approach from the kitchen.

'Aisling, I'm delighted you're back. Wasn't sure if anyone was going to show up for my session.'

Shit! The bread-making that had sounded like such a good idea when she'd signed up at the weekend.

'What time are you starting?' she asked, fiddling with the hem of her trousers to avoid looking up.

'We're about ten minutes away,' he said.

'Sorry about the sand.'

But Gerry had already turned to go back into the kitchen. 'Don't worry about that. I'll get the coffee on.'

She took the stairs at a run and closed the bedroom door with unintended force. Pacing the room, she went over Mick's 'confession'. Part of her couldn't believe it. Heather . . . and Mick . . . pashing it out in her back garden? She could phone Australia and have it out. But what would she say?

She tried desperately to think of a time they'd fallen out, any sort of disagreement. Yes, they'd been at odds over the education system; Heather was against private schools. They'd argued over Nick Kyrgios and if he deserved to even be on the tennis court. Who had shouted the last coffee – that was a regular battle. But as to hurting one another, Aisling drew a blank. Heather was a constant – steady, level-headed, a foil to her own weather-like personality with its ever-changing moods.

But Aisling had been there for her too. It hadn't been easy to be a single mother, working flat out with an ex-husband on the mainland, not knowing if he'd send through the money Heather needed to pay the bills. She had her widowed father to support, not least when he'd arrive unannounced and spend weeks licking his wounds in a melancholic daze.

Aisling imagined she was always the one going round to her friend's for a debrief about relatives, but Heather leaned on her too, shared the weight of all she would have other-wise carried alone. At least Aisling had Mick. And one kiss, at a time when she was at her most vulnerable . . . Wasn't Mick more to blame really? She thought about the physics of it now. Who moved in first? How did they even get close enough to touch?

She face-planted on the bed, pulling a pillow down around her head and seething into the duvet. 'Ugh!' she punched the pillow with a fist and waited to wail, but her tears had all spilled out on the beach and then on the drive back. Was he having similar thoughts about the *physics* of what she'd done with Brett Goodstone? Torturing himself by imagining what went on that night when he'd been home in Tassie minding their children, happy to think she was having a well-earned night out, oblivious to the fact she was having it off with the boss.

Mortified at the thought, she sat up and reached for her phone. They needed to talk. She could forgive him his moment of vulnerability with Heather, but would he ever be able to forgive *her*?

He wasn't answering. She knew better than to hound him. He would think this through in his own time as he did with any of the major decisions they had made in their lives. It was one of those qualities she loved and loathed about him. She was the spontaneous one. And look where that had got her.

She'd wait it out. But staying in her room while he mulled over the situation would drive her round the twist. No, she'd keep busy, go downstairs and make fecking bread.

—

Aisling padded downstairs in the thick woollen socks Ellen had provided, her hair pulled back in the ponytail she reserved for house-cleaning. After three and a half days, the relaxed vibe of the guesthouse had worn down her resistance to looking anything but her absolute best in public. She inhaled the floury smell wafting from the kitchen, hardly able to believe she was about to spend the next couple of hours making the kind of comfort food she usually tried to avoid.

Gerry had the sleeves of a blue shirt rolled up as usual, faded jeans under the denim apron tied at the front. A man in his element, sieving flour into a bowl, talking easily with Mia, Prue and Edwina. He was here to help them make bread. If there was anything else going through the man's mind, he didn't show it. Wishing she could shut out the furore in her own head, Aisling tried to do the same. She managed a smile for them and pulled on the neatly folded apron their host had set out for her.

First up, he told them, were French baguettes that would be made into garlic bread for dinner.

'Not sure if the French would approve of our variation on their staple, but you can't beat a bit of garlic bread with the butter melting off it . . .'

'Mmm,' Prue swooned. 'Did you know I met Ed in Paris, Gerry?' She spoke as if he was the only person in the room. He had that effect.

'That's amazing, Prue. Were you on holiday or what?'

He pointed to the collection of equipment and ingredients he had assembled at one end of the island. There was no sign of Katie Daly or Declan, but Aisling made no mention of it, not wanting anyone to ask as to the whereabouts of Mick.

'You'll need a bowl, scraper, spatula, sieve . . .' said Gerry, melding his conversation with Prue and instructions to the group with ease.

'We worked in the same language school,' said Prue.

He laughed as he handed round a bag of flour. 'There's hope for me and Ellen then.'

'What do you mean?' asked Mia.

'Working and living together, Mia. Doesn't always end well.'

The young woman laughed self-consciously.

'It's not for everyone, that's for sure,' said Aisling. 'Myself and Mick would kill each other.'

The comment was met with good-natured laughter, but no one argued with her. Surely there couldn't be any suspicion as to the state of her marriage among these near strangers. She dismissed the notion as she gathered a set of utensils, determined to concentrate on the task at hand.

Following Gerry's lead, they sifted the flour into bowls, adding yeast, salt and water and mixing as he did with the ends of wooden spoons.

'That's new,' said Prue, as she watched Gerry work the mixture into a ball of dough before having a go herself.

'Easier on the wrist, Prue.'

Prue, who made no secret of her preference for conversation over baking, gave the technique a go before declaring it hard work and handing over to Edwina.

It would take four forty-five-minute stints before it even went in the oven, but like a practised TV chef, Gerry had some he'd prepared earlier. Aisling was ready to flour the beautiful marble work top, but no, they were to wet their hands and work the dough that now looked like a glossy meringue for only a tiny minute before returning it to the bowls to rise under clingfilm.

Desperate for something to pound, Aisling was glad when they moved on to soda bread, turning out her homely-smelling dough this time onto flour and beating into it with both hands.

'Steady, Aisling,' Gerry cautioned. 'Only a light knead, enough to bring it together.'

'Damn!' She couldn't help herself. The other women laughed.

'Don't worry,' said Gerry, 'batch loaf next. That'll get out your frustrations.'

'Sorry,' she said but couldn't help a smile.

At every step, Gerry was patient. Prue had added a tablespoon of salt instead of a teaspoon. Gerry suggested she double the recipe. When Mia forgot to wet her hands before folding the baguettes and was nearly glued to the dough, he was there with a bowl of warm water and a towel so she could get unstuck. He reminded her of Mick, the easy way he had about him. Mick was nobody's fool and wasn't afraid to stand his ground in an argument, but he was kind. She was such an idiot!

<hr>

Mick lay face down breathing in the smell of some lemony concoction from a diffuser somewhere beyond the other massage table where Declan was snoring like a rhinoceros. The young man working the hot stones down his back was doing his best, but any kind of mindful meditative state he meant to imbue just wasn't happening. Mick's head was a torrent of images he wished he could turn off. He didn't even know what Brett Goodstone looked like and yet he pictured him tall, lean, six-packed, hands all over his wife at the back of some Melbourne hot-spot.

Why did it have to be wild passionate sex he imagined and not a straightforward vanilla encounter? What was wrong with the slow, comforting and yes, orgasmic sex they'd shared for most of their married life? The quiet kind of sex in bed of a night when they had the energy or snatched in the middle of a Sunday afternoon while the kids watched a movie. The kind Mick had believed to make him and his wife very happy. He'd do anything for Aisling, but he couldn't change what made him tick.

'Ah, that was marvellous, Mick.' Declan sat up on the bench, looking like a bear coming out of hibernation, the bags under his eyes drooping like the muffin top that hung over the fluffy towel he had wrapped around him. 'I'll need a dip in that pool to wake me up.'

They changed into borrowed swimming togs and plunged into a small pool that curved round an island where fountains of water spouted from the blowhole of a dolphin statue. *Natalie would love that*, Mick mused as he breaststroked round the smiling mammal.

'Karen would be in her element here.' Declan had caught up with him in the side-stroke his father had favoured. When he didn't respond, Declan kept talking.

'A great one for the pampering sessions.'

Mick found himself wondering what happened to Declan's marriage.

'Maybe that's where I went wrong . . .' Declan trailed off as he turned on his front and freestyled away.

After a couple of laps around the pool, Declan stopped to get his breath at the shallow end, taking in the well-maintained surroundings. With the place to themselves, the only sounds were of Mick's strokes and the echoey purr of hidden machinery powering the heat and light to the hushed space. *Karen would love this,* he thought, not sure why he kept thinking of his wife, soon to be very expensive *ex-wife* once the divorce got underway. There was that recurring pinching in his chest again. He would take a Valium later. He'd been trying not to take them, but at times he just needed something to calm down the catastrophising.

'It's great to relax,' he said as Mick pulled up beside him and leaned back with his elbows on the poolside. They talked about the accommodation and how everything about the place was conducive to getting away from it all. He mentioned the book nook he'd found on the top landing and the James Patterson thriller he'd started to re-read after twenty years. He'd fallen out of the way of reading with his Netflix and red wine habit. Karen was a great reader. It was one of the things he missed most, he realised – lounging around home on a rainy Saturday or Sunday when he wasn't working or on the golf course, swapping stories from the newspapers, reading snippets aloud to one another, setting the world to rights.

'I can't remember the last time I read a book,' he said.

'Life gets busy,' said Mick. 'Sure, isn't that what holidays are for?'

'Haven't had one of those in a while either.'

'Is that right?' Mick turned and looked at him, his face curious but with no hint of prying, no making light of his comment.

'My practice manager thought I needed a break. Tries to run my life.' He gave a tut, but it occurred to him that Mags Logan might be the only person still interested enough to do so. 'I'm separated since the summer.'

'I'm very sorry to hear that, Declan.'

'Don't worry.' He smiled. 'Between the comfortable surroundings and the seaweed vodka, I'm definitely starting to unwind.'

'Ah that's good,' said Mick. He reached his hands behind him to grab at the poolside and let his legs float up to the surface. 'I bet in all their plans for running the place, they never accounted for guests getting pissed on seaweed.'

Declan laughed, grateful for the company and the easy connection between them.

'The hidden treasures of West Cork,' said Mick, thoughtful. 'You said you had connections down here, didn't you?'

Declan nodded and looked down the length of the pool to where the rain blurred the sea view from the wall of windows, and took a moment to appraise the emotion welling up inside. Grief maybe, for the loss of a simpler life where success was measured on a different scale, the bar set only at the level of fun and enjoyment that could be eked out of every day. A place where his brother and he were loved for who they were, not how many letters they might gain after their names or how much they were likely to earn.

'My brother and I loved it down here,' he said, half to himself.

'You must have some great memories,' said Mick.

'The best,' he said, registering a cooling in his torso and ducking his shoulders under the warm water. 'I just wish I hadn't left it so long, you know . . . that I'd given my own boys the same experience.'

'Didn't you come down as a family?'

'No, sadly.'

Mick lolled in the water, but if he was surprised at the missed opportunities of Declan's life as a father, he didn't remark.

'Should make the most of the week.' He shrugged, not wanting to get too heavy. 'Let's get into that sauna. We'll be back on the treadmill soon enough.'

But as he sat in the steamy warmth, the acrid air pinching at his nostrils, Declan couldn't push down the emotion that came back at him like a heavy meal.

'Do you know dentists have one of the highest suicide rates among professionals?' There, he'd said it, voicing the issue that had been playing on his mind for months.

Mick's mouth opened, but no words came out.

'Sorry, Mick. I didn't mean to be so blunt,' he said, starting to shake despite the heat. 'I've lost a couple of dentist friends . . .'

'I'm so sorry, Declan.' Mick had no doubt seen it all in his line of work, but he made no judgement here, just listened.

Declan licked his lips and swallowed down on the blubbering he feared might cause them both embarrassment.

'Complete waste of life,' he sniffed. 'Perfectly good people. Not like me. Excellent dentists, great partners, friends . . .'

He couldn't help it. That graduation day photo appeared again, his mind's lens zooming in on the empty spot they'd made between a couple of them to remember Sam Roycroft. The shock he'd got the day his father broke the news. The utter gut-wrenching news of how his classmate had hung himself, two months before the final exams. He told Mick as much, registering the empathy he wished his father could have shown. *Foolish boy*, he'd said of his best friend. *Why couldn't he just have hung on with a great career ahead of him?* Even the unfortunate choice of words had been lost on the man.

'Then there was a colleague some years back.' He shrugged, sparing Mick the details of how James Boland had shot himself somewhere in Australia. To think he'd been jealous when they'd caught up at an association meeting and he'd announced he was emigrating. State of the art practice somewhere on the Sunshine Coast, he'd said. Time to gear down, enjoy the lifestyle a cousin had raved about after living there for years.

'Have you ever thought about ending your own life, Declan?'

It was a fair question after what he'd told him. He just hadn't expected the unassuming Corkman to be so direct. He hung his head and looked down to where his footprints were fading on the hot wooden slats.

'I don't think I'd have the balls,' he said. 'Never been what you might call a risk taker.'

Aware of Mick's concern at the grave turn their conversation had taken, he couldn't look at him.

'Have you talked to someone about it all?' asked Mick.
He shook his head.

'My boys thought that kind of thing would help, but no
. . . just threw myself back into work.'

Luke had suggested he get counselling when Karen walked
out, but he'd dismissed the notion. For lightweights, he'd told
himself and yet here he was confiding in a man he'd only
spoken to a handful of times, sport and politics the height of
their interactions.

In hindsight, he should perhaps have sought counselling
after Boland died. He'd gone into a kind of depression then.
The episodes were sporadic, but when they hit, it wasn't
pretty. The boys had already left home, steering well clear.
He'd put it down to a midlife crisis, dismissing Karen's concern.
He was just a bit down. So what if he wanted a good car,
hadn't he worked hard all his life, didn't he deserve a few
perks from the damn job? His staff did all right out of him.
Couldn't he treat himself to a few decent bottles of wine to
unwind of an evening? Karen hated his drinking. The drunk
calls to his sons hadn't endeared him to them either. He'd
reached out to old acquaintances. *Leeches*, Karen called them;
a crew of semi-retired, semi-married professionals he hooked
up with for the odd golfing weekend. It was the straw that
broke the camel's back. 'Right,' she'd said in front of the
entire staff that Tuesday after the June long weekend when
he'd managed to get himself to work, bang on eight as usual,
despite having gone from course to clubhouse, snatching two
hours sleep and driving down from Kildare. 'Marry *them*,

Declan Byrne! See how *they* like being abandoned when you get sick and tired of them.'

And just like that, he'd found himself packing up his home life and moving out. He'd tried to keep in touch with the boys, but the calls and texts had almost dried up. They too had moved on.

Declan heaved himself up from the sauna bench and opened the door, letting the cooler air wash over his clammy skin. He turned to Mick.

'Thanks for the chat.'

'No worries, mate,' said Mick, leaving him to do another few laps of the pool.

Regret was a terrible burden, Mick knew. How sad was it that Declan couldn't confide in anyone until he met a stranger in a B&B long after the events that caused his pain in the first place? He thought of his own marriage. Sure, he was shocked and angry at what Aisling did, but she'd told him. Five years ago, he'd kept his own indiscretion to himself, moved on. At least she'd had the guts to face him. If he made the wrong decision now, he might regret it for the rest of his life. He jumped in the pool and swam after Declan, tapping him on the foot.

'Do you mind taking me back?' he asked.

There was a brief look of disbelief, but if Declan was annoyed at having to cut their session short, he sucked it up.

In the changing rooms, Mick went to explain the rush. 'We've both done things we're not proud of,' he began. 'I need to talk it out with her, face it, you know?'

Declan looked up from where he was drying his sparse hair under a towel. 'You're a better man than I was, Mick.' Before Mick could dispute the comment, he went on, 'Karen did nothing wrong and I still let her go.'

Mick felt the lump lodge in his throat. *Poor bugger*, he thought. *Not so bad underneath it all*.

—

At Lizzie O's, Mick knocked on their bedroom door and stepped inside.

'Can I come in?' he asked to the shape of Aisling who had the covers pulled up over her head.

'You already are in,' she said in a muffled voice.

'I mean in there.'

She cocked her head out from under the duvet and stared at him.

'I suppose,' she said before resuming her position.

Mick lifted his side of the duvet and slipped in beside her.

'You smell of baking,' he said.

She turned a little towards him. 'And you reek of chlorine and something . . .' Propping herself up on her elbows, she gave him a serious look-over. 'Do not tell me you went to the spa without me.' He went to answer, but she was ripping a pillow out from under her. He felt the cool blow to the side of the head, before he could say 'massage'.

'You fecker,' she shout-whispered. 'I'm here crying my eyes out and you're there soaking up the essential oils.'

'There's flour in your hair.' He grabbed the edge of his own pillow in case. '*You* went to that workshop.'

She was in with another lash of the pillow. He pulled his own and held it up to absorb any ensuing blows, but she sat up in the bed and looked at him, mascara smudged like storm clouds under her beautiful eyes. In the unusual quiet, he could hear her deliberate breaths. Whatever she was about to say would be said without her default 'shoot from the hip' self-assurance. With the pillow squashed into her chest and her lovely chin resting on top, he realised he hadn't seen her look this vulnerable since those tense hours of labour when she'd had Natalie.

'I don't want to lose you, Mick Fitzgerald.' She blinked back fresh tears with her long eyelashes.

He sat up and propped the pillows against the headboard. She was tired, spent from the emotion of the day, not to mind the energy it must have taken to keep the cheating a secret.

'I love you, Ash.'

'I don't deserve it,' she said. 'I know what you did with Heather was bad, but what I did was unforgivable. I've ruined everything we had.'

'Hang on.' He reached out and put a hand on her sleeve. The merino jumper felt soft to the touch. She only bought the best. There were so many things he loved about his wife. All her quirks, her passion. 'Am I . . .' He faltered, but it had to be said. 'Am I too boring for you, Aisling?'

'Ah Jesus, Mick, no.' She scooted up the bed and leaned her head against his shoulder.

He took her hand and kissed it, gently, then held it to his chest. They were a good team, better together, but he needed to be sure.

'I hate what you did, but I don't want to lose you either.'

He'd set her off again, tears streaming down her cheeks.

'Mick,' she said, a tremor in her voice. 'I wasn't very nice to you five years ago.'

He thought for a minute but couldn't recall what she meant.

'We were at a crossroads, remember? I was desperate to move to Melbourne.'

'Ah!' It was dawning on him now, the fights, the emails she'd send him with properties from real estate agents. Tassie was too quiet for them, she'd argued. In the end, it had been Evan's resistance that swayed her. The boy nearly went in to decline at the prospect of another move after already leaving his friends in Ireland. He wasn't long into high school and had a good group of mates. Natalie was only seven at the time and had kept out of the arguments. All that interested her about Melbourne, she'd said, was the aquarium. Although she didn't say as much, Mick knew she didn't want to be the cause of any more discord. In the end, Aisling had let it go, but he wondered now if it was something that had never gone away.

'Do you still hanker for the city?' he asked as he held her close.

'I thought I did,' she said. 'But I read something online the other day that really made me think. It said, "Want what you have".'

He turned the phrase over in his mind. Such a simple but profound few words. 'Mm, I get that. But maybe you need to think about it, Ash.'

She turned her face to him and looked at him with those chocolate eyes he loved. 'I love you, Mick.'

When his lips met hers and he drew her into his arms, Mick was in no doubt, he had exactly what he wanted. He could only hope Aisling would always feel the same.

# Chapter Twenty

Katie's day had begun with an encounter she could have done without. The cleaner, who made herself known as Orla Maher from Goleen, accosted her just as she was leaving her cottage to drive to Cork. The annoyingly cheery woman insisted on trying to jog Katie's memory as to the relationship between her husband, Eamon Maher, and the O'Sheas who owned the guesthouse. She would have been there yet if she hadn't begrudgingly agreed to an invite to elevenses at the neighbouring house the following morning. As she jumped in the car, she mustered a smile, determined to keep peace with the locals on her mother's behalf. Phyllis Daly needed all the support she could get.

After not bothering with breakfast, she decided to stop on the way to give the Datsun a break in case it overheated. She feared the old banger would be hard-pressed to make it to the city, but she no had choice but to go. Her brother was busy, he'd said when she phoned him last night. He could squeeze in lunch if she was coming up to town. Despite having zero intentions of returning to the city she'd grown to hate, it was the only way she would have an opportunity to make Finbarr understand he needed to step up.

In Clonakilty, she sat in a small cafe far too brightly decorated for a Tuesday in winter. On her laptop, she connected to wi-fi and checked her emails. The usual suspects spamming her inbox and the one message from Stella that made it worth checking. Her business partner was full of questions. Katie sent a quick reply. Yes, she was coping. Her mother was grand. She'd fill her in on the details when she got back. No need to pick her up. She'd get the bus from the airport and walk home. Stella had enough to do; her life full of babysitting grandchildren and celebrating family milestones, on top of a full-time job. So different from her own life. And yet, the girl she'd met when first banished to the city all those years ago was possibly her only enduring friend. She paid for breakfast and drove on to Bandon and through the western outskirts of the city, rehearsing what she might say to the brother she hadn't seen in years.

～

It was Finbarr's idea to meet in the Kingsley Hotel as it was close to where he lived at Sunday's Well on the north-western side of town. Why she couldn't have just driven to his home, Katie wasn't sure, but she was here now wondering how the hell she'd recognise him. He was fifteen the last time she'd seen him. As she walked over the luxurious carpet and entered the riverside restaurant, her heart thumped in her chest and that clammy feeling spread across her palms. *Stop it!* she told herself, but the likeness to her father made her want to run out of there as fast as her legs could carry her.

'Finbarr,' she said to the man who had been looking straight past her. His face was a picture as he stood up from a tub-style dining chair.

'Katie,' he said, a hand rescuing the silk tie from falling into his coffee. She hadn't expected him to look so sharp.

'Look at you all dressed up,' she said, trying to make the painful reunion as light as possible.

A waiter appeared beside her. 'Here, let me take those for you.' She divested herself of the cape and hat and handed them to him.

'Must be doing well for yourself,' she said, sitting down opposite. She took another glance at the sophisticated surroundings and hoped he'd be getting the cheque.

'Not too bad,' he said, sitting back down, his face tinged with embarrassment. 'Will we order some lunch?'

The waiter was back with a couple of menus. 'Our specials today are wild-caught Atlantic salmon . . .'

Katie tuned out as he trailed on, scanning the menu as much for prices as courses.

'I'll have the soup of the day,' she told him, leaving Finbarr to question the origins of half the menu's ingredients before finally ordering the fish and another Americana.

She contemplated the Lee's steady flow alongside them beyond the deserted decking area and willed herself to calm down.

'How's things?' he asked, bringing her back from the moment's repose.

'Great,' she lied. 'Living away as they say.'

He shook his head and smiled. 'That's some twang you have on you.'

She smiled back. 'Years in the States will do that to you.'

He sat back and looked at her as though he was taking in every line, every freckle, double-checking it was really her.

'You've changed your hair,' he said.

'Beats the grey,' she mocked, nodding to his crew cut.

His face reddened again. 'God, I can't believe you're here . . .'

The waiter interrupted as he set the soup in front of Katie, together with a basket of breads. She'd missed her mother's soda bread, her brother's banter . . . but that belonged to another lifetime. This trip was starting to feel like she'd stepped through a force field. She wanted to be able to get back to her life without it closing in on her.

'So what have you been doing all this time?' Finbarr asked as he squeezed a wedge of lemon over his fish with a sophistication she hadn't expected.

'Mostly cleaning people's houses . . .'

'There must be money in it if the gear is anything to go by.'

It took her a moment to realise he meant her clothes. She wanted to tell him the Victoria's Secret jeans and cashmere sweater were from a thrift shop she sometimes went to on the Lower East Side, but he might have made all sorts of assumptions about her over the years.

'I get by,' she said, deciding to withhold the details of both her successful business and her frugal existence.

'Depends on the type of houses, I suppose,' he ventured.

It did, but she wasn't about to tell him how she'd come to work that one out.

'What about you?' she asked in an effort to move the conversation on from his obvious speculation as to her earnings. 'Mammy tells me you have two beautiful children.'

He took a shiny new iPhone from the table beside him, tapping at it with his thumb. The nail, she noticed, bitten to the quick. Habit of a lifetime. He turned the phone towards her and there they were, the nieces she'd never met, old enough to have children of their own.

'Wow, you must be so proud.'

'Ah, they haven't turned out too bad.' He laughed. 'Mairead must take most of the credit though. I'm usually working my balls off.'

She tucked into the freshly baked bread and let the comment rest. Looking towards the river again, she went over the lines she'd rehearsed on the subject of their mother. He was way ahead of her.

'Have you seen Mammy today?' he asked like it was the most normal thing to drop into the house of their childhood.

'No,' she said. 'I phoned Rita Kelly. She was going to call in this morning.'

'So you think she should go into a home?' His voice was steady, but his eyes had trouble in them.

She shrugged, taking her time to answer. 'I don't feel it's up to me,' she began. 'I haven't exactly been around.'

'She's still your mother,' he said, resting his cutlery on the side of the plate and clasping his hands under his chin as if waiting for her to enlighten him as to what they should do.

Not wanting to get into an argument, she decided to try and ascertain how *he* saw their mother's situation.

'When was the last time you saw her?' she asked, trying to keep her voice even.

He sat back in his chair and lifted his coffee cup in both hands. 'We had her up for Christmas.'

She smiled to diffuse the defensive tone. 'So you've seen how she is, mobility wise, getting in and out of bed . . .'

He shifted in his seat and set his coffee back down without drinking. 'Not really.' He took up the cutlery and started back into the salmon. 'Bernadette brought her up for the day. We had a bit on.'

'Sure.' She kept her facial expression neutral. It wasn't like she had earned the right to admonish him for not spending time with his own mother.

'Look,' he said, leaning forward and glancing round him. 'I don't have time to be driving up and down to West Cork. I'm running a business, you know, trying to make a crust.'

She felt herself recoil at the proximity of him. *It's Finbarr*, she told herself, but couldn't help feeling that the likeness to her father might extend beyond physical appearances.

'I wouldn't dream of criticising you, Finbarr,' she said. 'I'm sure you do as much for Mammy as you can.'

He set the knife and fork together on the plate he'd cleared and sat back, adjusting the knot of his tie. Katie let the mood settle before going on.

'You know I'm taking her for that assessment on Thursday?'

He nodded, seething under that starched collar, she suspected.

'I'll hear what the doctor has to say and let you know. Is that okay?'

'A home won't be cheap,' he said. 'Where's that money going to come from?'

She hadn't thought that far ahead. 'I think they have social workers to advise on all that . . .'

'You'll have to pay your share. You can't expect to swan back off to the States and leave me and Bernadette with all the hard work, not to mind the expense.'

'I didn't leave home willingly,' she began, but he cut across her.

'That's all water under the bridge as far as I'm concerned.' He looked away as he said it. 'Different times.'

He couldn't have hurt her more if he'd stabbed her. But at least she knew where she stood. Pushing out her chair, she caught the eye of the waiter and signalled for the bill. They both stood, Finbarr a good head and shoulders taller than her, just like his dad.

'I'll go so,' he said, putting a twenty euro note on the table and walking away. It was less than his share, but she let it go.

'I'll ring you Thursday –'

'Text me. I have meetings all day.'

She watched as he flicked out the collar of the suit jacket and closed the button, tucking in his goddamn tie. If the waiter saw the wobble she was experiencing, he had the discretion to leave her be. She plonked back down in the chair and let the shaking in her whole being subside.

*Swan back off to America!* Katie had never 'swanned' anywhere in her life. Every move she made was calculated, deliberated over, analysed ad nauseam. Her father and Martin Fox had seen to that. In the busy lunchtime hum, she gathered her bag and her hard-won resilience and went to pay the bill.

She could have gone straight back west, but decided instead to turn towards the city centre. With no idea whether or not the home would be still standing, operational, even accessible, she navigated the one-way system, taking in the once familiar streets and institutions. They had cousins in the city. An aunt, now dead, had been her favourite relative. It had struck her years afterwards that she loved the aunt for the normality that pervaded her household, the laughter and absence of fear. Perhaps she could have been a similar kind of aunt to Finbarr's children, but any chance of that was long past.

At the southern side of the city, she passed the supermarket where she and Stella would be sent on a rare errand if they had been 'good'. It was alive with shoppers going about their day. A bus stop she used to fantasise about standing at to be transported away from captivity, housed a handful of passengers bound for town or all the way to the Western Road. College students maybe, people with chances in any case, people with the kind of agency she'd been denied.

Parking the Datsun at the gated entrance of the home for unmarried mothers, Katie walked cautiously along the avenue, the skeletons of naked birch and beech trees lining her way. A car passed without acknowledgement from those within as if she were invisible. It was exactly how she'd felt here. Cast out of the family home and then punished all over again, scrubbing floors, feeding babies she was never allowed to hold. Girls came and went, relationships were fleeting. Only Stella became a friend.

Rounding a bend now, she heard a giggle. It reminded her of herself and Stella stealing a rare moment to joke around. She spotted the pram, a teenage boy pushing it, leaning into a girl the same age. Noticing her, they smiled.

'Hi ya,' the boy said with a warm friendliness Katie couldn't fathom. She said something in return, but as they walked by, she panicked, wanting to call out to the girl, warn her of what the nuns might do if they found her meeting a boy on the grounds. But as she rounded the corner where the grand house came in to view, there was another couple with a baby, taking selfies in full view of the imposing edifice, and those windows from where she and Stella had looked out over the lake and wished they were the migratory ducks that wintered there.

A sign for a day care centre caught her eye. Of course, the place must have moved on from the penitentiary it had been in 1985. A shame they hadn't dispensed with the grotto, she mused, as she spotted the statue of Mary with those eyes full of that expression – sadness, pity, shame? Yes, they were probably going for shame, whoever invented those things. The irony of it all; the world's most famous unmarried mother looking down on all those 'fallen' girls while their mothers and fathers prayed their hearts out that she would 'pray for us sinners now and at the hour of our death'. She could feel her body shake, remembering the pain, the back-breaking work the pregnant girls and the new mothers were made to do. Stella must have lost half her body weight here. A slip of a thing when Katie met her, by the time she gave birth to a son, she was bump and bone. How the child survived was nothing short of a miracle, if you believed in that sort of thing. Stella did, but Katie preferred to believe it was her friend's genes for determination and hope that gave that child a chance.

Pulling the cape tight around her, she turned to leave. Images too painful to remember welled up in her mind, the sounds of desperate babies left alone in cots, and like herself and others, crying themselves to sleep. The snide remarks from Sister Nasty – as they called her in what little privacy they had – as to how they'd come to be here in the first place. 'Sex, sister,' Stella would mock in a rare moment of abandon after lights out, on a night when no one was in labour or giving birth in the room along the corridor with the paper-thin walls that might as well have been loudspeakers.

# Chapter Twenty-one

It was close to five by the time Katie reached Schull on her way back to Crookhaven. The online phone book had listed a B. Daly as residing at Sea View Apartments. She found the modern building and went to pull into the parking bay that matched the number, only to find it occupied by a brand-new bronze Ford Focus. How Bernadette lived her life hadn't mattered much to Katie before this week. If anything, she'd been compelled to come to Ireland to let Bernadette *have* a life, at least a break from the monotonous, ageing-mother-minding one Katie had assumed she'd been living. Parking the Datsun in a vacant bay, she went to have a look around the Ford. Not a scratch, shiny as if it had just come out of the car wash. *Or valet service*, she thought as she leaned in close, cupping her hands around her eyes and taking in the spotless interior. She nearly jumped out of her skin as the car gave off a beep and the lights flashed.

'Can I help you there?'

Katie turned to where a petite woman in a business suit was tottering towards her on high heels, a leather tote over one arm, car keys in hand, one pointing at her as though ready to be used as a weapon if necessary. Any claim to having a right to be standing in her sister's space was evaporated by this woman's confidence. Closer now, she looked Katie up and down, 'What the hell are you doing here?' written all over her.

'I'm Bernadette's sister,' Katie started. 'I was just . . .'

'Ah . . .' A smile spread across the woman's face, softening the interrogative stare. 'Katie, isn't it?' She popped the keys into her bag and held out a manicured hand. 'Lucy Wells. I work with Bernadette. I'm so happy to run into you.'

Katie tucked her own hand back under her cape, at a loss as to what to say, but the friendly woman nodded towards the car.

'When Bernadette heard you weren't staying here, she let me have the place for the week. She's so kind.' There was a roll of her heavily made-up eyes. 'I'm based in head office in Dublin, you see. Just down here covering for her.' As she shoved the tote up her arm and moved in closer, Katie could smell the layers of cosmetics. 'Your sister does the job of three people, you know.' The feistiness reappeared as she lowered her voice. 'When I get back to Dublin, I'm going to tell our bastard of a boss he'd want to at least get her an admin assistant. I'm exhausted!'

'Tell him to throw in a new car,' said Katie before making excuses to get away from the woman who looked like she could talk all night. But as she sat back into the Datsun, she began to mull over the insight into her sister's life. Minding Mammy, working overtime . . . no wonder Bernadette had been desperate for a break.

The Datsun started on the third attempt, but as she drove into the darkness of the countryside, a whirring sound from somewhere in the front began to worry her. She didn't know much about cars apart from being able to drive one. Anxious to get to the guesthouse without incident, she put her foot down and kept driving. Ellen or Gerry would know someone she could call in the morning to fix whatever was the problem.

Conor Fox was shutting up shop when he heard the grating noise getting closer. Looking up, he spotted Bernadette Daly's Datsun struggling to take the rise in the hill. Remembering she was still in Spain, he realised it must be Katie. He watched as the car came to a stop on the other side of the road. Its irate-looking driver stepped out and slammed the door.

'Piece of shit,' she shouted, spitting the words with vitriol.

He glanced round to see if there was anyone else who might come to Katie's assistance, but Goleen was dead. Marit had shut her cafe hours ago and the few regulars at the pub were at home having their tea. There was nothing for it only to stride across there and help her out.

'What seems to be the problem?' He zipped up his jacket as a biting wind began to whip up.

She turned to him, but if he was expecting to see relief in her face, he'd been mistaken.

'I'm not a mechanic,' she stated. 'I have no idea what's wrong with it.'

Between the accent and the haircut, she could have been a tourist, a stranger. At least she looked warm.

'Could I try turning her over for you?'

She nodded and stood aside to let him get in. He tried several turns of the key in the ignition, but no joy.

'She's going nowhere tonight,' he said, stepping out of the car and handing her the keys.

'Will it be all right to leave it here?'

He gave a small laugh. 'I'm sure Bernadette has the rust bucket insured if anyone tries to damage it.'

But Katie wasn't laughing. The manly thing would have been to offer help straightaway, sort this for her, get her in out of the cold. He'd have done that much for anyone. Instead he found himself hesitating, wanting her to ask him. He'd spent over thirty years wondering where she was, what exactly happened all those years ago, why she couldn't talk to him, ask for his help. But looking backward on this icy night that would soon become tomorrow and the next day and the next, just as those years had trundled past regardless, was utter folly. He gave himself a mental shake. *Get away home, you eejit.*

'Come on. I'll get the car and take you –'

'The O'Sheas' place will be fine. I'm staying there.'

He knew that. Of course he did. Just like everyone else in the village who had mentioned the fact to him when they'd come into the supermarket, speculating as to why she'd come home at all if she couldn't stay with her poor mother. He led the way back across the road and up the hill past the church to the clutch of two-storey terraced houses where his van was parked at the kerb.

'I'd better go in and tell Da I'll be a bit late.'

He had the car keys in his pocket. It would have been easy to let her sit in the van and wait, but he wanted his father to see her with his own eyes. The gossipmongers had fed the old man stories of their own making. Conor was tired of it. At least if his father met her, he could stop with the assumptions.

—

Katie followed Conor in through the low gate and along the paved path to the corner house he'd grown up in. It was hard to believe he still lived here. His parents had run a shop out of a shed they'd built on to that house, before they'd branched out and bought the franchise for the supermarket. Goosebumps pricked at her arms as memories of the stone-floored shop came rushing back: the weighing scale with its brass weights in pounds and ounces; the potatoes that came out of a heavy-duty paper sack; Mrs Fox slicing a lump of ham on the stainless steel cutter; how she'd wipe her hands down the sides of her apron before doling out sweets from lidded jars; the agony of choosing what to buy with five pence long before the euro came to Ireland. If you had a pound, you were made. You only got that kind of money for your communion. Five if you were very lucky.

In their front room, Mr Fox sat watching the evening news, his tall frame folded in three; torso, thighs, calves, all clicking painfully into place as he stood up to greet her.

'Katie Daly,' he said, stretching out an arm, the shirt and jumper hanging loosely. 'It's been years since I laid eyes on you.'

Like her mother, the man had morphed into what was definitely a shadow of his former self. But there was still mischief in the watery eyes. In the shop, he'd never been without a joke to catch you out or cheer you up.

'Have you only a few months to live or what?' he said, a wry smile curling at his lips.

'What kind of a thing is that to say, Da?'

She turned to where Conor stood aghast in the doorway.

'I'm only ball hopping,' his father replied. 'Sure none of us know how long we have. I might be gone next week.' He winked at her and began to shuffle across the fireplace to a shelving unit beside the TV.

Katie held her breath watching the checked slippers barely leave the carpet as he made his unsteady way forward.

'Wait now till I show you this blasht from the pasht.'

Katie couldn't help smiling at the thick West Cork accent, but Conor interrupted.

'Dad, I need to get Katie back down to the guesthouse. They're on a strict schedule around mealtimes.'

She willed herself to be patient with the old man who had never been anything but kind to her.

'Don't worry, Conor. Ellen knows I'm always a bit late.'

She saw the tension in his shoulders. What was it to him if she was late?

'Here now,' said Mr Fox, making his way back to her with a framed photo. 'This wasn't taken today nor yesterday.'

She didn't need to see the photo to know what it was, but out of respect, she let him place it in her hands. Fighting the urge not to look, she saw her seventeen-year-old self in that white full-length dress, beaming up at Conor Fox. After the day she'd had, it was a wonder she didn't unravel. Without looking at him, she was aware of her then-boyfriend cringing behind her.

'Ye were a handsome couple,' said the old man with a rueful smile. 'You were mad to leave him.' He gave a chuckle. 'Rosarie, God rest her, always said you were a lovely girl.'

At the mention of his wife, Katie remembered her mother had told her of Mrs Fox's passing in one of her letters. How poor it must have seemed to them not to have sent condolences, but how many opportunities to reconnect with her old community had she let go?

'We'd better get moving,' said Conor who was making his way to the front door. 'I won't be long, Da.'

'Take as long as ye like,' said the old man. Then smiling at Katie, he added, 'You might call to me again.'

'I'm only here for another few days, Mr Fox, but it was good to see you.'

'Phyllis must be thrilled to have you home.' He touched her on the arm and lowering his voice, he said. 'Don't be too hard on her, girleen.'

⌐

There was no talk in the car on the way to Lizzie O's. As the wipers squeaked against the windscreen, Conor's head was fit to burst with possible conversation starters, none of them making it past the tip of his tongue. He sensed Katie's discomfort at having to be with him, but wondered if there wasn't a hint of the old curiosity in that impenetrable front she was doing a great job of upholding. The Katie Daly he knew, or at least had known, was curious, warm-hearted, shy yes, but not unkind.

'Is it the house you're in?' he asked.

'No, round the back.'

'I heard about the cottages . . .'

He followed the driveway round the side of the house and pulled in outside the cluster of low buildings. At least she wouldn't get soaked.

'Thanks, Conor.'

At the sound of his name, his heart did a little leap. It was a small triumph, but a triumph all the same.

'Will I get Dinny Kelly to have a look at her tomorrow?' He sensed her uncertainty. 'Bernadette can fix him up when she gets home.'

She looked at him now, a hundred questions in those green eyes he'd loved. How different she looked with the cropped hair under the brimmed hat, but the eyes were the same.

'If you don't mind . . .'

'No bother,' he said. 'I'll see what Dinny makes of it and ring you straightaway.'

He watched her run to the end cottage. She pushed in the door and turned, giving him a cursory wave before closing the door against the wind. Satisfied she was in out of the weather, he drove home, his head telling him he should be giving her short shrift, but his heart wanting to see her again. Touching the seat beside him, he felt the lingering warmth. Under that cool exterior, maybe the Katie Daly he'd known and loved was still there.

Declan was relieved to see a thawing in relations between Mick and Aisling. Maybe, despite nodding off in the massage and spending most of their time talking about his own troubles, he'd done some good. Oh, he thought he was doing good every day, treating patients, making people's lives better through his skills in oral health. But it had been a long time since he'd felt this warm fuzzy feeling that had spread across him since talking to Mick. A softening in his old age perhaps, or maybe allowing himself to reach out past the staid hardened bore he knew he'd become. He'd even thought of Karen without a bitter bile catching in his throat, admitted out loud she hadn't been at fault.

He looked around the table to where the strangers of Saturday were tucking into the garlic bread some of them had made together earlier in the day, passing pizzas round to a soundtrack of conversation that was coming easier now, midway through their week. Katie Daly had been last to the table, looking harried as usual, but she was down the end making an effort to listen as Edwina and Prue talked about their language school, their pride palpable. Karen had been the linguist of their family, encouraging the boys in their German and Latin studies at school. He wondered if it wasn't too late to learn a language at fifty-six. The Irish revival had intrigued him, but he'd done nothing about it. A language school upstairs from the practice and he hadn't given it a thought before now. God, he'd led a boring existence of late. He considered the two couples, Prue breaking a garlic baguette and setting a bit on Edwina's plate, Mick and Aisling brushing hands as they sat closer than on previous nights, past whatever stumbling block had come between them. Karen would have loved the liveliness in the room, the sharing of food and experience going on around him.

'Are we going to the poetry night at the pub tomorrow?' Mia asked him as if they socialised together on a regular basis.

He smiled at the young woman who reminded him of the sons he'd started to miss. 'Why not?'

Mia lay on her sumptuous bed, absently scrolling through her news feed. It had been a productive day. She'd seen two rental properties and made a few phone calls. Two seaweed farms had offered for her to come and visit, and while they had no work available at the moment, they'd sounded genuine about keeping her in mind for opportunities that might arise in the future. In the late afternoon, she'd taken the steps down through the garden and followed the overgrown path to the small cove to watch the sunset. She'd seen the dog man again there. As she'd walked along the jagged rocks fingering into the evening tide, she'd watched him striding down from the road with his charges, slipping off their leads, smiling as they went off in different directions, some barking at him to throw a stick, others going about the business of sniffing everything in sight and marking territories. When he spotted her, he'd waved, a cheery, open wave. She'd taken out her phone and gestured to it to ask if it was okay to take a couple of pictures. He'd given her the thumbs up.

She went to her phone gallery now and reviewed the photos. Those dogs were something else. Considering which to share, she zoomed in on one of the images that included Matt. The pixilation wasn't great, but there he was, looking straight at her, a broad grin spread across his rugged face. A funny expression. Admiration? She felt a tingle as she interrogated the image like she might the contents of a slide under a microscope. Yes, there was definitely something in that look. Zooming out again, she decided against sharing. It was bad enough that *she* was reading into the photo without her whole friend group speculating as to who the handsome dog man might be and how she'd come to being on a beach with him in the first place.

She set down the phone on the bedside table and switched off the warm lamplight. Pulling the duvet up under her chin, she drifted off, savouring thoughts of Matt and his mystery.

# Chapter Twenty-two

At breakfast, Ellen relayed the update from Conor Fox. The Datsun needed a new part that wouldn't arrive from Skibbereen for a couple of hours. He'd offered to come and get Katie or look in on her mother for her. She'd chosen the second option. The more people in the area that were aware of Phyllis Daly's predicament, the better. Once Saturday came, she'd be on a plane to America and her mother would be fending mostly for herself if Bernadette and the locals couldn't lend more of a hand. It was the only reason she was on her way to Orla Maher's now. She pulled her hat down over her ears and dipped her head against the wind that threatened to cut through her.

Orla was at the front door before she even got up the driveway, apron flapping in the strong gust coming down from Brow Head.

'Katie Daly,' she said, hands on her hips, looking a little in awe. 'It must be strange being back here after so long.'

'Thank you for inviting me,' said Katie, not sure how to respond. Neither Orla nor anyone else in this godforsaken outpost could imagine how it felt.

'Come in, come in. I have the fire on. There's a few scones just out of the oven.'

In the warm kitchen, Katie eyed the golden crusts on the well-risen scones resting on a rack beside the cooker. She was instantly jettisoned back to winter days when she and her siblings would come off the school bus and throw themselves down around the table, complaining of being starving. To her credit, Phyllis Daly never let her children go hungry. Teatime may have been a battleground, but it never had anything to do with the food. At least not in the eyes of her children. Their father on the other hand couldn't be relied upon to enjoy their mother's wholesome cooking. The only criterion to affect whether he deemed a meal good or bad was how many pints he'd consumed at the pub beforehand.

But she didn't need to be thinking about that now. There was a baby pulling herself up by the bars of a playpen, shouting in a fine strong gibberish to be taken out to join the party.

'Yes, Ava,' Orla told the child. 'I'll get you out in a minute to meet our visitor.'

Her host bid her take a seat at the table she had laid with a flowery tablecloth and set with pottery mugs and side plates in a design Katie recognised from a shop window in Clonakilty. There was a rich fruit cake on a fancy plate at the centre, a few thick slices next to a hunk of what must have been left over from Christmas.

'Help yourself to a bit of that porter cake while I scald the pot.'

It occurred to Katie that she might have brought a contribution. Her mother would never have called on someone empty-handed. Orla filled the teapot and brought it to the table, pouring for them both before sitting down opposite her.

'I should have asked if you'd prefer coffee,' she said, a worried look spreading across her face. 'Is it all coffee in America?'

Katie shook her head. 'This is grand altogether.'

Orla's face relaxed as she gave a small laugh.

'What's funny?' asked Katie.

'I'm sorry, Katie. I was only remarking to Eamon last night how you must be gone years, but the *Wesht* Cork accent is coming back to you.' She clasped her hands and leaned forward. 'Tell me, what have you been doing all this time?'

She was spared the impending inquisition by a knock on the door.

'Back in a mo,' said Orla.

The minute she disappeared from view, a wailing went up from the playpen. As the seconds dragged, Katie wanted desperately to calm the child, reach in and lift her out, but she was a stranger – it might make the crying worse. As drops of cold sweat pricked at her neck, she undid her cape and pulled at the top of her sweater that was starting to constrict.

'Whisht now, Ava,' Orla was saying as she returned with Ellen O'Shea coming in behind her holding a massive saucepan.

'Ah, Katie,' said Ellen. 'I didn't realise you were here.' She set the pot on the kitchen bench like she was a regular to the house. 'I was just dropping this back to Orla.'

The wailing continued.

'Come here to me, *leanbh*.' Much to Katie's relief, Orla went to rescue the child from her corral, the crying stopping in an instant and a broad smile spreading over the small face. 'Take her there, Ellen, while I make a fresh drop of tea.'

And just like that, she was passed easily between the women in a practised move the child didn't seem to mind one bit.

'Come here to your cousin,' said Ellen, sitting down and settling the child in her lap.

'Do you know I went to school with Katie's brother, Ellen?' Orla asked as she refilled the kettle.

Ellen raised her eyebrows without taking her smiling eyes off the child who she was now quietly communicating with, in that word-free language that people who were good with children were fluent in.

'I think I remember your youngest brother, Katie,' she said, 'but the rest of ye were a good bit older than me.'

Orla's face reddened. 'Poor Sean Óg, God rest him,' she said, making the sign of the cross.

Ellen looked mortified. Katie had heard she'd spent most of her life in Australia. She wouldn't have known anything of her brother's premature end, of how he'd fallen to his death on a building site in England when the scaffolding gave way and he hadn't heard his workmate shouting at him to try and save himself. Neither would she have known that it was their father's fists that had made him hard of hearing in the first place.

'Sean Óg passed away many years ago, Ellen,' she explained, shoving her grief down inside.

'Oh, I'm so sorry,' said Ellen.

Orla began topping up cups and setting scones on plates. Cutting into one and buttering it for Ellen, she swiftly changed the subject.

'How is your mother doing?'

Katie rested the warm cup in her hands and considered her response.

'Not too bad, thanks, Orla.' She'd like to have been more specific, but seeing Orla busy with her grandchild, she'd decided against asking her to call on Phyllis. These people had their own lives, running farms and guesthouses, minding families. The care her mother needed far exceeded the kind of dropping in by neighbours she might have thought adequate, even with Bernadette's best efforts around a demanding job.

'I see herself and Bernadette at Mass on a Sunday. I thought she'd got a bit frail this last while.' Orla looked thoughtful as they sat in silence for a moment drinking the tea.

'Is your brother nearby?' asked Ellen, who was only beginning to catch up with the Daly family whereabouts.

'He's in Cork all the time,' said Katie.

Ellen's face was full of concern and sympathy. She didn't know the stories of their intervening years, but Katie was long enough in the tooth to know there was no one untouched by family responsibilities. She had thought herself exempt from all of that and yet, here she was, thinking about the quality of her mother's future.

How strange it felt to be in a West Cork kitchen, chatting with women she hardly knew but felt connected to by some sort of divine sisterhood. There was no one judging her here. They could have quizzed her on why she wasn't staying with Phyllis, why she'd left in the first place, why she hadn't come back, but they didn't. It was, she had to admit, not an unpleasant situation. For the first time, she wondered what it might be like to move back. Would these women become her friends? Could she somehow regain her place, her birthright and even be free of what made her leave?

As Ava started to grizzle in Ellen's arms, she stood up and rocked the baby back and forth, but when the effect wore off, the wailing resumed.

'Give her here,' said Orla. Taking the child, she pressed her to her chest and began to sing softly into the down of her head.

'*Báidín Fheilimí d'imigh go Gábhla . . .*'

'Oh God, that takes me back,' said Ellen, smiling at the song they'd learnt as children about a small boat that sailed to Galway. She joined in with, '*Báidín bídeach, báidín beosach . . .*'

Irish words about the lively determined little boat, words that leapt onto Katie's lips from where they had been locked away along with so much else in a corner of her long-term memory. Hardly singing, more mumbling, she felt a tear trickle down one cheek. Oh God, she couldn't unravel now, not here, not with these women who were essentially strangers, not anywhere she could be seen. But as her pain registered in Ellen's eyes, a sob escaped.

'Is it a singsong ye're having?' A ruddy-cheeked man pushed open the kitchen door and paused mid-step as he took in the scene.

Katie thought he might back out, but Orla was over to him, thrusting the half-sleeping child into his arms. Katie wiped her face quickly on one of the serviettes.

'There's tea in the pot, Eamon,' said Ellen, turning to where the man was rooted to the spot, least of all by the weight of his grandchild. 'You'll remember Katie Daly?'

'Indeed I do,' he said, gathering the child and himself and stepping further into the room. He had a kind face, reminiscent of the O'Sheas of long ago. 'Sure weren't our grandmothers the best of friends?'

Katie could see the women now, smoking like troopers around the fireplace in one or other of their houses, places of retreat when she was young. Words failed her. She managed a smile but couldn't stifle the tears that spilled out over her cheeks.

'Oh, Katie, I'm so sorry if we've upset you,' said Ellen, reaching over and touching her arm.

'No, no, you're fine. It's not your fault.' She swiped with the serviette again. 'I think I should go.'

Ellen took her car keys from her coat pocket. 'I'll take you down, if you like.'

# Chapter Twenty-three

Katie's stomach growled as she sat into the Datsun, finding herself in close proximity to Conor Fox for a second time in twenty-four hours. To be fair, he'd managed to get the car back on the road and she was grateful to have her independence restored. Those women had been lovely to her, but she wasn't part of this community anymore. If they looked in on her mother once in a while it would be a bonus, but as she'd realised that morning, this place and its people owed her nothing. She had no control over her mother's circumstances. It would be all she could do to see the week out.

As Conor drove them to Goleen in silence, she made a mental promise to steel herself against the kind of nostalgia that had set her off in Orla Maher's kitchen.

'I'll let Bernadette know the damage once she gets back,' Conor said, smiling at her as he turned off the engine outside the supermarket.

'That's fine,' she said, wondering if he was going to get out or sit here for the rest of the afternoon.

He made no move to go and looked out into the drizzle. 'There's a bit of a poetry night down at the pub in Crookhaven later on.' His thumbs drummed on the steering wheel he was still holding. 'You should come.'

To be invited to a social event was the last thing she'd expected from the man she'd hardly been civil to since she'd arrived.

'It's not exactly Yeats . . . or Whitman . . .'

'Thanks,' she said, cutting in on the memories of Leaving Certificate poetry she could do without him dredging up. Still, he didn't get out. Only when she opened the passenger door did he take the hint. He could have left the keys in the ignition, but no. They crossed each other at the bonnet and he deliberately placed them in her hand.

'It's good to see you, Katie,' he said, head bent, looking her in the eye.

He was trying to be the bigger person here, she knew, the one who was willing to put whatever had come between them aside and offer the olive branch. God knows, maybe he still had no clue as to why she'd left.

—

'Ah, sure isn't Ellen very good to be thinking of me?'

You'd think it was Christmas, Katie mused as Phyllis went on and on about the containers of food her daughter was loading into the freezer. After a chat in the cottage, Ellen had insisted Katie come and help herself to the portions of leftover food she said they'd be delighted to give her mother.

'And plenty more any time,' Gerry had assured her as he'd packed the meals into a canvas shopping bag.

Ellen had been a revelation. Although Katie had told her she was perfectly fine on the short drive from Orla's house, once they'd pulled up at the back of Lizzie O's, Ellen had offered to come into Mussel Manor to make sure she was really okay. It had been in Katie's mind to decline, but her head had been that much of a washing machine of thoughts and memories, she was grateful to sit with Ellen in the chic open-plan space with its soothing greys and soft browns that had been a welcome retreat from her childhood home.

'It can be hard, coming back,' Ellen had said. It had been comforting to hear Ellen's story of leaving Ireland for Australia twenty odd years ago, of how she'd been pregnant with Gerry Clancy's baby without knowing and how she'd met a Greek man she'd loved and married, who'd raised the child as his own. In a way, Ellen too had been banished; her mother, Maureen O'Shea, warning her not to come back if she found herself pregnant. They were both victims of warped beliefs and a cruel patriarchal church that enforced them. Katie couldn't help but feel her heart soften as she'd heard how Ellen had made peace with her husband's passing and of how she'd rekindled her love for Gerry when he'd tracked her down in Australia only a little over a year before. And here the couple were, she'd marvelled inwardly, making a new life for themselves, picking up the stitches of past lives and knitting them into a future together.

'Isn't Conor a star getting the car fixed for you?' her mother was saying.

'Which one of these will you have?' Katie ignored the praise she was piling on the 'Knight in Shining Armour' she hadn't stopped talking about since she'd come in.

'Will we heat up a couple of those beef stroganoffs in the microwave?' Phyllis asked. 'I haven't eaten a bit of that in years.'

Katie hadn't intended to sit down and spend any more time with her than was absolutely necessary, but she was starving.

'Okay,' she conceded, and as if she'd given the woman an injection of cortisone or some other pain-numbing substance, Phyllis got up from the table and went about laying it with the good cutlery and ware Katie was sure hadn't been used in God knows how long.

'This is me daza,' her mother pronounced as she savoured the meal.

Katie found herself smiling at the expression, another one she hadn't heard in years.

'What's wrong wit you?' Phyllis grinned. 'Don't they talk like that in the United States?'

'No, Mammy. As you well know, they don't.'

Her mother scraped up the last of the sauce and sucked it from her fork. Smacking her lips in delight, she pushed the plate away.

''Tis great to have you home.'

Katie shifted uncomfortably in her chair and kept her focus on the remaining food in front of her.

Resting her elbows on the table, Phyllis leaned in.

'You could have come any time you liked, you know.'
Katie listened but didn't look up as she went on. 'You could
even have stayed with Bernadette. Didn't I always tell you
that in my letters?'

Part of Katie wished the ground would open and swallow
her, but despite her mother's ill health and advanced years,
she needed to stand up for herself, something she couldn't do
back then when her mother hadn't stood up for her either.

'Jesus, Mammy. Will you give it a rest?' She tried to rein
in the crescendo in her voice and focus on the food, but
her blood was about to boil. 'I wasn't welcome here when
I needed ye, but no, now that the shoe is on the other foot,
'tis an open house.'

Phyllis sat back in her seat and drew the top of her cardigan
up around her neck.

'I'm sorry, I . . .' Katie began.

'There was no choice back then,' said Phyllis, sounding
frail again. She looked away to the window where the rain was
running down in tiny rivulets from what must be a blocked
drain. Katie silently cursed her siblings for not having had it
fixed. Her mother looked back at her, a sadness in her eyes.
'The parish priest arranged it all.'

Katie didn't need to be reminded of the sequence of events.
She could still see the utter disgust on the face of the priest
as he'd left the house after convincing her parents to send
her away. No, they couldn't have that kind of scandal in the
parish. And the Foxes had enough to deal with after losing
a son. She was a disgrace to them all.

Her father hadn't looked at her after that. He hadn't laid a hand on her either, but the damage was done. Three months after the grads, she was shanghaied to Cork, period, end of story. It would have been bad enough to have been one of those girls who gave up their child and returned home to try and pick up where they'd left off, live on as normal or appear to do so. But she'd heard stories of girls like them suffering from the trauma later in life, like when they had other children, not being able to bond with them or not being able to even have the kind of relationships that let them start a family. Stella had been lucky in that regard. If it hadn't been for her friendship and Bernadette's help, Katie knew she would have ended up back here after the baby had been adopted. Her mother had been delusional to ever think that was an option.

'Getting pregnant was only the half of it, Mammy!'

Gathering up the ware, she shoved the chair out from the table, not bothering to right it when it crashed to the floor. At the sink, she turned the water on full blast and scrubbed savagely at the remnants of their meal. Aware Phyllis was shuffling towards her, she didn't turn round. Two sets of gnarled knuckles rested on the bench beside her. She could smell the talcum powder. In her head, she was in the bath with Bernadette, the three of them singing as her mother lathered them with Lifebuoy soap and kneaded the Johnson's No Tears shampoo through their hair. Those moments she'd learnt to compartmentalise. Moments where her mother was her hero and Bernadette her best friend.

'What are you telling me, girleen?'

'The night of the grads, Mammy . . . you and Bernadette went to Skib . . . Auntie Theresa was very sick . . .'

There was a slow nod, her mother's memory of the timing tallying with her own. Katie grabbed at the knives and forks and continued to scrub.

'Started out as the best night of my life, you know.' She gave a shake of her head but didn't turn from her task. 'My father and Martin Fox put paid to that notion.'

Phyllis made the sign of the cross. 'God have mercy on the dead.'

'Jesus, Mammy. You really have no fucking idea!' She let the cutlery clatter onto the draining board and wrung her hands dry on a tea towel, a tremor rattling through her whole body. 'Martin Fox raped me!'

Her mother's hand shot to her mouth, she steadied herself with the other. 'My God!' she gasped.

If this was elder abuse, yes, Katie was guilty, but it was hardly a crime after the years of PTSD she'd endured.

'Leave God and all your holy saints and apostles out of this, goddammit!' Katie could hardly look at her. The woman had spent the last thirty-five years unaware of this story or perhaps telling herself a different one. But Katie was damned if she was going to let her live a lie. Bracing herself, she went on with the truth of what happened.

'If it wasn't bad enough to be trapped in Martin Fox's car and he smelling of drink and fags and forcing himself on me . . . and I get myself in home, HOME where I should have been safe . . .' She gave a mocking laugh. 'I was no sooner into the bedroom, terrified, hardly able to take in what was after happening to me . . . the pain, the shock of it . . . and in my father comes, pissed, staggering about. "What the fuck were you doing out there with that Fox fella?" he asked me. He must have known I hadn't been willing but that didn't stop him. Can you believe it?' She wasn't speaking to her mother now, she was upstairs reliving it all again. '"I told you to be home long before now, not fornicating with the boys," and then he was shoving me on to the bed, punches raining down . . . and that dress . . . All I could think of was minding that fucking dress.'

'Oh Katie, my love.' Her mother's voice sounded as worn out as it did surprised. She bent her head and, closing her eyes, she said, 'I thought the child was Conor Fox's all these years.'

Of course she had. What else could she have thought? A wave of exhaustion came over Katie. She hadn't expected such an emotional day. Her plans to have a quiet week had been well and truly shattered. She wanted to sit down, but not here, not with this decaying woman who had once been kindness itself but who had cast her out when she'd needed her most.

'I'm so ashamed,' she was saying now. 'Why didn't you tell me?'

Katie went to grab her handbag, tugged the zip closed.

'Dad said he'd kill you if I said anything,' she said, 'and with the whole place in mourning after Martin smashed himself and his car to smithereens, I just kept it all to myself.'

A leaden silence sat between them. After the longest moment, her mother spoke again, her voice so small, Katie barely heard her.

'I killed your father.'

'What?'

As they stood there in the throes of truth-telling, a wild whistle went up outside like the cry of banshee. The wind, Katie knew, but she couldn't help considering the possibility of ghosts stirred up by the exchange.

'I'll have to sit down.' Phyllis made her unsteady way to the table and with her head bowed low, she told Katie, 'Drunk he was. Cursing me up and down, throwing his weight around, punches, kicks . . . Telling me I was no good, as usual . . .' She eyed Katie as though to check it was okay to go on. Katie said nothing, her mother's pain pricking at her own heart, tears starting to smart at the corners of her eyes.

'I suppose I'd had enough,' she went on. 'Years of it, thinking I was keeping him from hurting anyone else. But a person can only take so much.' She sat back and rubbed at the sleeve of her cardigan. 'Sure I couldn't even read a book and he'd be on to me, telling me 'tis his dinner I should be making and having the place clean for him.'

Katie remembered the way her mother had always read to her in whispers, like it was their special secret time. To this day, she couldn't read aloud. Now she knew why.

'Pushed him down his own stairs, I did.'

Katie could hardly imagine the frail woman ever having the strength, but she listened in stunned silence.

'Doctor Healy wrote down that he had a fall,' Phyllis continued, 'but he knew I pushed him.' She was looking unseeing out the window again. 'Pushed him with all my might,' she said louder, sitting up straight, raising her fists before letting them drop back down to her lap. 'Should maybe have done it years before, but I did it.'

Katie let out a long breath. 'Well, I'm glad you did.'

Her mother put a trembling hand to her mouth and leaned in over the table. 'I never told another soul.'

Katie pinched at her nose and sniffed back the tears she was loath to cry. She righted the toppled chair and sat down. Here they were, two wronged women, a lifetime of pain between them, a pain they couldn't share.

'I was trying to protect you, taking it from him,' said Katie. 'As it turns out, we both suffered, trying to protect each other.'

Her mother nodded. 'That night of the ball, Sean Óg told me your father got very drunk. He heard him go into your room –'

'Don't.'

Katie had relived it enough times. Her brothers had been in the next room all right. Sean Óg wouldn't have heard much, thank God, and Finbarr, well, he might have put a pillow over his head. She liked to think he had. And Conor Fox, who she'd thought to be her one chance of escape, had probably been tucked up in bed thinking he'd had the night of his life.

'Can I ask what happened to the baby?' her mother asked.

Katie shrugged. 'I saw her once. A tiny pudding of a thing.'

She thought of Ava and the love, the security that lucky child had around her. She'd always hoped the innocent child she'd borne had had the same. Stella's son had found her some years back, had a family of his own. They'd met and promised to stay in touch. He'd understood the times had been against her. There'd been a letter once. A woman saying she thought Katie was her mother. She hadn't replied. Best left alone, she'd thought.

'We can only pray to God she's all right,' Phyllis was saying.

Katie bit down on an urge to curse the church and a blind belief in a God that had made this happen, but it was probably the only thing that got her mother out of these four walls and away from their memories.

'We had good times too, Katie.' She smiled at her, a softening in her greying eyes. 'I always try and remember them.'

'We had, Mammy.'

So much had been unsaid, but as Katie saw the energy drain from her mother, she made to leave.

'I'll be up in the morning to take you for your appointment,' she told her.

'Thanks, love. I appreciate all you're doing for me.'

A pang of guilt squeezed at Katie's soul. For the first time, she imagined the possibility that if things had been different, she might have done a lot more.

# Chapter Twenty-four

'Declan, you're like a drowned rat!' said Gerry as he returned from what had been an exhilarating but somewhat ill-advised walk to Brow Head.

He'd come in via the mudroom, where he took off his walking boots and the jacket that had gone from a light red to a merlot by dint of the lashing rain that pounded him the three kilometres back down the hill.

Joining Gerry in the kitchen, he blew warm breath into his freezing hands.

'Would you like to change out of those wet clothes and have a drop of soup?' Gerry asked.

'That would be marvellous,' said Declan. 'I'll have a bath and come down for it.'

'I can take it up to you, if you like.'

'Erra no,' said Declan. I'll throw myself in front of the fire with it, if that's okay.'

'No bother,' said Gerry, leaving him to return to his loft room and thaw out.

In the seaweed bath the others had raved about, Declan
congratulated himself on banning the phone from the week
of R and R. He'd thought the anxiety had definitely subsided,
but he'd had to take a pill earlier after feeling that old twinge
in the chest again. Instead of self-medicating, he might just
go and see the GP when he got back, start to take better care
of himself, make a few changes. As much as it would be nice
to stay down here for longer, responsibilities would have to
be faced.

He'd always had Karen as a sounding board in dealing with
the practice. Not only was she an excellent dental hygienist,
she had always been heavily invested in keeping their business current and client-focused. Somewhere in amongst his
career success and personal insecurities, he'd lost sight of
the woman he'd once set on the pedestal she deserved. He'd
taken her for granted, without a thought to how he would
miss her if she wasn't around. Although he hated to admit
it, she'd had every right to walk away. When he considered
this holiday ending and the inescapable return to the grind,
it wasn't so much the dentistry that threatened to overwhelm
him, it was the loneliness.

~

In the parlour, he found Mia stretched out on the chaise longue
under the far window with that notebook she brought about
with her, surrounded by field guides and seaweed books. She
smiled at him, her youthful face making him feel a million
years old.

'Looking very studious there, Mia.' He wandered over to where he could see she'd been taking notes.

She sat up straighter. 'Look at these, Declan. *Irish Seaweed Kitchen*. This Prannie Rhatigan woman would blow your mind. You should see what she can do with seaweed.'

'You really have been taken by our little excursion, haven't you?'

She pulled her knees up to her chest, her face serious. 'When I moved to Ireland six weeks ago, I thought my life was coming to a bit of a dead end, that I was spinning my wheels, you know?'

He nodded, unsure if she'd indeed come here to travel around as he'd presumed.

'It's a long story. I won't go into it, but that seaweed tour has given me a spark of hope.' She tilted her head, waiting for his reaction.

What age did she say she was? Thirty-two? He wondered what he'd do if he was in his thirties again.

'Well, Mia, if I had my time over, I'd probably still be a dentist . . .' He registered the surprise in her eyes. 'I actually get quite a buzz out of fixing teeth.' He smiled. 'But if there was one thing I could do differently,' he went on, swallowing down a lump in his throat, 'I'd put more time and energy into . . . the people I love.' To his great shame, he couldn't remember the last time he'd told any of them he loved them.

Mia didn't speak, but her expression told him she was letting his latent wisdom sink in. He wished he could have such a captive audience in his boys.

'Your soup, sir.' Gerry appeared with the trolley, interrupting the moment. 'Ellen said something about Lindsey O'Leary phoning for you,' he told Mia.

The girl scrambled off the chaise longue, grinning with excitement as she followed Gerry to the kitchen.

Declan settled down to his soup and crusty bread with that creamy local butter, gazing at the fire, regretful, but more comfortable in his own skin than he'd felt in a long time.

⌁

Aisling left Mick to shower as she went down to dinner a bit on the early side and found Prue and Edwina sitting side by side at the table in the conservatory.

'Have you had a good day?' she asked as she took a seat opposite the couple, who looked like they were having a quiet moment.

'Oh, another excellent day, thank you, dear,' said Edwina, smiling warmly at her. 'Took a spin to Mizen Head. Hadn't been in years.'

'What have you two been up to?' asked Prue as she leaned down between their chairs and rummaged in a handbag.

Aisling's cheeks flushed. She was grateful Prue was distracted by her phone or whatever she was after. Edwina had enough tact to pretend to be interested in whatever it was her wife was searching for.

'We didn't go too far,' she said, trying to be honest without hinting at how she and Mick had spent most of the rainy day in their room in what had felt like a second honeymoon. As she tried to calm thoughts of the afternoon's passion that sent a fresh wave of tingling through her, Prue's head popped back up.

'You two getting along better?'

'Prue!' Edwina cautioned, but Aisling smiled. Obviously, the wide berth she'd been giving her husband hadn't escaped them.

'I hope you don't go in for the silent treatment,' said Prue. Stunned by the forthright comment, Aisling let her go on. 'Thrash it out, I always say. Don't sit there and let a problem fester.'

Edwina arched her pencilled-in eyebrows but nodded, obviously at one with Prue on how to navigate disagreements in a relationship. Aisling was grateful when the loud woman lowered her voice.

'Ed and I are lucky in that respect,' she said, leaning in as though to offer much-needed advice. 'Always been able to have it out, isn't that so, Ed?'

Without waiting for a response, she kept talking, openly declaring how Ed couldn't hide anything from her. She could read her like a book.

'Here,' said Prue, scrolling through her phone and turning it to show Aisling a photo of them, windblown but happy against the white arches of Mizen Bridge.

'That's a gorgeous picture of the two of you.' She smiled but couldn't help thinking of the day she and Mick had gone there and thanking God her husband had been big enough to forgive her.

The door opened and in he came, her handsome Mick, beaming at them before taking the seat beside her and reaching for her hand. Interlocking fingers with his, she held tight. There would be no more pushing this man away. She had hurt him in a way she could never have imagined when they'd exchanged vows fifteen years ago. She'd spend the next fifteen or however many years they would have trying not to take his love for granted. He was one in a million and he'd chosen her. She would always remind herself of that.

—

As the other guests trooped in, Aisling was grateful for the distraction from the emotional moment. Their butts had barely hit the seats when Mia was on to the evening's entertainment.

'Are you all coming to the poetry night later?' she asked as Ellen and Gerry brought in their starters.

'Is that in the local?' asked Declan.

'The most southerly pub in Ireland,' Gerry chipped in before wishing them bon appétit and leaving them to a discussion about who had already been there.

'You'll come down with us,' said Prue turning to Katie.

There was a lull as they waited for her to respond to what sounded more like a demand than a question. Katie put a hand to her hair and pushed the fringe tighter over her ear. Aisling suspected she had an urge to decline the offer of a night out with the group of people she was unlikely to see again, but maybe it was that very fact and Prue's manner that had her nodding her head as if someone was operating her by remote control.

Edwina gave a clap that started the others off whooping and clapping in response. There was an air of youthful delight at the prospect of a night out together, although from where Aisling was sitting, the look on Katie's face gave the impression their enthusiasm had the same effect as pouring oil on water.

For once Aisling was grateful when Declan started expounding.

'I could have written poetry today,' he began, 'up there on Brow Head in the wind and the rain, communing with my forebears, in the footsteps of Marconi.'

'Fascinating history,' said Prue, giving him his cue to regale them with tales of the Italian engineer who had come to Crookhaven and built a telegraphic station at Brow Head at the turn of the twentieth century. Oh yes, Declan was full of facts, including the one about Marconi being offered passage on the *Titanic* but opting to sail a week later on the *Lusitania*.

Right now, Aisling wished *Declan* had been given a ticket for the ill-fated ship, but she'd suck it up; her husband had credited a conversation with the dentist as the catalyst for their reconciliation.

'Maybe we could all go up there tomorrow,' Mia suggested. 'And you could be our guide.'

In her enthusiasm, the young woman had called Declan's bluff. If exercise was anything, Aisling thought, he'd be getting his money's worth this week. She only hoped her own calves would be up to it.

'Right, you lot!' Prue's voice bellowed over the hum. 'Best eat up and get down the pub.'

There were nods of agreement as they finished off Gerry's delicious Irish stew, forgoing dessert or the cups of tea and coffee that usually kept a few of them lingering in the conservatory. There were arrangements made about lifts. Aisling for one was happy to walk the short distance to the pub, already looking forward to the prospect of staggering home and falling into that comfortable bed with her love.

—

It amazed Mia that, in a tiny community, a pub could be packed on a weeknight in the middle of winter. A strange feeling had seeped into her since she'd arrived at Lizzie O's. Ellen had told them how she and her family used to go there for summer holidays and how she'd retreated there when life had thrown one of its curve balls. Mia had often wondered what it would be like to have taken the regular trips 'home' as Mick and Aisling talked about. Since her mother died, the Montgomerys' farm had been the only place where she'd had a sense of home, but she was about to give all that away. Stepping out of that comfort zone seemed like a massive undertaking, but she'd thought long and hard, given Harry all the leeway she could. It was time to move on.

As she stood at the bar, the lively strains of a fiddle played over the crowd from where a group of musicians were jamming in a corner. If Harry were here, she'd have found them somewhere to sit and guarded the table while waiting for him to return with a wine. Tonight, she thrust a ten euro note over the counter until it caught the eye of the barman and for the first time in her life, she ordered a pint.

Happily standing and tapping a foot to the music, she didn't notice the dog man approach.

'G'day, mate,' he joked, nearly making her spill her drink onto the new shoes she'd treated herself to that afternoon between viewings.

'What are you doing here?' The question was out of her mouth before she could take it back. 'I'm sorry, I was thinking about the dogs . . .'

He gave her a quizzical look. She kept talking, trying to explain herself.

'I just imagine them like toys coming to life once their owners have gone to bed, getting up to all kinds of mischief . . .'

If he thought her mentally deranged, he would be within his rights to walk away, but he smiled and dipped his lean frame down to where his face was level with the top of her head. He smelled of toothpaste and tobacco, the mix of self-care and self-destruction adding to his appeal.

'Don't worry,' he said, those bright blue eyes looking into hers, 'they're being well looked after.'

God, he was gorgeous. And she was married, she reminded herself. He wouldn't be the first man she'd found attractive since marrying Harry, but she'd never been unfaithful. No, as it turned out, she'd been too faithful.

'I'm Mia,' she said, reaching out to shake hands.

'Matt, Matt Summers,' he said, swapping his jacket onto the other arm and taking her hand. 'My mate Tom's minding them,' he explained.

They were interrupted by a man adjusting a microphone to one side of the bar, who introduced himself as their MC. Matt took a roll of A4 paper from the back pocket of his jeans and rocked on his ankles.

'Are you one of the poets?' Another question Mia had voiced with an incredulity she wished she'd toned down.

His cheeks flamed as he sucked in a breath. "Fraid so.'

⌐

Given the collective enthusiasm for her to join the group in their outing, Katie couldn't back out of spending the evening at the pub she'd been too young to frequent when she'd left. She would have preferred to have made its acquaintance under quieter circumstances, over a pot of peppermint tea perhaps and definitely alone behind one of those stained-glass divider affairs. No such luck tonight after Prue and her boombox of a voice had momentarily deprived her of the ability to make a rational decision. But she was here now, imagining what it might have been like if she'd stayed, perhaps strolling through those doors on what might have become a regular kind of Wednesday in winter after a day working somewhere in the local area, teaching maybe in the primary school as she'd once dreamt.

'Myself and Prue spent a lovely few hours holed up here the other day,' Edwina was saying.

The woman had hardly stopped talking about her honeymoon since they'd commandeered one of the long tables up the couple of steps that at least gave a good view of the proceedings. Katie half-listened, scanning the joint for signs of Conor Fox, who thankfully was nowhere to be seen.

'Ladies and gentlemen, welcome to Crookhaven's Annual Poetry Slam . . .' The voice of the MC broke off Edwina's commentary. 'Judges will be chosen in the usual way.'

With a wry smile, he turned to a young woman who scrabbled in a bag and began lofting sweets into the audience. A pop to the side of Katie's head was met by whooping and a round of applause. As a Werther's Original fell to her lap, she managed a nervous smile as her face flamed in what felt like the worst hot flush she'd ever experienced. Beside her, Edwina was batting her tinted eyelashes, congratulating her. She'd gone along with this night out thinking she could disappear in a quiet corner. Now she had to pay attention and actually choose winners in what she hadn't even realised was a competition.

Declan caught a Fox's Mint like a rugby pass and declared he too had been chosen. Someone went about handing out whiteboards as their host explained how they were expected to score. Prue was shouting encouragement to them from near the bar. So much for retreating to a quiet corner, Katie mused as she readied her pen and whiteboard, hoping she could concentrate enough to give the as yet unidentified poets a fair score.

Such was her consternation at having to actively participate in this circus, she didn't spot Conor Fox until he was called upon to perform. He looked nervous as he took his place behind the microphone and a hush came over the crowd. The last person she'd imagined would have the balls to get up and stand in front of people, Katie wondered if this was something he'd done before in that other life she wasn't a part of. The only consolation was that he didn't look at her.

'This isn't a sad poem
This isn't a mad poem

Just a love poem
From the bottom of my heart poem . . .'

He certainly had the crowd's attention. She'd heard of slam poetry, listened to a bit of it online in the quiet hours when she'd given up on a boring book or been too tired to keep her eyes open to watch TV. As far as she was aware you had to breathe around the lines, let them run from your mouth like a train, carrying the audience with you on a journey that made you look out the window and see something in the fleeting images that flew past, something you'd never seen, or at least would look at in a different way. Conor Fox was doing that now in a poem she would never forget.

'You left me all those years ago
My heart was shattered by the blow
Who could tell at seventeen
That I would never leave Goleen?
I might have left had you asked me to
But you were gone before I knew
The whisper network still resounds
With speculation about what grounds
Made you a castaway, a couldn't stay
I always hoped you'd return one day
A thousand questions filled my head
At times I wished I could be dead
But for the hope that times of old
Times of fun and stories told
Could be renewed and lived again

I held on tight unlike some men
And women too who all too broken
Leave unspoken words of truth, of troubled thoughts
That might have spared their precious lives
God knows we all deserve to thrive
I bear no grudge for who am I to judge
The last thing I would do is pressure you to make this
    any better
Helping you was all that mattered
But not one word, not a letter
Can we sit down without the frown
Just be civil, no agenda, would hate to offend ya
But I'd love to tell you what's been happening
Share your stories morning glories
The memories that connect us
Before you jump on the next bus
Suitcase pulling at your arm, hair hanging limp
    behind you
I can still see you, that look in your eyes
Like your spirit had left you.'

# Chapter Twenty-five

Mia felt compelled to start the applause in the hesitant moment where the audience decided whether or not the poet was actually finished. Declan raised a whiteboard with 9.5 over his head and if she was not mistaken, tears glistened at the corners of his eyes. She was sure Katie was only copying him, as she caught her glancing over and quickly scribbling on her board before turning it round for the judges to get the briefest glimpse and wiping it clean again.

The next couple of poems were thankfully lighter, satirical in nature, with the poets letting rip their thinly disguised frustration at political figures, most of the references unfamiliar to Mia but the themes universal. Matt looked like he might burst a blood vessel, such was the chest-hugging with his arms crossed around him and the grip he had of the paper he twirled between his fingers.

Finally, it was his turn. She pulled at his jacket in an offer to mind it. With a grateful grin, he thrust it into her arms, shoved the paper into his back pocket and strode to the microphone. Mia thought she too might rupture something, such were the nerves she had for him, but her worries were unfounded. With a hilarious poem that managed to mention nearly every dog breed known to man, he brought the house down. She whooped and clapped as the whiteboards went up with scores between 9.7 and straight 10s. There was no disputing who'd won, but that didn't stop Matt shaking like a leaf as he left the makeshift stage and made his way through the cheering punters, many patting him on the back. It was obvious the Kiwi was well known among the locals. She couldn't help wondering how he'd managed to endear himself to the kind of small community where, she knew only too well, it could be hard to integrate.

Somebody shouted to let him know his name was on a pint at the bar. After thanking them, he collected the drink and appeared beside her.

'You were amazing,' she told him, turning to take in the humble expression, beads of sweat starting to run down his face. Taking the end of his T-shirt, he drew it up over his forehead to wipe at the moisture. The toned abs and the waistband of the Bonds underwear caught her off guard. She looked away, hoping no one had seen her jaw drop.

At thirty-five, Harry was already developing a belly. *Older than his years*, her mother might have said had she met him. It had been part of the attraction. The safety of it. Standing beside Matt tonight, safety wasn't something Mia craved. No, this dog-loving, poetry-writing outdoorsy individual held a very different kind of attraction.

He did that dipping thing again. 'There's a spot over there if you want to sit,' he said, gesturing with his glass to where a couple were just about to vacate a table.

Surely there were others he'd prefer to debrief with? But she wasn't complaining. He was easy company, not to mention the best-looking bloke in the pub.

'Okay,' she said, handing him back his jacket and letting him lead the way. The butterflies in her tummy were doing a jig in time with the music. *It's a drink and a chat,* she told herself. *Nothing more.*

Sitting in a pub with a man who wasn't her husband brought with it a sense of daring. She could never have been called the cautious type, but her life so far had been about risks taken to suit others. Taking a risk on her own behalf was new. This week had already taken her way out of what she thought was her comfort zone. There was no need to make a big mistake here. She could go back to her normal life on Saturday, Harry none the wiser about her adventure. But eyeing this man over her pint glass, she knew she'd already moved on. She wouldn't allow herself to feel guilt or shame, she decided. It would be foolish to rush into a new relationship, but equally, she wouldn't close herself off to the possibility. Her future would be on no one's terms but her own.

'So what brought you to Crookhaven?' she asked.

'Ah,' he began, taking a gulp of the pint and setting it down on the table. 'Bring a man down to earth after his big win.'

She went to apologise, but he winked to reassure her he wasn't serious.

'I'd much rather hear about you,' he said. 'Not sure you really want to listen to my sob story.'

On the contrary, more than anything right now, Mia wanted to know everything about him. In fact, she'd be happy if he told her what he'd had for breakfast, such was the thrill of sitting here with this handsome Kiwi, surrounded by jovial conversation and fantastic live music. She gave him what she hoped was an encouraging smile.

'It's simple really,' he began, leaning over the table, his voice low. 'I met Rachel, a Crookhaven girl, in sunny Nelson about six years ago.' He paused to check she knew where that was.

'Top of the South Island?'

He nodded.

'That's where I'm from.' For a moment, a look of longing crossed his eyes, but he took a breath and continued. 'When her holiday in NZ was over, I followed her here and fell in love with the place.'

'And with her?'

'Eh . . . yes. That's why I came.'

Mia looked down, embarrassed to have sounded so naive. He rubbed at his stubble, the leather bracelet loose on his wrist. This had the potential to throw a bucket of ice-cold water on any designs she might have had on the dog whisperer. As nice as this was, she didn't want to look like a fool.

'So where is she now?'

He grabbed his glass and before taking a drink, he said, 'Somewhere in Southeast Asia, I believe.'

Her eyebrows narrowed, not understanding.

'Got itchy feet, decided she wanted to do more travelling.'

'And you didn't go with her?'

'No. Things weren't as rosy as I thought they would be once I got here.' He gave a shaky laugh. 'An old boyfriend kinda got in the way.'

Mia imagined a not-so-old husband getting in the way of anywhere this might be going but pushed the thought aside.

'And you didn't want to go back to New Zealand?'

He shook his head. 'It was Tom that kept me here in the end.'

Her question was written all over her face she knew, but she'd pried enough already. Any ideas she might have had about this Matt dude were quickly dissolving. So what, he was gay now?

'You can meet him if you like.'

Oh lovely. Exactly what she'd planned for tonight. A good reason to forget she'd ever fancied him. But maybe this was exactly what she needed – gather the facts before diving head-long into something she might regret.

'Sure, I'd love to,' she said with as much enthusiasm as she could muster.

'Great.' In one move he'd jumped up, downed his pint and grabbed his jacket from the back of the chair.

*Oh, he means now.*

There was nothing for it but to follow as he led the way out the door, dodging calls from locals to stay on and leaving her to wrestle through the throng, barely managing to make eye contact with Declan and let him know she was going.

Outside, as she jogged to keep up with Matt's long strides, Mia cursed the freezing cold wind and driving rain that ruined any chance of conversation on the stretch of road out from the village.

'Here we are,' said Matt, pointing to an overhanging sign lit up by what looked like an old-fashioned gas light.

'Digz for Dogz,' she read. 'Cute name!'

As he opened the front door of the house, they were met by a flash of white as a West Highland terrier yapped and sniffed about their ankles.

'Hello, Winnie,' he said, bending down and scooping up the dog, who proceeded to lick at the back of his ear.

A chorus of barks went up from inside.

'Your favourite poet has returned,' Matt shouted over the din. 'I've brought a visitor,' he said as he threw his parka over the end of the bannister. 'Let me take that for you.'

He took her jacket and put it on a proper coat hook beside a mirror in the hallway where she caught her dishevelled appearance.

When she turned, there was a young man standing in a doorway beaming at Matt, dogs milling around him, tails wagging at the excitement of their arrival. He lifted the latch on one of those childproof gates that kept the dogs corralled and came out, carefully closing it behind him.

'Tom, this is Mia. Mia, Tom.'

She took his outstretched hand. 'Hi, Tom. Nice to meet you.'

If her face was a million questions, she tried to smile through them.

'Have you had a cuppa?' Matt asked him as he walked towards the back of the house.

'I was waiting for you,' the young man replied, a hint of good-natured scolding in his voice.

Mia followed them into the kitchen, Winnie in tow. It was a space she would have described as rustic but homely. A worn table that looked like a recycled door served as both a dining and work area, by the look of the pile of papers Matt was stacking together and shoving on to a laptop towards one end.

'Where you from?' Tom asked her as Matt put on the kettle and washed a few mugs that had been sitting in the sink.

Mia told him a little about herself, aware Matt was taking it all in. Apart from the obvious fact that Tom had Down Syndrome, she was at pains to figure out where he fitted in to Matt's life, and why this gentle young man had made the Kiwi stay when his home was nearly twenty thousand ks away.

'He smashed the poetry comp,' Mia told him, anxious to get off the topic of herself and nodding towards Matt, who was setting mugs and a teapot on the table. She liked a man who used a teapot, she decided.

'Well done, mate.' Tom's delight was tangible.

Matt gave him a high five. 'Couldn't have done it without you, mate.'

Mia smiled at the contagious warmth between them, the kind of bond she'd always craved as an only child.

Over the tea, Tom gave a detailed account of the evening. He knew every dog by name and behaviour. There'd been a scrap between the over-friendly Bernese and a cranky old shepherd who'd brought him in to line. The collie had thrown up on the carpet after eating too much grass that afternoon, but Tom had cleaned it up, had it all under control, he assured them. After finishing the tea, he started to yawn.

'Best get to bed, mate,' Matt advised.

'Okay.' Tom yawned again. 'Nice to meet you, Mia.'

Mia smiled as he gave Winnie a goodnight pat.

'Night, Tom,' she said as he left and went upstairs.

'Rachel's brother,' Matt explained, lowering his voice. 'The parents are getting on a bit. Can hardly look after themselves . . .'

'So you look after him?'

'Someone had to step up,' he said. 'Don't think I'm any kind of hero here. Anyone would have done it. He's a fantastic worker. Brilliant with the dogs . . .'

Mia could hardly believe that someone with no connection to the place other than an ex-girlfriend would do something so selfless.

'Which came first?' she asked, wishing she hadn't sounded so judgey.

'The kennel was a dream for me and Rachel,' he explained. 'I did farm work around the place when I first arrived, but when she left and I decided to commit to looking after Tom, I just went for it.'

He shrugged as she took in the risk, the love, the commitment it would have taken to set up this business and offer job security to the young man who, as far as she could see, he had come to consider a brother.

'Enough about me,' he said, getting up and going to refresh the teapot. 'It's more comfy over there.'

He gestured to a low sofa along one wall, a collection of throws and cushions strewn across it. Mia hesitated, not sure if it was wise to get too comfy with someone she hardly knew. But as she took a seat at one end of the sofa, Winnie, who had finally calmed down, climbed up beside her, making Mia's right leg a cushion of her own.

Matt tutted as he brought the mugs and handed one to her.

'Sorry I can't offer you anything stronger.'

'Tea's fine,' she told him, grateful to have drawn a halt to the alcohol after consuming her first pints. She would keep her wits about her.

'So, holiday girl,' he said, sitting down with her new best friend between them, 'what's your story?'

At the other corner of the sofa, he stretched his long legs out onto a worn leather pouffe.

'I'm actually not on holiday,' she began, hoping he wouldn't think less of her for misleading him. 'I moved here six weeks ago with my husband.'

His mouth opened to say something, but there was no sound, just an intensity in his eyes that made him look intrigued.

'It's over,' she said. 'I just need to tell him.' It was only fair. However much she might be attracted to Matt, she didn't want to deny Harry's existence. They both deserved so much more.

He leaned an elbow on the back of the couch and rested his head in his hand. 'Well you're here and I'm listening.' He smiled. 'Life story. Go your hardest.'

'Are you sure you want to hear it?'

'Positive.'

She tugged at the sleeves of her jumper, pulling them down over her knuckles. 'I grew up in Melbourne,' she began. 'Unfortunately, my parents died in a horrific accident when I was young.' She looked down at her hands and worried at the nail polish that was starting to chip, aware of him watching her. 'I had no living grandparents or any rellies that could take me, so I was put into care.'

Matt drew a hand over his face. 'Oh God, I'm so sorry, Mia. I didn't mean to –'

'No, I don't mind telling you . . . if you don't mind hearing.'

He nodded, his face serious, encouraging her to go on.

'The school they sent me to had some really good teachers. They looked out for me. Took no shit from bullies, you know? Mum used to say I had a good brain. I hung on to that. Ended up getting a scholarship for uni.' She stroked at the soft silk of Winnie's coat. 'That's where I met Harry.'

Matt took a drink of his tea but didn't take his eyes off her. She hadn't spoken this much about herself in years. Both at home and in company, it was Harry who did most of the talking.

'Harry was a few years older than me,' she went on. 'He was doing a PhD. Used to help out in practical sessions to get extra cash. We began seeing each other, spending weekends at his parents' farm . . .' She could see them in her mind's eye, the kind of people she'd fallen asleep fantasising about as a child, a distraction from the uncertainty of how long she would spend with any particular foster carers. She screwed her mouth over to one side at the thought. Those days and nights were in the past. There was no way she would ever go back, and yet they stayed with her.

'It was his family I fell in love with,' she said, looking down at her hands again. 'They fed me the best meals, gave me the warmest bed, listened to me stressing about exams, cheering me on when I'd get a good grade on an assignment.'

'Did you love Harry?'

Matt's question sounded so simple, like she could answer yes, or no. Mia shook her head.

'I thought I did. Honestly, I thought he was the best thing that ever happened to me.'

And he was, for a time, she realised.

'When I became a regular fixture, his parents began hinting at wedding bells. To marry into a family like Harry's felt like a dream come true.'

She couldn't deny being swept along by Kaye and Trevor's enthusiasm. She'd married their son on the farm. A small wedding by Kaye's standards, massive by Mia's. She reckoned they'd put the invite out over the outback airwaves, such was the sea of dusty utes parked in the front paddock. The Country Women's Association would have been proud of the small army of women who catered with a high tea served in the huge marquee. Harry spent most of the day trying to introduce her to people, half of whose names he'd forgotten. She didn't mind at the time. She was Mrs Harry Montgomery, soon to be a doctor's wife of sorts. Her parents would have been pleased.

'So where did the game of happy families go wrong?'

How disloyal she felt even thinking it hadn't worked out. Harry was self-absorbed, yes, but he wasn't all bad, and Kaye and Trevor the best in-laws anyone could wish for. And yet, since she'd found herself in that charity shop weeks ago suspecting her marriage might be over, she'd become more and more sure that marrying Harry and expecting a happy ever after had been a mistake.

'I married a family,' she said, the truth sounding at once simple and oh so complicated.

Matt let the comment sit between them.

'Poor Harry.' She shook her head. 'I think he was a bit coerced by his parents and me. Harry Montgomery, my hero, rescuing me from an awful past. Sometimes I think he'd like to end it too. Probably feels responsible for me.'

'So what do you think you'll do?' Matt asked.

She paused before answering, the reality of what she was about to do starting to weigh heavy.

'I'd like to breathe on my own for a while.'

Matt leaned a little closer and reached out. Her stomach did a leap that made her wish they didn't have the snoring dog between them. All that resolve around not jumping into anything romantic threatening to crumble at the touch of his hand.

'I've got some experience in that department,' he said. 'I'll help if you want.'

He made it sound so easy, the scale of the mammoth tasks that lay ahead diminished in his laid-back, caring presence.

'I have an interview on Friday,' she said, 'Lindsey O'Leary at the seaweed centre ... I'm nervous as all hell.'

'Beauty!' He interlocked his fingers with hers. 'I think you'll go just fine, Mia.'

As he walked her back to the guesthouse, it felt good to have off-loaded, to be listened to in a way that made her feel special. It was time to step out of Harry Montgomery's shadow. She had an ally in Matt, and if the stars aligned, who knew where it could lead.

# Chapter Twenty-six

Breakfast was a muted affair. Katie hadn't slept a wink after she'd slipped out of the pub once the poetry competition was over and driven back to the haven that was her tiny cottage. Despite the warmth that reached the mezzanine from the modern fireplace downstairs and the lush linen and throws on her bed, she couldn't escape from the lines that Conor Fox had so passionately delivered. Whether or not anyone in the audience linked the poem to her was impossible to know, but she was in no doubt as to exactly what he meant to convey. Had he really spent all those years awaiting her return, even remembering her, when she herself had spent so much time and money trying to forget?

Edwina was quiet this morning, but nowhere as rough-looking as Prue, who was obviously nursing a hangover. Gerry's offers of Irish breakfasts were met with low groans unlike the enthusiastic reactions they'd evoked on previous mornings. Even Declan – who she could have sworn was on that low-carb beer all night – looked the worse for wear as he shook out his napkin and tucked it into the collar of his shirt.

'All set for our guided walk?' Mick asked him with a pat on the back and a heavy hint of sarcasm as he and Aisling joined them.

Declan rolled his eyes and lifted his coffee cup. 'Let me get this into me first and I'll get back to you.'

Mia sat down with a plateful of pastries.

'Did you enjoy the poetry, Mia?' asked Mick.

The younger woman yawned and gave a smile Katie knew had a story behind it. But she gave nothing away.

'A great night, thank you,' she said before starting into what was definitely a deviation from her usual healthy morning meal.

A comfortable hush fell over the table as they ate. Katie had to concede the misgivings she'd harboured at the beginning of the week about her fellow guests had been unfounded. Each of them had their own cross to bear, she'd suspected, and was grateful to have been left to deal with hers in private. She watched bemused now as Declan cleared his plate of the sausages, bacon and Clonakilty black pudding.

As he wiped up the last of the egg with his toast, he asked, 'So who's up for a brisk walk?'

A few muted responses went up around the table.

'Not me, sorry Declan,' Katie told him. 'Big day for my mother.'

If any of them were surprised at her volunteering personal information, they didn't say it. There were a few nods and good lucks before she left them to plan their expedition.

It was in her mind to confront Conor Fox before she left on Saturday, tell him to get a life, forget about her, but today was about minding her mother and making plans of her own for the woman's future.

Phyllis was all dolled up when Katie arrived in time to take her to her appointment. *Must have got up at the dawn*, Katie thought as she helped her on with the good coat and let her link arms from the house to the car. Her mother had always dressed in her Sunday best for doctor's appointments, down to the lipstick Katie could smell in amongst the talc and the same soap she'd put to her nose when she'd used the bathroom. After their previous conversation, Katie wished she could separate her mother from the discomfort she must have felt in the house and like a cardboard cut-out, lift her from the picture, leaving behind the background and all its bad memories.

Her mother was quiet as they drove down the curving hill to Goleen.

'So this is it,' she said in a small voice.

'What do you mean?'

Out of her peripheral vision, Katie could see her head bowed.

'They'll tell me I have dementia or Alzheimer's and I'll be thrown into a home.'

Katie parked her car behind the surgery and killed the engine. Turning, she could see defeat threatening to overwhelm the eighty-two-year-old. She reached out a hand to where the blue veins and brown age spots coloured the rice paper skin. It felt cold to the touch. Katie squeezed.

'Let's not cross our bridges, Mammy.'

Her mother looked at her. There was a shine in her eyes Katie recognised as hope.

—

'Phyllis, you made it on time today.'

If Katie felt like punching Doctor Smit, she didn't let on. No point getting him offside before the assessment was done and dusted. The sooner Doctor Healy was back from holiday the better, but they were here now. She sucked in her dislike for the man and pushed back in the extra seat where her mother was visibly shaking beside her.

'No need to be nervous, Phyllis. I'm just going to take you through a few tests, fill in some paperwork.' He held up the stapled sheets of paper that would determine her fate. 'We gathered a lot of the important information on the physical side of things on your last visit, so it won't take long.'

He launched into a series of questions about where they were, what time of day it was, how she would spell 'world' both forwards and backwards, could she identify objects he placed on the desk. The more he asked, the more exasperated Phyllis became.

'Do you think I have a screw loose, doctor?' she asked.

Katie stifled a laugh as he bent his head over his documents. She was sure he too was trying not to smile.

'I may be one foot in the grave,' her mother went on with a strength Katie hadn't expected, 'but I can assure you, Doctor Smit, there is nothing whatsoever wrong with my brain.'

Katie wanted to cheer her on but sat waiting for the doctor's opinion.

'Mrs Daly,' he began, sitting back in his chair, 'I am inclined to agree with you.' He made a steeple with his fingers and rested his chin on top. 'The problem remains, however, that you are a danger to yourself alone in that house.'

The feisty moment was past. Phyllis gave a defeated shrug. There was no denying the fact she was too frail to mind herself.

'So what are you going to do with me?'

'We have some very good aged care facilities in the county,' Doctor Smit was saying, taking brochures down from a shelf and setting them in front of her mother.

Averting her eyes, Phyllis pulled her walking stick close into her, obviously wanting to leave but looking trapped. Katie couldn't stand it. For the first time since she'd come back, she wanted to take her mother in her arms and hold her. The woman had suffered her whole life, and now she was to be handed over to strangers.

'We'll take them away and have a look,' she told the doctor, leaning forward and gathering the brochures to her chest. He got out of his chair and helped her up, at last showing a little of the compassion she deserved.

'She'll need more than someone looking in on her,' he said to Katie as Phyllis made her unsteady way out the door.

Katie swallowed. 'I know. Thank you.'

—

In the supermarket, Katie wished she'd let her mother dictate a list so she could have torn round the aisles, filling the trolley and getting the hell out of there. Phyllis, however, said she'd love to go in as the place kept her in touch with the community and made a welcome change from sitting alone in the house. It would have been mean to deny her the outing. They took slow steps as she leaned on her walking stick and kept a hand on Katie's as she shuffled along, directing her as to what to buy. Despite the pain she'd suffer later in the arthritic knee, Katie knew this was exactly the kind of activity that would keep her going.

'Is that you, Phyllis?' came a voice from behind them. Katie turned to see Rita Kelly beaming, a basket filled to near overflowing weighing down one arm. 'I was going to call up to you later. Will you be in?'

'I will, Rita.'

Katie could almost feel the lightening in her mother's demeanour.

'Katie had me at the doctor's for that assessment I was telling you about.'

Rita regarded Katie with a look of measured admiration.

''Tis an awful shame you're so far away,' she said. 'You'd be a great comfort to your mother.'

Katie wasn't sure what to say and gave what she felt was an inane smile. She knew Rita was genuine, with only her friend's best interests at heart, but she couldn't help feeling guilty at the prospect of leaving her mother to the decisions Bernadette and Finbarr would have to help her to make. Spain or no Spain, she'd have to phone her sister later and talk it out.

As luck would have it, Conor Fox was at the checkout when they'd got everything they needed.

'Phyllis, nice to see you in here.'

If she wasn't imagining it, Katie was sure he was keeping his head down, avoiding eye contact as he exchanged a few pleasantries with Phyllis about his father and the weather. *Jesus Christ*, she couldn't leave Saturday with even more guilt on her conscience. They needed a conversation to set all that stuff in the poem well and truly behind them.

'Thanks again for sorting the car out,' she began, handing over her card to pay and gathering up the bags. She took a deep breath as their eyes met. 'Would you have time for a drink later?'

He looked at her, holding her gaze for longer than was necessary.

'I would.'

Shoving down her doubts, she pressed on with the arrangement. 'Eight in O'Sullivan's?'

'Right.' He said the word slowly as though he were sceptical as to whether or not she was serious.

Her mother had made her way almost to the door. With a couple of strides, Conor was out from behind the counter and holding it open for them.

'See you tonight so.'

Katie nodded. She left the shop with the image of his shy smile playing in her mind. Tonight couldn't come soon enough. He didn't need to be getting any ideas. She just needed to set him straight.

# Chapter Twenty-seven

After breakfast, Mick sent his mother a message. With all that had been going on between himself and Aisling, he hadn't been in the form to check in. Besides, he knew she'd have been in touch if there was anything wrong. When she messaged back straightaway, he decided to call.

'You're up late, Mam.'

'Can't sleep for the heat.' He could hear a big yawn. 'But I'm not complaining. The weather is glorious. Are you having a good time, love?'

'Yes, all good here. Very grateful to you all for a wonderful week.' He would spare her the details. It was no secret she considered Aisling a firecracker and they didn't need to tell each other everything to show they supported each other. 'How are the two?'

'Grand. Evan is working a lot. I hardly see him. Poor Natalie got her period, God love her.'

He thought of his baby girl becoming a young woman. He didn't want her to grow up so fast but accepted the inevitability of it all.

'She's okay,' Lilian went on. 'Myself and Charlie looked after her.'

He could see his mother's warm smile. 'Better let you get to bed, Mam. We're about to go for a hike here.'

'Sounds good. Enjoy yourselves.'

Aisling came out of the bathroom and found the new trainers she'd bought in case of any athletic activity.

'Was that your mam?'

Mick nodded. 'Natalie got her period.'

Aisling sank down on the side of the bed. 'And I wasn't there.'

Typical! She'd missed all of her daughter's milestones – first steps, first words. Even on her first day at school she'd been at a trade fair and Mick had had to go with her. He used to take her to playgroup when he was off, experienced so many of the special moments Aisling missed out on.

He gave her shoulder a squeeze. 'Mam looked after her, don't worry.'

She shrugged his hand away. 'I know that, but I wanted to be the one to mind her. It's always the same. I get time off – nothing happens. I'm working and miss all the important stuff.'

*Lily Fitz*, she fumed to herself. That woman got all the attention. Ever since her daughter was small, when Lilian came to visit or they went home, Natalie would always head into her grandmother's bed when she woke up. The two of them thick as thieves, reading stories, telling yarns. Mick loved the lie-ins, but Aisling hated being abandoned. Her only girl and she favoured her mother-in-law over her.

But there'd been enough arguments this week. If she let rip now, Mick would be within his rights to say what did she expect, she was always busy. She leaned into him and felt his warm jumper wrap around her, breathed in the scent of him. Lynx Mick Fitzgerald – they should patent it. No, forget that. She wanted him all to herself. Maybe she was too busy, flitting around the state, back and forth to Melbourne, climbing some endless ladder. The thought of going back to it all filled her with dread. Her foolish encounter with Brett Goodstone had seen to that. She hugged Mick in tight.

'What would you think of me opening a shop?' she asked, not looking up.

He held her a little away. 'Didn't we have that discussion before? About taking something on when you already have –'

'*Instead* of my crazy job,' she cut in. 'I know it's risky, working for myself, but I'd be close to home. There are a few vacant retail properties in Shearwater . . .'

'I think you'd do a brilliant job.' She could see the cogs whirring in his mind. 'It would mean some financial wrangling, for sure, but we'd be fine. We don't need much, you and me, Ash.'

She cuddled into him again, her heart swelling in her chest at his belief in her. It wasn't in her nature to be idle but running a shop might be enough for a while. Natalie might even help out after school or on weekends when she got a little older. She didn't need three hundred staff and the Brett Goodstones of the world to make her happy. She had everything she needed in their wee corner of Tasmania.

Lilian tossed and turned in the guest studio, wide awake again after speaking to Mick. She got up and slipped her light silky dressing gown over her chemise, not needing to tie the belt, it was that warm. In the lounge, Charlie eyed her from over the edge of his bed and began to stretch. Despite her efforts to ignore him, he got up and gave a meow.

'You'll wake the house,' she told him as he came and rubbed his soft fur against her leg, no doubt expecting a midnight feed.

She peered into the fridge and decided to pour herself a glass of the white wine she'd opened the night before. Taking it outside, she set it on the low table at the front of the house and lit a citronella candle to deter the mozzies before settling back into the comfy two-seater she imagined her daughter-in-law using as a great vantage point for keeping an eye on her neighbours.

*So peaceful*, she thought, listening to the wash of the waves and the low thump of a wallaby foraging along the nature strip. Letting her head tilt back against the cushion and her mind clear of all the random thoughts that were keeping her up, Lilian didn't notice the lone walker until she heard a cough from somewhere close by. Her eyes took a moment to adjust.

'Doug!' She gathered the sides of her dressing gown, fumbling for the belt she'd sat on.

'Sorry to disturb you, Lilian,' he said in a low voice. 'I couldn't sleep either.'

In the awkward silence that followed, Lilian didn't know whether to invite him to sit or make excuses to get back inside. Her wineglass was still full. What was the harm in offering him a drink?

'Would you like to join me?' She gestured to the glass.

He hesitated in the open gateway.

'If you don't mind my company.'

In the house, she retrieved the bottle and an extra glass. No, she didn't mind his company one bit. In fact, since the day on the boat, she'd realised he could actually be quite pleasant to be around. When she came back outside, Doug had settled himself in the two-seater and was looking out to where the blue-black sea shimmered in the moonlight.

'Thank you,' he said as she poured, aware of his eyes resting on her ageing décolletage. Not wanting to give him the wrong impression altogether, she sat down as far away from him as the seat would allow.

'Any word on the house?' she asked. What Doug and Heather did with their money was their business, but she was at a loss as to how else to avoid a painful silence.

When he gave an embarrassed smile, she thought she'd overstepped the mark, but he leaned a little towards her.

'That's why I hoped you were up,' he began. 'Heather was thrilled when I told her about your advice.' Lilian was still considering the notion that he'd walked past hoping to see her, but she listened as he went on. 'Cheryl didn't sound overjoyed when we spoke to her, but she accepted our offer. I think she's strapped for cash . . .'

'That's wonderful!' Lilian sat up a little. She would have hugged Heather if she'd delivered the news, but not wanting to overwhelm the man in her enthusiasm, she clinked glasses instead. 'Congratulations!'

Doug looked down into the pale gold liquid, thoughtful again. 'I must apologise,' he said.

As the warm sea breeze played at the bare parts of her skin, Lilian waited for him to go on.

'I haven't been quite myself for some time.'

She stifled a smile of relief. Maybe the person she was sharing her wine with wasn't the grumpy old boatman she'd met at the garage.

'After Celia died, I thought I'd never come right.'

She wanted to say, *Join the club*, but let him explain.

'She was the extrovert of the partnership. Always planning trips, parties, remembering kids' birthdays . . .' He trailed off and took a drink.

'It's hard, isn't it?' she said. 'You think your life is over. And it is in some ways. At least the life you knew.'

He nodded and for a moment she wondered if he would say anything more.

'I don't want to sound like an idiot, Lilian,' he said, finally meeting her eye, 'but you're an amazing woman.'

The serious expression in the piercing grey-blue eyes made something wobble inside her.

She laughed and brought her glass to her chest in both hands. 'What's in this wine?' she asked, unsure of where this was going.

'The way you handle those teenagers of ours for a start,' he began. 'Your help with the house loan was invaluable.' He paused. 'I've even been feeling a bit more myself . . .'

'And who exactly are you?' she asked, not wanting to dismiss the compliment, but not wanting to make a fool of herself either.

'Douglas Campbell MacDonald, born in Fort William, Scotland,' he said, sounding more relaxed. 'My father wanted to make a statement . . .' Seeing the puzzled expression on her face, he explained, 'The clans, Campbell and MacDonald? The Glencoe Massacre?'

She raised one eyebrow at him. It was a bit late for a history lesson.

'He was a peaceable soul, wanted to get out of Scotland, away from the sectarianism –'

'We know all about that where I come from,' she interrupted.

'Of course you do.' He smiled. 'We came to Australia in '62. Same boat as Jimmy Barnes.'

'Who's Jimmy Barnes?' If this was another dose of history, he could forget it. She had enough history of her own. It was the present that interested her. She watched as he took out his phone and began to scroll. Some video or other appeared on the screen. He turned it towards her.

'I'd play it only I'd rather not wake the street,' he whispered.

Leaning in, she recognised Tina Turner but not the man beside her. Whoever he was, he must be pretty talented if he was singing with Tina, she conceded. But it wasn't some Australian singer she wanted to know more about. It was the enigmatic individual beside her. She took a gulp of her wine and swung her feet up under her on the sofa. Her nightie inched up over her knees, but she didn't adjust it. With her head resting on her hand, she gave him her full attention.

'So tell me, Douglas Campbell MacDonald, who were you before you turned into a grumpy old man?'

His face reddened, but she kept her eyes on him. They were too old to play games. He returned the phone to his pocket and clearing his throat, he turned to her, pulling a hand through his thinning hair as he began to speak.

'I was an ordinary bloke . . . happily married . . . worked for Holden all my life.' He paused to check if she understood the reference.

She nodded, remembering a Christmas song the children used to sing about Santa in a rusty Holden ute. She could have listened to them all day, nearly knew their Aussie songs by heart by the end of their holidays.

'That factory was my life. Worked there since I left school.' There was a sadness in his eyes. 'It took years to finally close the place. We all knew the writing was on the wall. Matter of time . . .'

Lilian listened, hearing echoes of what happened to Cork's Ford factory in the eighties. Her eldest brother had twenty years service when, along with hundreds of others, he'd been forced to join the dole queue. 'Money talks', their father used to say. It was the same everywhere.

'Being laid off was bad enough,' Doug went on, 'but losing Celia a year later nearly finished me.'

They sat in silence. Lilian knew exactly how he felt but saying it wouldn't make it any better.

He gave a shrug. 'I wonder how you do it? I don't think I've ever seen you without that beautiful smile.'

She drew a flap of the dressing gown around her, shaking her head. He really had no idea, did he?

'You should see me at home,' she began. 'I have my meltdowns.'

He kept his eyes on her as she spoke.

'When Jack died, I fell apart. I grieved sure, like anyone would, but when I retired . . . it was like I'd lost him all over again. Every morning, I try to be grateful, you know. Pull those curtains open,' she made a sweeping gesture with an arm, 'let in another day.' Her shoulders slumped. 'Some days ain't so easy, but then I might see a message on my phone or pick up a photo of Natalie, I don't know, just something to keep me in the game of life . . .'

He was smiling at her now, a playful smile. She tousled her hair and looked away.

'You've still got great legs,' he said.

She went to cover them up a bit more, but he reached out a hand and rubbed it gently along her thigh. God, she hadn't felt this rush of hormones since the change.

'My legs might be well preserved, but I'm afraid the rest . . .'

But she didn't want to talk. Inching closer to this quiet man whose eyes held something that made her want more, thoughts of Jack, her family, flashed through her head. What would they think? But she drove those thoughts away, wanting to own this moment, keep it for herself. The image of Doug diving shirtless into the aqua water came to her. She hung on to it as their lips met and she kissed him for all she was worth, letting his lovely weather-beaten hands run over her body and cup her breasts through the silky chemise she'd hoped to feel good in. My word, she hadn't expected to feel this good. Not on the outdoor sofa of her daughter-in-law's beachside bungalow.

'Night, Gran.'

They drew apart, stunned to see Evan walking straight past them and into the house. When the door closed behind him, Lilian gasped, but as they dared to look at each other again, she let out a laugh.

'Oh God, that was embarrassing,' said Doug. 'I'm sorry, Lil –'

'Don't be.' She stood up and went to tie up her dressing gown. 'That was shaping up to be something very special.'

Standing beside her, he took her hands in his. 'When your son gets back, would you like to come up the coast with me . . . for a night or two?'

Lilian hoped her heart wouldn't give out, such was the excitement she was trying to keep a lid on. 'That sounds like a really great idea. But right now, I'd better get in there and smooth the waters.'

He bent his head and kissed her once again before he left. She blew the candle out and stayed a moment longer, savouring the thrill of what had just happened. There were no guarantees, of course, but there were possibilities. The rest of the year could wait, she had a hot date right here in Tasmania.

Inside, Evan was fixing himself a cool drink.

'Sorry about that, Evan,' Lilian began. 'I thought you were gone to bed.'

He made a stop sign with his hand as he sculled back his drink, his face puce with embarrassment.

'You don't have to explain, Gran.'

'I know,' she said, leaning on the kitchen bench. 'I just don't want you to think I was doing anything wrong.'

He looked at her now, his expression puzzled. 'You're an adult, Gran. Isn't that the bonus of being grown up? You get to do what you want?'

She smiled at his youthful take on life.

'I wish it were that simple,' she said, 'but I wouldn't want to hurt anyone.'

'Like Dad?' he asked, her reservations dawning on him.

'Or Granddad, even if he's not here anymore.'

'Oh Gran, we all just want you to be happy.'

And out of the blue, the once podgy toddler reached out, and encasing her in his skinny frame, gave her an awkward but most welcome hug.

'Love you, Gran.'

'I love you too, son. Always will.'

# Chapter Twenty-eight

At least the rain had held off for their expedition to Brow Head. Halfway up, Mick had to smile as Prue laid her hands on Edwina's shoulders and literally began pushing her up the narrow road where grass waved about on both sides. The pair of them were like teenagers, such was their good humour and obvious affection for one another.

'Piggyback?' he asked Aisling hopefully.

'Get away.' She laughed. 'I'll beat you to the top, no bother.'

And she was off, defying the headwind for a brief sprint before coming to a stop and turning back to where they were making a human trail up the hill.

'The calves aren't what they used to be,' she shouted back to them. It was so good to see her smile, having shaken off the disappointment about not being there for Natalie. 'Come on, Declan,' she urged their guide. 'This was your idea.'

Mick couldn't help feeling a bit sorry for the dentist who had the look of a man who might be regretting doing this hike two days in a row. All work and no play was how

he'd described his life in one of their chats that had been
a welcome distraction while Mick had been going out of
his mind wondering what was up with Aisling. Declan had
certainly gone from woe to go with this holiday.

Mia was the fittest of them, capable of keeping up a conversation as they took the sharp incline. It was the only time
Declan hadn't been the one to do most of the talking. Not
only had Mia brought down the average age this week, but
she'd been so enthusiastic, encouraging them all to take part
in everything from the food to the local activities. He imagined Natalie travelling in years to come and having adventures
of her own.

At the top of the hill, they hopped over the stile beside a
five-bar gate, grateful to be met with a wide expanse of flat
land that spread out towards the sea. Standing for a moment
to let Declan and Edwina catch their breath, they took in
the buildings Declan had told them about: the tower shedding its slates over years like a snake's skin, what must have
once been a grand house where echoes of the past hurtled on
the wind through glassless windows, a clutch of other dwell-
ings and outhouses, moss growing around their crumbling
edges and remaining chimney breasts, all left to the ravages
of nature.

Mick slipped an arm around Aisling and held her close as
they pointed out the road curving round to Barleycove, the
hotel and apartments nestled above the beautiful beach where
rollers pummelled their way in from the Atlantic.

'It's even more spectacular from over there,' said Declan,
tramping his way towards the cliffs. The others followed.

He was spot on. As they crossed the headland, they could see to the opposite side where surf crashed against rocks below the cliffs, and houses sat like white boxes dotted along the finger of land that poked into the raging waters. A screeching broke through the gust as a flock of seagulls soared above them, searching for prey.

'Black-headed gulls,' Declan shouted. 'Look at that plumage!'

'There,' Prue pointed to where a bigger bird was diving from a height, wings streamlining to its sides. 'Cormorant, isn't it?'

'Beautiful,' said Aisling as she leaned into Mick and watched the show.

'What's that one?' Mia was looking to where a clutch of birds with unusually smooth feathers in an odd matt brown bobbed on the waves.

'Guillemot,' said Declan, obviously a man in his element.

Mick smiled to himself as he tried to reconcile the portly nature lover with the squeaky-clean image he had of Declan in the clinical environment of his surgery. Shame he couldn't do more of this, he mused.

⌁

Katie returned to Lizzie O's to find Ellen and Gerry in the kitchen preparing dinner, in sync as usual, one chopping fresh herbs while the other mixed the oil and vinegar that would no doubt form the basis of one of their amazing dressings.

'Sorry, guys. Just wanted to drop these off,' she said, setting the Tupperware containers on the island. 'Mammy was thrilled with the stroganoff.'

'Ah that's brilliant,' said Ellen. 'How is she getting on?'

She was about to answer when they heard what sounded like a helicopter.

'Sounds a bit close . . .' Gerry stilled his knife as the noise grew louder, closer now as though it would crash into the house.

Ellen darted to the window. 'It's over Brow Head.'

'Are they making a film up there?' asked Gerry.

Katie hoped he was right. A phone vibrated on the island bench. Ellen reached for it.

'It's Orla,' she mouthed to them, listening again before relaying the details. 'There's been an accident . . . Someone went over the cliff.'

'Is it a local?' she was asking.

They couldn't hear what Orla had said at the other end, but as Ellen hung up the phone, Katie saw her face blanch.

'It's one of the guests.'

'Jesus.' Gerry looked as shocked as Katie felt.

'Eamon's gone up to give them a hand,' said Ellen. 'Orla's on her way.'

She went to gather throws and blankets and get the fire going in the parlour. They'd be frozen by the time they got down, she said. Before she knew it, Katie was taking directions from Gerry, slicing bread and finding fillings for sandwiches. Orla was with them within minutes, her oblivious grandchild in tow.

'I couldn't stay home on my own,' she said. 'I said I'd be better off here, helping.'

'We're grateful to you, Orla,' said Gerry. He put her in charge of defrosting soup and getting the trolley ready for serving hot drinks.

With Ava happily chewing on a teething ring, Orla pulled on an apron and made a quick sign of the cross. Katie caught her eye. She could see the worry.

'Eamon always answers the call,' Orla explained as she went to the freezer. 'Volunteers for the lifeboats.' She turned away, digging in amongst the tubs of frozen food. 'His father was out helping the night of the Fastnet.'

Although Katie had been very young, she knew well the story of the 1979 Fastnet Race when so many lost their lives, their yachts engulfed by a summer storm the like of which they'd never seen. She shivered at the memory. *The Wild Atlantic Way* was well named. In amongst the stories and lore of the event, there'd never been mention of her own father stepping up. She dismissed the thought of him and focused on making the best sandwiches of her life.

━

Aisling had hardly let go of Mick's hand since they'd stood watching, helpless, as the coastguard helicopter winched Declan from where he'd fallen what must have been at least ten metres down into the gully. She couldn't bring herself to touch the brand-new iPhone she'd left in her coat pocket, the one they'd used to take the selfie that should have been a treasured memory of their holiday. It was all playing in her mind: Mick turning to look at the camera after warning Declan not to go too close to the edge, Prue doing a half squat so Edwina could be seen behind her, Mia's chin jutting over Edwina's shoulder and Declan grinning at the back, the wind whipping up their hair as she pressed the button, taking several shots before Declan screamed and fell simultaneously. They'd all turned to where he'd tumbled, his sack-like form ricocheting off rocks towards the sea that splashed and sprayed like a wild angry animal below the ledge where, by some miracle, he'd come to a stop.

'You okay?' Mick whispered softly into her hair now.

She nodded. But she was far from okay. She pulled the blanket round her shoulders and watched as Ellen stacked logs on the fire in the parlour where they were all hunkered down together in the aftermath of what had started out as a simple hike.

'You were brilliant,' she whispered as she leaned into him.

He shook his head and gave her hand a pat. *All part of the training*, he'd told the paramedics who'd arrived on the scene and were still around, having ferried them down the hill and back to the guesthouse. Locals too had come to their aid. She had an overwhelming urge to hug Natalie and Evan close, but Mick was here. She was grateful for that.

Mia was sitting with Edwina on the chaise longue. The poor girl couldn't be consoled, claiming the accident was her fault. 'If I hadn't suggested the walk,' she was saying between heart-wrenching sobs.

Prue stood at the mantelpiece explaining the sequence of events to Katie. '. . . Mick's quick thinking . . . could have been a different story if he hadn't been airlifted . . .'

It was true. Her husband's call to the emergency services requesting an air ambulance had given Declan the best possible chance of survival. She could see Mick now, talking to the operator in that calm collected way he had while the rest of them stood clutching at each other as they looked on helpless at the man splayed out on the rocks below.

'What made you think it was a heart attack?' she asked now as her teeth chattered despite the warmth in the room.

He put an arm around her and drew her back against the sofa cushions.

'I'd noticed him putting a hand to his chest when we got to the top of the hill and stopped for a rest. We were all puffed but he was sweating more than the rest of us. I was thinking how unfit he was for someone who likes the outdoors. Then when I looked into the camera, I caught him clutching his chest again, not so much smiling as doing a kind of grimace. As I went to turn round, he was already falling over the side.'

He interlocked her fingers with his own, rubbing a thumb at her wedding ring. Turning her face into his chest, Aisling vowed to remember that Mick was her hero each and every day.

⁓

Ellen and Orla appeared with the trolley loaded up with scones and sandwiches, pottery mugs, a huge teapot and cafetières. Despite the smell of fresh bread and roasted coffee, Mia couldn't think about food. As hot drinks were passed around, Edwina urged her to eat, but she only took a cup of tea.

It had been her idea to go up there, not Declan's. He'd only been up the day before. She shouldn't have put it on him

to undertake the hike again so soon. Edwina tried to ease
her anxiety, telling her it was a freak accident, hopefully he'd
pull through. But Mia couldn't get past the helplessness she'd
felt as she stood looking down to where the red jacket made
him stand out against the dark rocks, the gruesome sight of
blood and bone where he'd smashed his leg on impact. She
could only hope they'd got to him in time. A lifeboat would
have had to come from Baltimore or Castletownbere, the
paramedic had explained. If Mick was right and he'd had a
heart attack, it would have been too late. Just as well they
had someone trained in their party. She gave a shudder as
she brought the steaming mug to her lips and drank in the
healing tea.

At the Cork University Hospital, Declan lay on the stretcher
they'd flown him out on, aware of the buzz of a medical
team prepping him for theatre. As the anaesthetic started to
kick in, a nurse held his hand and told him they would be
operating soon. The reassuring tone of her voice sent him to
a place where he could see Karen singing to one of the children. Luke or Robert, he couldn't be sure, but just before he
went under, he prayed to God he'd see them again.

# Chapter Twenty-nine

Conor pulled on his leather jacket and took a last look at himself in the mirror above the fireplace. He'd tried to look presentable but not over-the-top flash or anything.

'What's that shtink?' his old man mocked good-humouredly from where he was eyeing him on the armchair he would occupy until Conor returned.

He smiled. 'Will you get away outta that.'

'Ah well, 'tisn't every night you meet your old flame . . .'

'Dad, don't let the aftershave fool you. We're only having a chat.'

'Of course ye are.'

Conor wished he could share his father's lightheartedness. He would tread carefully with Katie Daly. Underneath the tough exterior, he sensed a brittleness. But look, it was she who'd asked for the meeting, hardly a date he'd had to admit. She could take the lead. Perhaps he had been a fool to think of her in some romantic sense all these years, but he was ready if there was any hope for him. At least his last-ditch effort with the poem had had an effect.

Parking his car outside the pub in Crookhaven, he took in the fine night, a sprinkling of stars visible between wisps of cloud passing over a crescent moon. They'd had their share of rain and storms these past few weeks. A stretch of settled weather was certainly due.

Inside, the place was quiet. Like being in a different pub, he told the owner as they moved on from the morbid topic of the afternoon's accident to the great turnout the night before. There was no sign of Katie, but scanning round, he saw Matt from the kennels gazing into the eyes of a girl he didn't recognise.

He went to turn back to where the owner was pulling him a half pint of lager when the door opened. And here she was, the girl he'd never forgotten, nodding to him as she pushed in the door and headed straight towards him. There was no cape, no intimidating trilby, just her in a pair of denim jeans and a warm cowl-necked jumper, a string of large beads dressing up the otherwise casual ensemble. He tugged at the neck of his good shirt, opening the top button. She wouldn't know, but the chinos he'd worn for the poetry slam as well were brand new.

'What would you like to drink?' he asked, parroting the line he'd practised in front of the bathroom mirror.

'A Diet Coke is fine,' she answered, sweeping her eyes past him and looking around the bar.

Of course, she'd be worried about who might see them together, but they were here now. She went to unzip her purse.

'On the house,' the owner announced as he placed the drinks on the bar.

'Thank you,' said Katie, taking her drink.

They took a seat in the secluded corner Conor had hoped would be free.

'Here's to you,' he said, raising his glass to her but receiving only a weak smile in response. He'd talk about the events of the day. 'Terrible thing to happen to that fella from Cork.'

She nodded.

'The last time you were in these parts, we were underage,' he tried again, looking at his pint.

'I was underage for a lot of things.'

There it was, that edginess. If there was to be any kind of reconciliation, regardless of what she thought he had or hadn't done, he'd need to keep this friendly.

'You did a great job last night,' he began, 'with the judging . . .'

'I didn't have much choice.' She gave a wry smile and brought the glass to her lips. 'If I'd known, I'd have run a mile.'

As she sipped her drink, he took in the lines around her mouth and eyes. It was a face with a story he wanted desperately to know, but he wouldn't push.

'Well, you always knew a thing or two about the English language,' he said. 'Weren't you always getting As in English?'

She set down her glass and sat back against the cushioned wall, a tinge of red in her cheeks.

'What about that composition you wrote in fifth year on silence?'

She shook her head. 'I can't believe you remember that.'

Yes, he remembered. '"Silence is silver, not golden, and only silver-plated at that . . . "'

'Okay that's enough,' she said, waving a hand at him. 'And what about you with your poetry?'

He shrugged. 'Ah, I dabble a bit now and then.'

They remained quiet for a moment, the content of the poem playing in his mind, but he'd managed to lighten the mood. It was progress.

'Conor,' she started, sitting forward and pushing her hands between the legs of her jeans. 'I hope you haven't . . . I don't know, held some kind of torch . . .'

'Don't worry about it,' he said, taking a drink of his pint. 'Let's just have a chat, like two old . . .' He wanted to say friends, flames perhaps.

'So, what have you been doing?' she asked, her expression less serious.

This was good. She was still here, being normal. He could do this.

—

Conor Fox was a pillar of society. Nursing his mother through her long-term battle with MS, running the shop with his father, taking over and running shop and home once his mother had passed and his father was no longer able. He'd had his own place for a while, but it hadn't been practical. Yes, his relations pitched in when they could. She'd remember his cousins. They were great for phoning and calling down.

He'd moved on to the amateur theatre group. A couple of personalities they'd gone to school with were in it with him.

They put on a production every year, sometimes a musical, or maybe something deeper if they felt up to it. He'd been so quiet in school, but after his poem, she could imagine him treading the boards at the community hall. Everything else had aged, but his voice was still strong, with the kind of timbre that made you listen, like he had something important to say. And yet, the most important thing remained unsaid. As much as Katie wanted to hear of his life, she didn't want to leave without saying her piece.

When he returned from the bar with another round, she knew it was her turn to relate the milestones of her past thirty-five years. Listening to him tonight had certainly taken the edge off her anger, but she still needed to set him straight. He really had lived all those years in oblivion, remembering her as a kind of first love, dating a few women in between but, as he'd said, never finding *the one*. After all this time had passed, she was hardly *the one*.

'Conor, you need to know I've made a life in the States,' she said.

He shrugged. 'So tell me all about it. What do you do over there?'

There was an innocence in his expression, an expectation that moving away from here had been all about escaping to some wild exciting life. Was he thick as the wall or what? Could it be possible he didn't know she'd been sent away? What kind of line had they spun to make him so curious about her life? He watched her now like a child ready for a bedtime story. It seemed cruel to dive into the details of the knock-on effects of their night at the grads. She needed to work up to that. She'd start with Stella.

'I made a great friend in Cork,' she began, glossing right over the circumstances of their meeting. 'She had rellies in London, so we went there, working for a while before we went to the States on Donnelly visas.'

He was nodding, remembering the much sought-after tickets to America.

'Another aunt of hers had a hotel in New York. Gave us both jobs. We were just housemaids, but we loved it. Eventually started our own cleaning business . . .'

She took another drink as she thought of how to make her life sound full and exciting, the kind of life he'd think she was in a hurry to get back to. 'Stella met a guy who used to come and do the maintenance . . . They've been married years, have three beautiful children.' If it hadn't been for Stella, she might be dead by now, but he didn't need to know that. 'She's a grandma twice over.'

Conor listened attentively, but she knew he'd heard enough about Stella.

'Did you meet anyone yourself?'

She wouldn't bore him with her string of failed relationships. Men didn't last long around her. She was too much like hard work, she imagined.

'I never married, if that's what you're asking. Never needed to.'

She was definitely the repelling end of the magnet when it came to relationships. It was one of the reasons Stella did all the talking when it came to clients while she took care of the book work. They had a squad of cleaners to do the physical work these days, Stella doing most of the hiring while Katie only rowed in for the occasional firing. But he didn't need the gory details of how she'd come to build a successful business. She would tell him what she came here to tell him, no less, no more.

She looked towards the bar, taking a moment to consider how to broach the elephant in the room. There was no getting away from their history if she was to tell him the truth. But here he was, the same Conor Fox she'd fallen in love with, dreamt of having a future with, those gorgeous honest brown eyes regarding her with that same admiration as long ago. They said you should keep a man who looks at you that way. For the first time in a very long time, she found herself wishing she'd kept in touch with him.

'Conor, I didn't ask you here to bore you with my life story.'

The puppy-dog look was gone. He knew. On some level he knew this was complicated. She took a deep breath as tears welled behind her eyelids.

'We learnt our trade at the unmarried mothers' home.' She couldn't look at him but was aware of the shadow that crossed his face. 'Those nuns saw to it that we were experts by the time we left. Hands and knees stuff too; none of your fancy machines for us fallen girls.' She sniffed back a sob. 'Floors you could see your face in,' she went on, almost feeling the bulge of her unborn child dragging down over the herringbone of the parquet flooring, smelling the lavender-scented polish. To this day, she couldn't stand lavender.

She pushed the fringe away from her face. 'Rose was the child . . .' She'd been over this, gone to counselling, talked enough times to Stella about the whole experience, but saying it out loud to Conor brought with it a whole new wave of grief. There was anger too, but an anger she didn't have the energy for. She thought she'd go mad at him, have it out, how he'd been implicit in the ruination of her life. But he was kind then, he'd been kind all his life, Son of the flipping Year, God damn it!

He was looking around for something to dry her tears.

'I've got some,' she told him, plunging a hand into her jeans pocket and retrieving a tissue. She wiped it across her eyes, grateful for the partition that shielded them from the rest of the bar. She lowered her voice all the same. 'The baby was Martin's.'

'What?'

She looked up and saw the shock, mouth agape, a frown pinching at the bridge of his nose.

'What are you telling me?' he asked again.

'That night, while we were at the grads . . . my mother was called to Skib. Auntie Theresa had taken unwell. It was only Dad and the boys at home . . .'

He listened, looking desperate to understand. She could see the beads of sweat pricking at his hairline.

'We all went back to your place . . . the after party . . .'

He was nodding, but still had no clue as to what went wrong.

'You'd arranged for Martin to drive me home, remember?' His cheeks flushed and the Adam's apple bobbed in his throat. 'You were all cool about the whole thing. You kept telling me he'd be back soon. I didn't need to worry. I didn't even know my mother had been called away, but I sensed that I needed to get home.'

He was giving her his undivided attention, but she couldn't look at him. Focusing on a knot in the wood of their table, she went on.

'Martin got me home all right. Just wouldn't let me out of the car . . . until . . .' She flipped a thick lock of hair against its natural fall, beyond caring how it looked. 'I couldn't stop him . . .'

'Jesus Christ, if I'd known . . .'

'What Conor? What would you have done?' She shrugged, clasping her hands in her lap. 'I blamed you at the time,' she said. 'In fact, until tonight, I've held you responsible for starting the whole series of sorry events.'

Conor buried his face in his hands, but she wasn't finished.

'It's funny what the brain blocks out and what it remembers.' She gave a small wry laugh, stifling tears. 'I remember getting in the door, taking off the white high heels, creeping up the stairs so as not to wake my father. Must have been the one night he wasn't passed out from the drink.' She wiped at her nose with the tissue and took a breath. 'No, he'd seen it all from the window. Or at least what he thought he'd seen. "Dirty whore", he called me. At one point in the beating, I thought he'd actually kill me.' She shook her head. 'There have been times I wished he had.'

'Oh God love you, Katie. I wish . . .'

She looked at him now and saw the tears rolling down his cheeks. Gathering himself, he eased closer to her, moving his glass out of the way and clasping his hands on the table.

'I'm so sorry, Katie. If I could turn the clock back to that night –'

'Don't. It wouldn't help. My father might have done what he'd done regardless. He abused my mother for years afterwards.'

Conor's jaw dropped open. Yes, it was incredible what went on behind closed doors.

'Too many secrets we had. I couldn't look at you after that night. Too traumatised, the psychologists tell me. I've had a few of them and all.'

She could have gone on for hours if she started down that road, but she figured they'd had enough for one night. When the barman came to clear their glasses, she gathered up her purse, grateful to let the lock of hair fall and hide her tear-stained face.

'We'd better go,' she said, exhausted and raw from the reopening of old wounds.

'If Martin wasn't dead, I'd kill him,' said Conor. He was talking half to himself. She could see the whitening of his knuckles as he curled a hand around a tight fist, the horrific turn of events still sinking in.

'Just drop me home, Conor. What's done is done.'

<hr />

As they sat again outside the cottage at the back of Lizzie O's, Katie could hardly move, such was the weight of what sat between them.

'I wish I could make it all up to you,' said Conor, breaking their silence.

'Thank you.'

With no point speaking in platitudes around keeping in touch, she let herself out of the car and listened with her back turned as he drove away. Inside, she made it as far as the leather lounge and collapsed on to the cushions she pulled in tight to absorb a lonesome howl.

Conor let himself into the house where his dad was nodding off in front of the television. The old man had spent half a lifetime mourning a dead son who had dishonoured them all. His mother had been more pragmatic. She'd done her grieving, no doubt about that, but she'd let it rest. In private moments, when his father was in the shop and it was just the two of them, she'd say the crash had shocked her at the time, but that Martin had always had a taste for danger. Fast driving and fast living, she'd say, shaking her head and saying a prayer for his soul. They said no one knew you like your own mother. He could have done with her counsel now.

Katie Daly was a wronged woman. How hard it must have been to come back. Their young innocent dreams had been shattered by his own brother. He was lucky she had the grace to speak to him at all.

The old man stirred and looked around, his lined face breaking into a smile. He sat up in his chair.

'Well, how was your date?'

Conor smiled. There was no point enlightening him as to what had gone on. Katie would go back to America in a few days and they would go on as normal.

'Ah sure, we had a chat about old times,' he told him.

Pleased with the response, his dad eased himself out of his chair.

'A shame she can't stay for a while,' he said. 'But sure life goes on.'

It did and it would, Conor reasoned. But it would be all the poorer for having come so close to reconnecting with the one person he'd ever truly loved.

—

In the kitchen, Mick took the untouched Baileys cheesecake they'd all declined at dinner from the fridge and carefully arranged two slices onto the side plates their hosts had left to hand. Lizzie O's was starting to feel like a home from home, especially comforting now after what happened to the man who had become an unlikely ally in a week that would go down as one of the most challenging of his life. With the kettle almost boiling, he didn't hear the front door open.

'Channelling your inner Nigella, Mick?'

He spun round to find a smiling Mia.

'Jesus, Mia, you nearly put the heart crossways in me.'

'Sorry, you wouldn't have heard me come in.' She nodded to where the kettle had switched itself off on the bench. 'How are you doing?'

Mick dropped teabags into two mugs and leaned on the island opposite her.

'Ah sure, I'm grand.' He shrugged. 'Just hoping Declan pulls through.'

'Me too.'

'And what about you?' he asked, fixing the mugs and cake on to a cheery melamine tray. 'How are you faring?'

She stood with her hands in a parka jacket he hadn't seen her wearing before. Something about it made it look borrowed, but he didn't remark.

'Okay.' She nodded. 'It's been a crazy week for me anyway, but Declan's accident just blindsided me completely.'

When she didn't volunteer an explanation, he turned to make the tea and asked, 'Good crazy, bad crazy week?'

'Life-changing crazy, but I don't want to jinx myself by talking about it, do you know what I mean?'

'I do indeed, Mia,' he said, giving her a sideways nod. 'Speaking of crazy weeks, I'd best return to my wife with the promised goods.'

'Do you think he'll pull through?' Mia asked as he picked up the tray and walked past her towards the door.

'We can only hope for the best,' he said, with that practised reassuring smile he'd spent years perfecting.

—

Declan opened his eyes to the sight of a very tanned Luke. Karen was beside him, her eyes full of concern. He was about to drift back into what must be a dream, when he heard the familiar voice.

'Dad.' Though spoken softly, the word held an urgency, a fear, if he wasn't mistaken.

He went to respond, but his lips failed to play their part. His hand moved instead, making the line in his arm register. The context came to him now, the stripy curtains, the vaguely unpleasant smell, West Cork, the photo. My God, how long had he been out? He went to sit up but was halted by the stabbing pain in his chest.

'Take it easy, Declan.'

He turned his head at the unexpected sound of Karen's voice. What was she doing here? The last time they'd spoken, hadn't she asked for a divorce?

'You've had a stent put in,' she was saying. 'You'll be in here for a week or so.' In the fog of his brain, he tried to remember the procedure. A stent? His uncle had had one put in his heart. 'They fixed your face up as they were at it.' She smiled as she said the last bit. 'Might keep you quiet for a while.'

He touched a hand to his face and felt the row of stitches running from above his left eyebrow to the top of his jawbone. No wonder his mouth hadn't wanted to move. He went to wiggle his toes and realised his right leg was somewhere under a heavy plaster cast.

'We're here for you, Dad.'

Luke was at the other side of the bed, the worry on his face almost tangible. Declan had an urge to wrap him up in a bear hug like the ones he would have given the boys as toddlers. But he'd long stopped showing them that kind of affection. Emotion threatening to get the better of him, he was grateful when a nurse stuck her head round the curtain.

'Ah, Declan, you're awake.' She smiled. 'No sudden movements now. We'll come and help sort you out in a minute.'

He could only imagine what that meant he couldn't yet do for himself, but she was giving Karen and Luke the eye to let them know they needed to leave.

'Take it easy, Dad.' As Luke left the ward, Declan noticed the look that passed between him and his mother.

'We'll come back later, Declan. Get the nurses to contact me if you need anything.'

'Kar . . .' It hurt to speak, but there was so much he wanted to say.

'Don't say anything,' Karen urged. 'I know I'm probably the last person you expected to see when you woke up, but when the police phoned . . .'

She reached out and touched the blanket, tears pooling in her eyes. He wanted to listen, stay focused, but with his head feeling like a cannonball, his eyelids drooped.

'Get some rest,' she whispered. 'We'll talk later.'

As he lay there losing the battle to stay conscious, he wished he hadn't caused her so much pain.

# Chapter Thirty

Katie woke herself up with a scream. She'd had a dreadful vivid dream about falling from Brow Head, Conor Fox calling out her name, straining to reach a hand out to save her as she fell in slow motion, getting further and further away from him. Shaking off the nightmare, she got out of bed and pulled on the robe and slippers that came with the cottage, the irony of the salubrious accommodation not lost on her. Anyone else would sleep like a baby in the place.

Downstairs, she made tea and took her laptop to the sofa, grateful for the heat from the recessed fireplace that kept the place good and warm. Thoughts of Declan swirled in her head. She hadn't had much to do with the man over the course of the week, deliberately avoiding him as much as most of the others. But she felt for him now, hoping he'd pull through. Did he have family, she wondered, people to help him? If it had been her, who would have come to her aid?

Distracting herself from morbid thoughts, she checked her emails. An invitation to have a look round a local care home got her thinking about her mother. She'd sent an expression of interest after their visit with Doctor Smit. The photos on the website had made the place seem appealing enough – clean, fresh-looking, with staff and residents smiling, at least for the camera. Phyllis would no doubt be popular with them all. Perhaps Katie could phone her every week and hear how she was faring, keep in more regular contact with Bernadette too. But she had to admit that even if her siblings were in agreement, it was not what their mother wanted. More than anyone, Katie knew what it was like to be sent away against your will. And if what she'd learnt about Bernadette was true, her sister would be just as busy driving back and forth to visit their mother regardless of where she was to live.

When she'd arrived here on Saturday, Katie had been determined to do what she came to do and get back to her life in the States as quickly as possible. Sitting here a week later, she found herself rethinking that plan. She'd unearthed truths about her mother's life she might never have known had she not come home. As for Conor Fox, she'd learnt a few truths about him and all, not least his complete ignorance as to why she'd left.

*Home.* She played the word over in her mind. Yes, there were people here who cared about her. People who would come to her aid if she fell off a proverbial cliff. But help worked both ways. Maybe it was her turn to reach out a hand. Maybe it was time to consider coming home.

Mia couldn't believe the change in Katie. As they discussed West Cork real estate over breakfast, she had to wonder if this was indeed the same gruff woman who she'd hardly spoken to for the entire week, not so much in any deliberate way as to never having been given the opportunity. Yet here she was, consulting her about rental prices and proximity to shops and services. There was no denying the collective surprise when she'd mentioned having a mother in the area the day before. Mia wasn't sure what the Irish American was up to, but there was an urgency in her voice that made Mia want to help out. Housing, she realised, had always been a source of anxiety in her life, both before and after she'd married Harry. Whatever this Katie's circumstances, she certainly wouldn't hold back in providing any information she could.

Just the day before, Mia had secured a rental in that lovely street at the back of Crookhaven. Matt had promised to go and see it again with her later. There was still the daunting task of telling Harry, but she wouldn't think about that just now. Today she had an interview with Lindsey. Declan would be so supportive if he knew. They still hadn't heard.

Tucking her phone in her pocket, Katie let herself out of the conservatory and took a walk over the little wooden bridge that led to the garden. Breathing in the crisp sea air, she went over the monumental decision she'd made as she'd stared at those care home photos in the stillness of the early hours. A robin redbreast twittered from the branch of an old hawthorn tree she'd climbed as a youngster when she'd come here, hand-in-hand with her grandmother to visit Lizzie O'Shea. So much had changed, but more had stayed the same.

Looking out towards the Fastnet, she put all the doubt and second thoughts to the back of her mind and took out her phone.

Her sister answered straightaway.

'Bernadette, it's Katie.'

'Oh Katie. So good to hear your voice. How is it all going? Is Mammy okay?'

'Everything's fine here. How are *you* doing?'

Katie listened as Bernadette gushed about the wonderful week she'd had, the sightseeing, the food. The Spaniard, who turned out to be called Miguel, sounded like he was shaping up to be way more than the passing fancy Katie had imagined. There was an earnestness in her sister's voice that made her hope this Miguel was sincere. It reminded her of the self-belief in the tone she'd used with their father when he'd belittled her dreams of going to university. Maybe Bernadette had been inured to him in a way Katie had never managed. There were still so many things she didn't know about her sister. Things she'd found herself longing to discover. Sure, she could go back to America as planned and retreat to her small life in Brooklyn, but there was an opportunity here she might regret not taking, a second chance to connect with the people who had always cared.

'Would you like to stay on for a while?'

There was a pause before Bernadette answered. 'What about Mammy?'

'I thought I might help out for a bit longer,' Katie began. 'Give you a chance to . . .'

Bernadette didn't let her finish. 'Oh, Katie, you have no idea how much that means to me. Are you sure? I wouldn't want to –'

It was Katie's turn to interrupt. 'Bernadette! I owe you a great deal and until now, I've never done anything to pay you back.'

'Sure what do you owe me for?'

'For everything you did back when they sent me to the home.' Thirty-five years and it still hurt to say those words, but Katie pushed down her grief.

'I only gave you a few pounds,' Bernadette was saying, 'organised a birth cert –'

'You gave me a chance to get away.' Katie heard a sniffle. Her sister didn't need to be breaking down and she in the middle of a romantic getaway. 'Now will you do as Mammy would say,' she said, her tone lighter, 'and don't be looking a gift horse in the mouth.'

She laughed. 'I've missed you, Katie.'

'Shhh, would you go on and enjoy yourself with Miguel.'

Bernadette started to set dates, talk of coming home, but Katie assured her there would be time for all those arrangements. Yes, she would sort out the house, keep her siblings informed at every step, but for now at least, she would make sure her mother was safe and minded.

~

It was later at dinner, when they'd all gathered in the conservatory that Gerry and Ellen brought the news they had been
hoping and praying for all day. Declan would be fine. He'd
had a stent put in his heart and surgery to set a fractured
femur. Aisling shuddered at the memory of him pinned to the
rocky outcrop, his bone visible through the jeans and they
all helpless, looking on. But tonight was about celebrating
his survival.

'So, a double celebration,' said Gerry, with a wink as he
brought a bottle of champagne from where he'd hidden it
behind his back.

Aisling smiled and felt herself coming over all teary when
the other guests cheered and whooped as their hosts filled
flutes with the bubbles and handed them round.

'To Aisling and Mick on their anniversary,' said Gerry,
raising a glass to them.

'Aisling and Mick,' the others chorused.

Mick turned and kissed her on the lips, right there in
front of the people who'd been strangers only a week ago. She
even wished Declan could have been here. They'd visit him in
hospital before they flew out. Mick would like that. She took
a teaspoon from the table and tapped the side of the glass.
There was a hush as the guests looked on, ready for a speech.

'Thank you so much, Gerry and Ellen, for making our
anniversary special. We do have one more thing to celebrate,
however.' She paused, feeling her husband cringe beside her.

'My lovely husband and I got married on his twenty-fifth birthday, which makes him –'

'Forty!' Mia shouted to whoops of surprise and delight as Ellen wheeled in a cake alight with candles.

As Mick regaled them with tales of their wedding and the double celebrations they'd had over the years, Aisling sat back with her bubbles and inwardly toasted her husband and the wonderful love and life she was lucky to share with him.

⌁

'Can I have a word?' Katie asked Ellen as she left the party in the conservatory after congratulating Mick and Aisling once again.

'Of course. What is it, Katie?' Ellen dried her hands on a tea towel as she came towards her.

'I'm wondering are you full up this week?' she asked.

Ellen shook her head and smiled. 'I've had a cancellation. A couple had to postpone after a grandchild came early.'

Katie took a breath. She was committing to forfeiting her flight back to the States and stepping into a very uncertain future. 'Could I stay on?' she asked. 'I can't be sure for how long.'

'By all means,' said Ellen. She put a hand on Katie's arm. 'Are you staying on for your mam?'

Katie shrugged. 'I think I'm staying on for myself.'

'If there's anything I can do, anything at all . . .'

'Thank you,' said Katie. 'You've been a great help already.'

⌁

Katie could hardly believe she was knocking at Conor Fox's front door at half-past eight at night. As she stood in the freezing cold, she remembered how herself and Sean Óg would play runaway-knock along the few houses up from the shop on a Sunday, more to combat the boredom of waiting for their father to come out of the pub after Mass than to make mischief.

Conor appeared now, looking as surprised as she was to find her on the doorstep.

'Is everything all right?' he asked.

'Can we talk?'

He made to look in towards the living room. 'Give me a sec.'

She saw him reach behind the door, retrieving his jacket before looking in on his father and saying something to the effect that he wouldn't be long.

Without needing an explanation, she followed him up the side of the house, past the shed where the shop had been and the grassy path that led to where they used to play as children around a clump of boulders that doubled as a den and lookout.

With the light of a full moon illuminating their way, the words of a Mary Black song came back to Katie. 'Once in a Very Blue Moon' had never failed to make her tear up and miss Conor Fox on those nights she'd lain awake in the house in London, wondering what might have happened had circumstances been different. She'd worked hard at putting the past behind her, but this week had whittled away at that resolve.

When they came to the rocks that looked smaller than she remembered, they sat down. Conor took a woollen hat from his pocket and pulled it on. She hoped it would keep him warm long enough to tell him her plans.

'I'm thinking of hanging around for a while,' she began, her breath visible in the chill air as she spoke. 'Bernadette does her best, but she has no life between her full-time job and minding Mammy.' Conor looked surprised, but she went on. 'The neighbours are great, but . . . I . . . I'd like to help out, you know?'

'I thought you'd be dying to get away from the place,' he said.

It was an honest assessment after the way she'd behaved this week.

'That's exactly how I felt until I realised . . . that my mother,' she stuttered over the admission, but carried on, '. . . and you . . . you weren't to blame.'

As he pulled the jacket up around his chin, she caught herself noticing the once familiar shape of his hands. He was an older version of the dark lean boy she'd loved as a teen, but he could still make her look. In the strange moment where time leap-frogged over their lives, connecting past and present, she knew she'd miss Conor if she left.

'I need a friend,' she continued. 'I'm not the easiest person to get along with . . . I know I'm not the same person that –'

'Katie,' he interrupted, 'you're not the only one who could do with a friend.'

A warmth rose in her cheeks in stark contrast to the cool night. The circumstances that had caused their lives to diverge could never be undone, but it was enough to know he cared, that despite her attempts to avoid him, push him away, he had persevered. Reaching out a hand from under her cape, she linked his arm.

'Let's get out of here before we freeze,' he said.

At the Datsun, they stood looking into one another's eyes. Katie didn't trust herself to break the silence of the moment. In her mind, she was back at the grads, swaying to the music, wrapped in her partner's embrace, 'In the Air Tonight' fading out as he'd bent to kiss her. Maybe it was a case of telepathy, but she felt that old embrace now as his hands curved around her back and held her close. When their lips met, she was at once transported back in time and catapulted into a future she could never have envisaged. A tear trickled from the corner of her eye.

'Oh Conor,' she began, pulling a little away, 'you don't know how broken I am.'

As he drew a hand to her face, she felt the most gentle touch to her cheek.

'What you are,' he told her, 'is everything I've ever wanted.'

# Chapter Thirty-one

Mick stood at the bedroom window, surplus to requirements, as Aisling packed the last of their things into those vacuum bags she'd insisted on buying for their trip.

'Looks like our Yank is ready to go,' he said as he watched Katie Daly greet the driver who had alighted from the front seat of the Mercedes Benz. Perhaps she was just in better form, but there was none of the formality of her arrival the weekend before. Funny how he'd judged her to be some kind of celebrity, he thought, smiling to himself.

'She's not going far,' said Aisling. 'Her mother is only up the road in Goleen. Katie's staying on to mind her.'

*Katie*, Mick mused. You'd think she and Aisling were best friends with the knowledgeable way his wife told him what the stranger was doing. Only a few days ago, she'd been all speculation about why the American-sounding woman had come here. They were welcome to their drama. He'd had enough drama this week to last him a lifetime. A nice settled phase of marriage was the only thing on his agenda. They'd swing past a couple of rellies on their way to the airport, check in on Declan who thank God seemed to be improving, and it would be back to Tasmania to the good life they'd worked hard to build.

'Will you take them so?' she asked when everything was zipped up and the only task remaining was to put their suitcases in the hire car. Yes, he had his uses.

In the hallway, Prue and Edwina were thanking Ellen and Gerry, Edwina throwing her arms around the couple with her signature enthusiasm.

'Let me take one of those for you, Mick,' said Gerry, extricating himself from a bear hug and relieving him of the heavier case, which was of course Aisling's.

Without complaint, their host hefted the case out the front door and set it down on the gravel along with a collection of other luggage. As he veered past Ellen and the honeymooners, he saw Mia and Katie bent over their phones, exchanging numbers if he wasn't mistaken. At the sound of Prue's voice, he turned to where she was stepping out into the chilly morning, a leather-gloved hand flicking her big scarf across one shoulder.

'Safe home now, Mick.'

He bowed slightly and beamed at her. 'You too, Prue. Look after yourself . . . and your lovely wife.'

Edwina blushed as she joined them.

'What a smashing group,' she said, scanning the party. 'Just a shame Declan couldn't be here to say farewell.' Her eyes glistened as she looked up over the stone façade towards the top of the house where Declan had stayed.

'Oh, Ed.' Prue reached out an arm and tucked her in close. 'He'll be fine.'

Aisling gave Mick a worried look as she came and stood beside him, but in her calm tone, Ellen reassured them.

'His son rang earlier. Himself and his brother are coming down for the Lexus later today. They said he's starting to come round from the anaesthetic.'

There were murmurs and smiles as they stood for a moment in shared relief. The family were rallying round. Mick knew it was everything Declan would want.

'We'd better get on the road,' he said, reaching out to shake hands with Gerry and Ellen. 'You've been incredible hosts.'

'It's been an absolute pleasure to have you all,' said Ellen.

Behind him, Aisling was doing a round of hugs for both of them. He was about to make for the car when Mia came towards him, arms outstretched.

'Give Declan this from me,' she said wrapping him in a warm hug.

He laughed. 'He'll think I've lost it if I do that.' As if inviting the man to a spa day hadn't been bad enough.

'Okay.' She smiled as she let go. 'Just give him my love.'

'I sure will.' Looking into the eyes of the young woman who'd kept him company over otherwise lonely breakfasts, he nodded. 'Take good care of yourself, Mia.'

As they drove away with the group dispersing and the grand old farmhouse diminishing behind them, Mick reached out to Aisling.

'Onward and upward, my love.'

She didn't say anything, but the squeeze of her hand was all the reassurance he needed. Tough week, yes, but they were definitely back on track.

—

'Are you right, Mammy?'

At this hour of her life, Phyllis Daly would never be ready in a hurry. But that was fine. They had all day. William ran a chamois over the Mercedes, the bonnet shining like a starling's wing. Katie had phoned the car company requesting the same driver and vehicle if possible. Although she'd been at pains to arrive in Crookhaven unnoticed, she couldn't help a twinge of pride at being able to give her mother a day out with a little luxury. Sure wasn't the money she'd saved through her own blood, sweat and tears paying for it? Money she'd had little to spend on but had squirreled away for a rainy day.

There was no telling how she'd fare in the new chapter of her life that was about to unfold. But that was all to be discovered. She would take one day at a time, and today she was taking her mother to see a house. Mia had saved her so much time in trawling real estate websites. Turned out the young Australian woman had spent much of the week doing the leg work in an effort to find a new home of her own. With any luck, Mammy would agree to sell the family house of horrors and move in as soon as the cosy two-bedroom that looked perfect for their needs was available. For all Katie cared, her siblings could divide the spoils. She would stick around for as long as her mother needed. Who knew what lay in store for any of them? At least she wouldn't be alone. Conor would see to that.

She'd reported back to Stella and let her know she'd forgiven her mother and rediscovered her other best friend. Stella had video-called to make sure she had the right Katie Daly, laughing and crying with joy at the news.

Declan was sitting up reading *The Examiner* when his visitors appeared.

'Dad.' His eldest son nodded.

Declan watched as Robert pulled out a chair for Karen beside the bed, equally attentive towards his mother as Luke had been. It came to him, not without a pang of guilt, that they would have rallied round her after the break-up, even from a distance.

'Hello, Robert. Long time, no see.' It was out before Declan could retract the inane statement. Robert's face was serious. Declan thought he was standing extra tall like he was facing down an enemy.

Mustering as much of a smile as his injured face would allow, he held out a hand to the lad who came closer and shook it gently, a tinge of red in his cheeks. *He'd never have made a dentist*, thought Declan as he felt the clammy hand of his nervous-looking firstborn. But he'd try at least to be gracious. It had been months since he'd spoken to Robert, something he resolved to put right. In West Cork, when he'd taken the time to look back on the mistakes he'd made in his life, he hadn't been proud of the way he'd raised, or failed to raise, Robert. They hadn't always seen eye to eye and if he was honest, he'd largely left the boy to his mother. He'd taken the easy way out, which hadn't been fair on either Karen or the boys.

But Robert was here now, stepping up when he needed him. It was an olive branch he would be foolish to decline.

'Are you staying down for the weekend?' he asked, working his bruised and battered jaw around the words, but determined to say something positive.

His son looked him squarely in the eye. 'I came down with my partner, Dad. We're staying at his mum's.'

Declan knew he must have looked like a rabbit trapped in the headlights, sitting there in the hospital gown that took away all of his status. He glanced at Karen, whose eyes were beseeching him to be kind. His own father would be horrified at the revelation, but he wasn't his father.

'I'd like to meet him,' he managed, biting down on old ill-informed beliefs.

It was all dawning on him now: the near estrangement with his son, Luke's pushing to have him vote Yes in the referendum on gay marriage. Karen's face said it all, willing him to give their boy space to be himself. He thought of Prue and Edwina and the sheer happiness that radiated between them. It was right in front of him all this time and he'd failed or refused to see it.

'I'm sorry I wasn't there much for you, Robert,' he began, but the boy shook his head.

'We can talk when you're better, Dad.' He smiled but Declan could see the hurt in his eyes. 'I'll get on,' he said. 'Luke's making dinner.'

Of course he was. That was Luke all over, the glue of the family he had taken for granted. He couldn't help a tear as he watched Robert disappear from the ward.

Karen leaned in closer and took his hand. He hadn't expected her support, let alone her touch.

'They're great boys,' she said. 'We can be very proud.'

She went to take her hand away and get up, but Declan held on, desperate to tell her what he should have told her long ago.

'I wanted to talk,' he slurred, his jaw smarting at the movement, 'wanted to say . . . how sorry I am . . .'

Tears pooled in her beautiful eyes as she let him go on.

'You're a better person than I could ever be,' he said. 'I've been so selfish . . . the drink, the stupid golf . . .'

She shook her head to stop him, but he needed to be honest. God alone knew if she could ever forgive him.

'If you could give me another chance, I could try . . .'

She gave an embarrassed smile, sniffing back her tears. He wanted to take her in his arms like he might have done when they were young, to make love to her like there was no other woman on the planet he'd rather spend his life with. But here he was, smashed up, washed up, a lesser man than he should have been, compromised on so many fronts. But if he'd learnt anything from his week at Lizzie O's, it was that everyone had their troubles. And wasn't that why they needed each other?

He brought her hand to his lips, kissed the soft skin, breathed in her signature smell and held it there to him.

'Come back, my love.'

She smiled as the tears toppled down over her cheeks.

'What I was trying to tell you when I first came in . . .' she began, swiping at where her mascara was starting to run. 'When the police showed up at my door, I knew I couldn't stand the prospect of losing you forever.'

He listened, still holding on to her hand, not wanting to let go.

'I know our marriage wasn't perfect, Declan, but I never stopped loving you.'

For once, words failed him. It was all he could do to look into those kind eyes and let her love wash over him like a balm that might, in time, help both their wounds to heal.

Grateful to be home, Aisling let her bare feet sink into the warm sand on Hawley Beach. From the comfort of her camping chair, she took in the gathering of the neighbouring family and her own. Mick and Natalie fossicked in the rock pools while Evan, Ruby and Darwin swam out to the rocks that provided hours of entertainment having been the launch pads of spectacular bombs and bellyflops over the years. Even Lily Fitz was in the water, being coaxed out by a rather swarthy Doug, who looked so much happier in himself than he'd done on previous visits. There was talk of the pair of them taking off up the coast. She would have to get the lowdown from Heather later on how that had happened.

'This is the life.' Heather handed her a glass of bubbles and took a seat beside her.

'To the good life,' said Aisling, raising the glass to her friend.

'Is everything all right now, Ash?' Heather's frown spoke volumes, but there was no need to go over their indiscretions. She'd had a message from the lovely doctor telling her the blood test had come back clear of any of her imagined illnesses. There was no denying the week in West Cork had been one of the most challenging of her life, but her marriage had survived. It was all that mattered.

'More than all right,' she said, giving Heather a smile.

It was a new year with new possibilities. She'd already emailed her resignation. Her offer on the property she wanted had been accepted, and she'd started to source stock. The clothes shop would be enough for now. They might even expand later on. Who was to say they couldn't open a chain? But Mick didn't need to know any of that just yet.

'Mum!' The call went up from where the wind was whipping up the small surf sloshing about the rocks. 'Come in,' Natalie called, waving a hand vigorously to get her attention.

Aisling set the glass down. 'Mind that for me,' she told Heather. And without as much as a thought to how she might look in the bikini she'd agonised over buying, she threw off the sarong that had been covering up her jiggly bits and ran down over the wet sand, launching herself into the cool sea, gulping for air as she surfaced and found her daughter's body wrapping around her in a heartfelt hug.

'I missed you, Mum.'

'I missed you too, love.'

Out of the corner of her eye, Aisling could see Mick watching, a loving smile spreading across his handsome face, the face she realised that no matter where they were in the world, would always mean home.

# Acknowledgements

Feeling utterly privileged to know that this book has found its way into the hands of a reader. I hope you have enjoyed it. My sincere thanks to Rebecca Saunders for giving me the opportunity to share my stories and for helping me to take out the ráméis (Irish for rigmarole). They say you know you're Irish when you can't make a long story short, so I am immensely grateful to both Rebecca and author/editor Dianne Blacklock, who together had me kill several darlings but ultimately made the book a better version of early drafts.

The writing is only the half of it and I am so grateful to the entire Hachette team for all their various expertise in making this book a beautiful thing to behold and bringing it to readers far and wide. Special thanks to Karen Ward, Christa Moffitt and Sarah Holmes.

You can't know everything, but thankfully I had friends on hand who generously shared their knowledge and experience.

Frances Gallagher, the seaweed queen, thank you so much for the inspiration and taking me back to our zoology days in Cork. John Holland, my nephew, for advice on issues of a medical nature, so proud of you. Ursula Shannon, for conversations around unmarried mothers, a theme that continues to resonate with me. Arlene Moon, for answering my random queries across the miles. Karen Murphy and Helen Crockett, for the memories woven into this book. Norma McNeil, for a borrowed story. Helen Sibritt, for getting married on your birthday. Royce Kurmelovs, for your insightful book *The Death of Holden*.

Special thanks also to Marie Isaacson, for much-needed encouragement at a wobbly moment in what has been a steep learning curve, and to Kristen Lang for keeping me accountable when my word count was terrifyingly low.

For my family and friends, near and far, who continue to cheer me on – it means the world to me. My children, thanks for sharing in all of this. Finally, my husband, to whom this book is dedicated, thank you for your honest feedback and steadfast support.

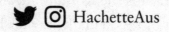

hachette
AUSTRALIA

If you would like to find out more about Hachette Australia,
our authors, upcoming events and new releases you can visit
our website or our social media channels:

hachette.com.au

HachetteAustralia

HachetteAus